THE CITY — SIDEWAYS

Lyn McConchie

Hadrosaur Productions, Mesilla Park, NM

The City—Sideways
Hadrosaur Productions

ISBN-13: 978-1-965313-02-2

Hadrosaur Productions
P.O. Box 2194
Mesilla Park, NM 88047-2194
www.hadrosaur.com

CONTENTS

THE CITY — SIDEWAYS

URBAN LEGENDS

"There's a working bee to tidy up the Bolton Street Cemetery again," Nerida informed her mother. "Are you going?"

Patti smiled. "I always do."

"I know you always do – and I always wonder why."

Patti shrugged. "I just do."

"Mum, you're sixty. It's exhausting work with all that bending and I reckon it's time you quit. Tell them to find someone else."

Patti Paiwai looked at her daughter. "No, I'm still fit enough and I like to do it," she hesitated. "I owe a debt."

Nerida looked at her. "I've always thought there was a story behind your going on that working bee every single year for as long as I've known about it. Isn't it about time you told me?"

"Maybe it is. Make us a cup of tea, love, and sit down. I'll tell you and perhaps you'll laugh, but as Granny Ngaire always says, there's some strange things happen in the city and if you're smart you don't try to convince yourself you didn't see them. Lie to other people if you must, but never lie to yourself. I've kept quiet on this story most of my life but she's right, and I know it happened."

Nerida brought the teapot and mugs. They settled comfortably at the old kitchen table and Patti began.

"I was sixteen in 1962. My old man was a drunk – not the sort who hit any of us, but he spent every penny he could lay his hands on. My mother cleared out with my little sister and my brothers and left him a year earlier and in another year, I'd had enough of him too. I left school and got a job as an usherette in a movie theater, along with my best friend; we each had a room in a big old house up the back of the university, and we went out most nights around the coffee bars to have a good time.

"I wasn't sleeping around at all, but I was out with Rosemary at the coffee bars every night, dancing until midnight when a lot of them shut, having a good laugh with all my friends – and it's possible some of the boys thought that I was available. Some girls in the coffee bars had that reputation then."

* * *

She remembered one boy in particular. A tall, good-looking boy named Douglas who'd come down from Auckland about six months earlier. The talk was that his parents had money. Whatever the truth of that was, he always had a pound or two in his pockets and he seemed willing to spend it on her for a few months. Until he found that she wasn't planning on paying him back for it in the way he'd hoped.

"Aw, come on, Patti. It'll be good. I know what I'm doing, you'll like it."

"No."

"Look, I'll be careful, I've got condoms. You won't get pregnant, honest."

"No."

"Aw, come on!" His hands were all over her and he was trying to push her down on the grass of the zigzag footpath. "It's dark. No one will see. Just let me." He was getting angry.

"No!" She thrust him away savagely and he yelped in frustration.

"Hell, I've spent money on you for months, what did you think I was taking you out to all those places for?"

"I didn't think you were trying to buy me, that's what. I thought you liked taking me out."

"I did, but jeez, Patti. A guy expects a girl to come across sometime. We've been going out for five months. It isn't as if I was trying to get you into bed the first time we met."

"You wouldn't have said no if I'd agreed then though."

He stared at her. "Of course I wouldn't. But everyone said

you're a nice girl so I gave you time. I've waited, taken you places, let everyone see we're together. Now, how about it?"

"No."

He groaned. "For God's sake, can't you say anything but no? If you aren't going to, then I guess you and me are done. I'm not wasting any more time and money on a tease."

"I'm no tease, Doug Spence, and you know it. I told you the first time we went to the pictures that I don't put out. I'm not going to be like my mum, pregnant at fifteen and married. She was stuck with a house full of kids the rest of her life while my dad did whatever he wanted to do and left her alone with four kids every evening and no money in her purse."

Doug Spence gaped at her. "Married! Who said anything about us getting married? Look, Patti. I like you, but you're only sixteen an' I'm nineteen. I'm not getting married until I'm thirty an' I start to slow down."

Patti glared at him in exasperation. "I know. That's what I've just said. You don't want to get married, and I don't want to get married either. But mistakes have a way of happening. I daresay Mum didn't mean to get pregnant and have her father make the guy marry her either, but it's not going to happen to me. Got that?"

"Yeah yeah, all right. I get it, and I'm gone."

He turned on his heel and left her standing in the street. Patti looked wistfully after the tall figure, then shrugged. Plenty more fish in the sea. She'd liked his taking her out, they'd usually had a good time together, but she knew he'd been expecting her to sleep with him sooner or later and she wasn't going to. She'd been expecting him to give her an ultimatum eventually too, and she'd already known what she'd say. Oh well!

"Hey, Patti, where's Doug these days?"

"Gone off me," Patti said briefly. "I wouldn't come across so he dumped me."

"Hell, guys are pigs!"

Patti grinned at her best friend. "No, they're just guys. All they think of is what's in their pants and how they can get it into your pants instead."

"Yeah. So, you want to come down to the Cobweb or the Beachcomber tonight?"

"Why not?" Dancing all night was a good cure for a heart that wasn't broken at all – but maybe just a little bit scratched.

Patti put on her white outfit, long skin-tight jeans and a white Emma Peel top with polo neck and cutaway armholes. In it she felt really good. She flipped her hair up into a beehive, put on generous mascara and eyeliner, and painted her mouth with a dark pink lipstick. She dabbed "Evening in Paris" perfume behind her ears and on her throat and went to meet Rosemary.

"Wow, you look great!"

"Thanks." It must have been true because she danced all night and she was never short of partners. She laughed, danced, talked, and accepted their offerings of Coke and toasted sandwiches. But at midnight she headed home with Rosemary as her only companion.

"Let's take the short cut?" They both had rooms in a large house on the other side of the cemetery and cutting through the place halved the time it took to walk home.

Rosemary shivered. "I'm not going through there. I've heard some funny stories about that cemetery."

"Ah come on. It's all nonsense. So the university students have parties there sometimes."

"On the gravestones."

"So what?"

"My dad says that's disrespecting the dead and they don't like it."

Patti grinned. "They probably did the same when they were alive and students too. I don't think they'd mind."

"They say there's a coven meets there every full moon."

"That's true." Patti confirmed. "My cousin knows one of them. They're all women and they aren't doing black magic. It's some sort of earth magic thing. They're white witches. They wouldn't hurt you and anyhow, like I say, they're all women."

"There's the statue there. My cousin told me that the guy it's of used to practice black magic and when he died the Devil dragged him off to hell. It's dangerous to go near it after dark. He'll drag your soul into hell with him if you get too close."

Patti loved Rosemary. She was her best friend – but she didn't read much, in fact not at all since they'd left school, and Rosemary listened to the weirdest stories. What was more, she sometimes believed them. Patti could even work out where some of this particular story had come from.

"Your cousin Joe told you that?"

"Yeah, so?"

Patti giggled. "So he goes to music school and they've been practicing for that big end-of-the-year recital they're planning on doing. They're going to have it in the town hall and they're starting to sell tickets next month. His lot are doing *Don Giovanni*."

Rosemary was baffled. "I don't get it, what's that got to do with the Bolton Street Cemetery?"

"That's the story of the opera that Joe's doing. All about a statue that comes to life and drags a wicked man down to hell. He's been having you on, Rosie. Teasing you. The opera isn't real either, just some old tale that they put to music. And anyway, that statue's of one of our Prime Ministers."

Rosemary inhaled once, loudly. "Next time I see that Joe—"

"Yeah. So? Are you coming?"

Patti had to admit that the cemetery was spooky at midnight. It was silent, just the faint rustle of the trees in the light breeze, and the loom of pale gravestones. That damn statue ahead of them did almost seem to move nearer to the path when they got closer. But she knew it didn't really, it was Joe and his stupid stories and Rosemary believing them. There wasn't anything here, and she wasn't going to pass up the best shortcut home.

"Let's go this way." It avoided the statue, Patti knew, and while she wasn't Rosemary to swallow Joe's stories, the place was eerie and she wouldn't mind avoiding the statue herself.

"Okay." They giggled their way down the path, cut along the back of the cemetery and arrived at their rooms in the big old house on Salamanca Drive at the back of the university. Rumor had it that in a year or two the landlord was putting the houses here on the market. More rumors said that the university was going to buy the places and use them as an extension of the campus. Patti hoped it would take longer than that, she quite liked her room and the price was better than that of a lot of other rooms she could have rented.

The next morning Rosemary knocked at her door. "I'm just off to work, but are we going out tonight?"

"Let's go to the Picasso. I love that place."

She did, and with its being in Upper Willis Street they could just cut up the zigzag there and skip using the cemetery shortcut. Rosemary would appreciate that.

"Yeah, me too. Okay!"

Patti grinned at the enthusiastic response. She knew part of that was having an excuse to walk home another way. But they had fun that evening, she seemed to be dancing all the time, she never had to buy her own Coke the whole night and two of the guys offered to walk her home, one suggesting that they go on to another coffee bar.

"That's all right. I'm walking with Rosemary, and it's work in the morning again. I have to get my beauty sleep."

She made it stick although they did seem very keen. She had a sudden thought and smiled to herself as she and Rosemary walked down the street. Maybe Doug had been moaning about how she was hard to get and some of the guys thought they'd have better luck. They wouldn't, but it was fun having them so keen. She'd dance with them all they liked, drink the Cokes they bought her and eat the food offered, but she'd still walk home with Rosemary. She wasn't for sale, and if she had been, it would have been for a lot higher price than a large Coke and a toasted ham and tomato sandwich.

Work itself was boring, Patti thought the next day as she took tickets, tore them in half, and passed people into the theater. But they didn't pay her that badly, it was good working with Rosemary and the other girls were nice, and she saw all the movies here for free. You could even let your friends in free now and again – so long as you didn't do it too often and always at the matinee sessions when the place was half empty anyhow.

"Yes, madam, just here. Intermission's at nine-thirty for this film."

She liked the old Majestic too. It was close enough that she and Rosemary could sometimes go home between the five o'clock and the eight o'clock sessions when there was a spare hour and have a cup of tea and make their own dinner. A tin of braised steak on toast and a good cup of tea. That was a lot cheaper than buying something from one of the cafes in the theater block.

Her room was bigger than Rosemary's and she'd quietly bought herself a cupboard that locked. In it she kept a couple of pots, a frying pan, a toaster and hot-water jug, and a single-element miniature cooker along with some cutlery and crockery. The landlord didn't know about any of that. It wasn't allowed – but what the eye didn't see the heart didn't grieve over, as her dad always used to say. Anyhow it was really handy to be able to cook meals for Rosemary and herself sometimes, so long as she was careful.

Intermission came around, she showed the stragglers in the audience back to their seats, and then she and the other usherettes were free to finish for the night. That was one of the good things about the job. It didn't start until one-thirty in the afternoon, she could go to a coffee bar after the eight o'clock session's intermission – around nine for most films – dance until late, and then sleep in. Rosemary and she usually had breakfast about eleven and then they went uptown for a while before they were due at the theater. If they met a boy, they could have lunch with him before they had to go to work.

"Hey, you daydreaming? I said, what say we go to The Beachcomber tonight?"

"Okay. But I'm not walking home from there. We get the last bus."

"Jeez, Patti, that leaves Courtney Place at eleven-thirty. By the time we've walked down there from the 'Comber, we'd have to leave at eleven."

"If I spend all day on my feet, and half the night dancing, I'm not walking for miles after that."

"Marty will probably be there. We could ask him for a lift?"

"If he is."

"He is most nights. Look, I'll tell you what. If he's there I'll ask him and if he isn't or he says he can't take us home, then we leave early and catch the bus, all right?"

Patti nodded. Towards the end of the week, her feet started hurting. As an usherette she had to stand a lot and when she was dancing, she never noticed, but walking home for miles made her feet burn at work by Thursday and she still had Friday to go.

The Beachcomber was good. Marty said he'd take them home and that meant they stayed even longer dancing, knowing they wouldn't have to walk at all. Marty dropped them off right outside the house at two a.m. and they staggered inside.

"Come and have a cup of tea before you go to bed," Patti offered. Rosemary nodded, following her friend into her room and watching as Patti made tea and brought out a packet of biscuits.

"Wish we could have stayed a bit longer."

Patti agreed. It'd been a really good night. Though, Doug had been there dancing with someone else for about an hour and he'd completely ignored her, making sure she knew it. It hadn't bothered her at all, and she knew she was over him. She said that to Rosemary.

"Better than being under him." Rosemary could come back with a smart line when she wanted to.

"Yeah."

"You ever going to do it?" Patti knew Rosemary did sometimes – if she really liked the guy, but she was a good friend and she never expected Patti to do anything just because she did.

"Of course. But not until I want to. Maybe in a couple of years when I'm eighteen. And my first time's going to be with a guy I really like. Not some bloke who thinks he's got the right because he bought me a Coke." Without intention her voice had become edged and Rosemary responded.

"Yeah, what a wanker that Doug is. You see him tonight? Swanning about with Lois Marama. Bet he was into her pants before he even *bought* her a Coke an' a sandwich."

Patti had a mental picture of Doug holding a large glass of Coke in one hand and a toasted sandwich in the other, while trying to work out how to get Lois's pants off. She began to laugh.

"What's so funny?"

Patti told her and Rosemary laughed so hard she almost fell off the bed.

"I can see that, yeah. Guy's a loser. You're better off without him. Jimmy Gillespie likes you. A bit of encouragement and he'd ask you out."

"I might. He's nice, and he doesn't think he's bought you just because he's got you a meal or something."

Patti found it the more surprising, then, that when she did go out with Jimmy on her night off, he took her to a live play at the town hall and in a dark doorway as he walked her home, tried to get his hand up her skirt. He was pushing her back against the door in the shop alcove, panting like a dog, kissing her neck urgently, and using his free hand to hold her upright against the door as she writhed away and protested angrily. She freed herself and snarled at him.

"Hey, what do you think I am?" In the light from the shop sign she could see that he was looking at her oddly. She couldn't place the expression at first but she finally understood when it changed to rather shame-faced embarrassment.

"Sorry, guess I got a bit carried away. Didn't hurt you, did I?"

"No." He looked like a smacked puppy and she relented, reaching up to kiss his cheek. "It's all right. But none of that stuff. I don't do it. You know that."

"Well, yeah, but…"

"But nothing, James Gillespie. I never let you think I would and if you expect me to, then you don't have to take me out."

This time his expression was one of plain relief. "I'm sorry. I know you don't. An' it's okay, I like taking you out anyway. You're a nice girl, Patti."

She was briefly puzzled by the tone of those last words. As if he were affirming something he'd always thought before – but the belief had somehow been temporarily shaken, and now he was happy that it was restored.

"And don't you forget it."

"Promise. Look, what say I take you dancing tomorrow night?"

"Okay. How about you get your mate, Ken, to ask Rosemary and we can all go together."

Ken had a car. It was only an old bomb but it went and if they used that, they could maybe go dancing out at Lower Hutt and not have to worry about getting the bus home.

Jimmy was nodding and Patti smiled at him. He was a nice guy really. Rosemary quite liked Ken too so they'd have a good night. She told Rosemary about it while they were changing into their usherette uniforms at work the next afternoon.

"Fine by me so long as Ken wants to ask. How was it with Jimmy?"

"Pretty good. We saw that live play at the town hall and he walked me home afterwards..." Her voice trailed off." Rosemary looked at her.

"Something happened?"

"Well, sort of. He tried it on and I had to really shove him away from me. He got me pinned in that doorway by the newspaper entrance."

"What?" Rosemary was looking furious. "What'd he do? I'll kill him!"

"It's okay, he didn't hurt me, but it was disgusting. He was holding me up against the door, trying to get his hand right up my skirt and into my pants and he was sort of gasping and all excited. I made him stop it and I had something to say to him, I can tell you. He said he was sorry and promised to behave. But Rosemary, he knows I don't. What made him think I would – and in a doorway in Willis Street?"

Rosemary had a thoughtful look on her face. "I don't like to say it, and I know you won't like hearing who could have been saying stuff, but I think I have an idea."

Patti stared. Rosemary nodded. "Yeah, Doug Spence."

"You think— "

"I reckon he's been going around telling the guys that you an' him did it. He probably gave some reason why it was him dumped you after that. Maybe said you were no good, or that he got bored with you wanting it all the time."

Patti took in a deep breath. She could feel her eyes almost sticking out, her face going red with fury, and she'd just bet that Rosemary was right. It would explain why she'd been getting such a rush from the guys ever since she'd dropped Doug. It was the sort of lying lousy thing he'd do and she wouldn't stand for it.

"So I left home," she said in a hissing whisper, "but they love me and I go back every few days to see Mum and my little sister. I've got two big brothers and a whole bunch of cousins and they won't let him spread that kind of talk. I'm going straight to Mum's tomorrow morning to tell my brothers before they leave for work."

"You don't want to do that," Rosemary cautioned. "I could be wrong and if you make a fuss, it's you that looks bad. It's better if we go out with Ken and Jimmy tonight and you get Jimmy alone and ask him. Make him tell you. Then when you know for sure you can maybe ask Marty too. He's a decent guy. If Doug's been saying that sort of thing Marty will tell you if you ask him straight out. Then you tell your family and with Jimmy and Marty to back it up that that's what Doug's been saying, you're in the right."

It made sense to Patti. "I'll do that." She gave her friend an impulsive hug. "Thanks."

"No trouble. Now let's get some customers ushered to their seats before the boss comes to ask us what we're doing wasting the time he pays for."

The film was a good one that night. Patti found herself easily distracted on the surface, but underneath she was still seething. Oh, yes, she'd talk to Jimmy – and Marty, and then she'd do a lot more talking to her brothers and some of her cousins. If Doug Spence thought he'd get away with trying to wreck her reputation he had another think coming.

It was quite easy to separate Jimmy and Ken. After they'd danced at The Beachcomber for an hour, Rosemary suggested they go outside to enjoy the cool night air for a while. Then she took Ken by the hand, led him around the side of the building and started kissing him. As both youths expected, Patti promptly led Jimmy away so that they strolled down the Parade until they reached a bench where she sat.

"Jimmy, I want to talk to you about something."

"Look, if it's the other night, I said I was sorry."

"It sort of is. Jimmy. You know I don't go all the way, but you – well – for a minute there I was scared you were going to rape me and…" she allowed her voice to trail off and shivered visibly.

Jimmy sat up sharply. "Jeez, no, Patti. I wouldn't have. I guess I got a bit – well – you know, worked up. But I wouldn't do that, I swear. I'm sorry if I scared you."

"I know, I've always trusted you, that was why I went out with you after Doug wanted me to go all the way and I wouldn't. But Jimmy, are you sure it was your fault? Are you sure Doug didn't say something to you and the other guys about me?"

"Um, you didn't? With him?"

"Of course not. That was why we split up. He kept wanting me to and I kept saying no and then one night he got rough about it and I told him I wasn't ever going to, not with him. So he called me names and dumped me. He said he'd spent money on me and he expected something back for that. That wasn't how you felt, was it?"

She could see his face turn towards her. His voice was low then, and ashamed. "I gotta say, Patti, it sort of was, but not until Doug kept talking about you. I should have known better. He's a loudmouth any time, but after you and him split up he kept talking about how he'd had you at all sorts of places. Up on the zigzag, behind a couple 'a coffee bars, an' in his friend's car. I sort of knew it couldn't be true but..."

"But you hoped it was because if I'd done it with him, I might do it with you," Patti finished for him.

"Yeah. I guess so. You don't hate me, do you?"

She considered the question, and decided no, she didn't hate him. She just felt let down, disappointed that he'd been prepared to try it on, on the basis of a story he'd admitted that he was pretty sure wasn't true anyway. She said so and saw his face redden.

"I know. That Doug, I was a fool to listen to him an' I'll say so next time I see him."

Patti smiled. It wasn't a very pleasant smile, as Jimmy could see in the streetlights. "Don't bother. I want to have a word with one of the other guys then I'm going to tell my brothers and a couple of cousins. You keep quiet about that too. Promise?"

"Yeah, okay. He's got anything coming to him that they'll do I reckon."

Patti walked back along the Parade, collected up Ken and Rosemary and went into the coffee bar. Once inside she scanned the dancing crowd until she saw her quarry. She pounced.

"I need to have a word with you if you've got time?"

Marty studied her and nodded. He was older by seven or eight years than most of her crowd and a decent, reliable man.

"I can guess what about." He opened the side door, took her through then turned to shut it behind them, before facing her. "You've finally heard what Doug's been saying. Who told you? Jimmy?"

"Ah huh."

"And you want me to tell you that Doug definitely has been saying stuff about you and if I had to guess any further, I'd say you want to know what?"

"Ah huh."

"All right then. This is what he's been spreading." He spoke quietly for a few minutes while Patti listened, her expression hardening. He concluded with the comment. "I'll tell you, Patti. I never believed it and I told him when he started talking, that unless he was a complete idiot he should shut his mouth."

"But he didn't?"

"Around me he did, but I know he was still talking to some of the other guys."

"Then that's all I need to know. Thanks, Marty."

"No trouble. Listen; be careful if you try some scheme to get back at him. I've heard this and that about Doug Spence and I don't think he's a good enemy to have."

Patti nodded. "I'm going home. In the morning I'll be telling all this to my brothers and a couple of my cousins. They'll probably make it clear to Mr. Spence that he shouldn't come anywhere near me again, and he definitely should keep his mouth shut."

Marty said nothing but opened the side door, saw her through to meet up with Rosemary and their friends, then went back to his car. He didn't like any of this, the Paiwais were a large extended family and they hung together. Patti might not live at home any longer but to her brothers she was their little sister and they wouldn't take kindly to what Doug had been saying – particularly since none of it was true.

Doug Spence had no worries about that. So far as he was concerned Patti wouldn't have a clue about what he'd been telling the guys around half of the city's coffee bars. And what did he care if she did find out? She lived in a cheap room and worked as an usherette at a movie theater. It wasn't as if she was going to sue him for slander or anything. What could she do?

He discovered that two nights later. Three big men loomed

up out of the darkness at him as he walked home. Before he could yell for help, he was hauled into an alley, a fist hit him in the stomach and he had no breath left to call out. More fists landed wicked body blows as he twisted, attempting to avoid the impacts. The blows drove him to his knees and then to the pavement – where he discovered that kicks hurt even more than fists.

He tried to protest, to tell them that he wasn't whoever they thought he was. Until the largest of his attackers leaned down to where he lay on the filthy pavement and spoke, and Doug discovered he was wrong – yet again.

"You've been talking to your mates about my sister. A couple of them don't like you so much and didn't believe a word of it, so they were happy enough to tell us that it was you spreading the rumors. Just in case you've been making a habit of it so you aren't sure what girl I'm talking about, I'm Rangi Paiwai; this here's my brother, Tamati, and our cousin, Piripi. If you go talking about Patti again, you'll get a lot worse than we've given you this time. Next time we break something. Understand?"

A foot thudded into his ribs to underline the question. Doug moaned. "Yes, yes. I understand. I'm sorry." There was a grim chuckle from the speaker.

"I reckon you are. Just remember that you'll be a hell of a lot sorrier if we have to come looking for you again." A final kick wrung a gasping shriek from Doug.

Footsteps padded off down the alley and their victim managed to roll over. They were gone, thank God! He crawled to his feet, hunched over against the flaring pain between his legs, and realized something else; not one blow had landed on his face. No one but he and Patti's family had to know what had happened.

It occurred to him then, in a flash of thought, that it could be that if something were to happen to Patti – if it was the right sort of thing – she would keep quiet too, at least initially. God, he hurt! He thought he might have cracked ribs, and it felt as if he'd been castrated. Slowly, gingerly, he straightened up and began to walk.

"That cow," he muttered softly as he winced his way along the empty street. "That bitch. I'll make her sorry. I've got friends too. She'll find out. She won't be so keen to go running to the police when I'm done with her, and her family can all go to hell. I'll fix the cow and be right onto the overnight bus back up North."

His mouth worked as he spat viciously. His family had money; he could buy a plane ticket to Australia here in Wellington before he got on the bus. Once overseas he could vanish into the Sydney crowds and her family wouldn't even know where to start looking. Maybe he'd go on to England for a year. He had family there and his father had a branch of his business in London.

He spent nearly two weeks holed up in his flat while the bruises healed and the pain subsided. Then went out and bought a seat on the bus to Auckland, a plane ticket to Sydney, and an expensive wig. What he planned would bring the cops looking too, but he'd see to it that they had no proof. Anyway, he'd get a couple of other men involved, if anything happened, his father would get him a good lawyer and all the blame would go onto the other guys. He'd say that he was just a boy led astray by older men.

"I'm telling you, she's a professional tease. She makes a habit of it. The bitch gets a guy to spend a fortune on her taking her out to restaurants, buying her pretty clothes and jewelry. He's showing her a great time, then when he expects something in return, she smiles at him and says she doesn't do that. She needs to be taken down a peg."

He could see both of the men liked what he was suggesting. They just weren't sure it was safe for them.

"What about the cops?"

"Come on. You ever been at a rape trial? She's got to prove it was rape. It's three against one, if the cops come asking you—" whoops, nearly gave his escape plans away there, "—we ... just tell them she was willing, even asked us for money. We don't have to hit her. We just grab her. Two of us hold her while the other one's busy. Turn about and she hasn't got the black eye, the split lip that'd make the cops believe her an' take it to court."

"Who is she?"

He wouldn't give Patti's real name. This pair lived in the city, and they could know the family.

"Patti Jackson. She's a real little tart. I reckon if you did pay her, she'd roll over anyhow. But I've spent enough, I want it for free and you get it free as well. No one's going to listen to her if she talks. The police won't even bother. And I'll give you ten pounds each to celebrate afterwards."

He saw the hungry gleam in two pairs of eyes and bit back a triumphant smile; ten pounds was a week's pay to these men. That'd clinched it for him. They'd help. They could have her after him and he'd be able to watch that pride of hers crumble. She could take her "I don't do that, and I wouldn't with you anyway" arrogance and stick it. He smothered a giggle. On the contrary, he'd stick it for her – right where the monkey hid his nuts.

"Give it another two weeks to let the bitch think she's got away with it. Then you stay by the phone in your boarding house every night around ten o'clock. If I find her and she's going to be alone I'll ring you. Then when she leaves, I'll ring you again. You grab a taxi and meet me at the Bolton Street Cemetery, the entrance just up from the cenotaph. She often goes that way home as a shortcut after she's been in the coffee-bar."

It was easy enough to arrange. Patti knew her brothers and cousin had given Doug a thumping, and no one had seen him since then. When, after two weeks, he did show up he steered well clear of her. That suited Patti. The truth – that he'd lied about her – had quietly spread and no one was much surprised when Doug kept his head down. Five weeks after Doug's beating, Patti was in the coffee bar on her own. Ken had had a bit of luck, he'd found a wallet, handed it in to the police, and been given the reward of ten pounds. To celebrate he'd taken Rosemary out for the night, just the two of them.

There'd been a customer complaint about Jimmy's work and he was doing overtime on the annual stocktaking. Doug heard Patti talking about both events and sneered to himself. Stupid tart thought it was all a big coincidence. Doug had spent time and good hard cash to arrange both events and he'd get his reward in a couple of hours.

It wasn't much fun on her own, Patti thought. Well, an earlier night than usual wouldn't do her any harm. She'd gone with a group of friends to the small coffee bar down near the railway station – someone had suggested it, saying they'd heard that there was a good folk singer there tonight – there hadn't been, but they'd had fun anyway. From here she could just cut up through the cemetery and be home in half an hour at the most.

"See you tomorrow night."

"Yeah, take care, Patti."

She walked along the road past the cenotaph with its stoic lion statues who seemed to know all, to the curve in the road where the steps up to the cemetery started. Drat Rosemary's cousin, Joe, and his urban legends of walking statues, and that other stuff she'd heard about seeing places in the city that were long gone. All that rubbish had made her jumpy even though she knew perfectly well that none of it was true.

It was spooky under the trees. She thought she heard footsteps behind her once as the path leveled out, but when she looked, she couldn't see anyone. It had to be her imagination working overtime. She stepped out a bit more briskly though. A man stepped silently past the tree behind her. Two hands grabbed and Patti found that with one arm about her waist and the other over her mouth she was unable to scream or fight.

"That's it, get her down on the ground."

She felt her skirt pushed up, cold metal against her leg and heard a tearing sound. They were cutting off her pants. Oh, God! She knew what they were going to do. If her struggles had been strong before, they now became frantic.

"Christ, it's like trying to skin a bloody eel! Hold her still."

She knew that voice. Doug. She didn't know the others and she'd bet they didn't know who she was either. If she could just get her mouth free? She bit. A man yelled in pain and Doug, moving more quickly than he'd ever moved in his life before, got his wadded up handkerchief stuffed into her mouth before she could speak. That'd been close! At least his wig hadn't fallen off.

Patti twisted violently, squirmed, struggled, and kicked with all her strength. She was snapping at them like a dog. She'd make them leave marks; no one would be able to say she'd agreed to this. But she was weakening. In her mind she screamed for help, there were stories about this place. They said strange things happened here. She could do with one of them now. *Please, someone, help me!*

Behind and above her, standing on his plinth as he'd stood for decades, someone heard. Slowly, stiffly, the statue descended, strode to where three men held a frantic girl on the ground and tapped the shoulder of the nearest. The man turned. In the dim light, he didn't at first know what he was seeing, only that some fool was interrupting their fun.

"Mind your own business or..." He hit out viciously as he spoke. His fist crashed against an unyielding substance. His hand broke and Patti's would-be attacker howled in startled agony. His friend straightened.

"What the hell..."

He punched, and in turn he also screamed and doubled over his smashed hand. "God, what are you?"

The person facing them moved, and a shaft of moonlight lit face and figure. Douglas Spence screamed too then. His cry of terror was echoed by his friends' howls as they fled. The statue took a slow pace towards the third man, frozen where he stood. This time Doug's shriek cut through the Thorndon night like the cry of a goosed banshee. He snapped out of his terror-stricken trance and departed in haste, not so much running as low flying. He fell down the steps towards the road, scrambled to his feet and continued his flight.

His two partners were long gone and he didn't care about them. He was heading for the bus, then the mid-morning plane. He'd keep moving after that as well. The further away the better, in Doug Spence's opinion. Alaska wouldn't be far enough, even Outer Mongolia would be too close to a city where cemetery statues walked up to interfere with a man's pastimes.

Patti staggered to her feet and looked dumbly at the statue. What did you say to something that'd come to save you when you needed it most? Well, she could think of one thing.

She managed a small, trembling smile. "Thank you. Thank you very much!"

The statue of Dick Seddon, one-time Prime Minister of New Zealand, nodded politely, climbed back on his plinth, assumed his usual position, and froze as if he had never moved. They'd said a lot of things about Dick Seddon over the years, but he'd never been the sort of man to stand idly by when a woman begged for his help.

* * *

"And," Patti said to Nerida as she finished the story, "just before he became a statue again, he winked at me. I went home and never told anyone but Granny Ngaire about the statue. I told people I'd been attacked and managed to get away. I reckon Doug's still running and I never found out who the other two were. But they'd have heard who I was and they probably left the city as soon as they did. My brothers would have killed them if they'd found them."

"So you help with the working bee every year?"

"I owe him." Patti told her. "I've never forgotten how much. Every year I go up there to the working bee. Yes. I take a bunch of flowers with me as well, lay them on his pedestal and say thanks again."

Nerida drank her tea, and walked home, but before she reached her house, she went to a florist's, bought an expensive bunch of roses, and stopped by the statue. She looked up at it and nodded.

"That was my mother you saved that night. "When she gets too old to do the working bee I'll come in her place. Thank you."

She laid the bunch of yellow roses on the statue's plinth beside its feet, straightened up, and nodded politely to it. Somchow she could have sworn the statue winked at her too then, and Nerida winked cheerfully back before she walked away, smiling to herself. Paiwai family debts owed would always be remembered – and just as faithfully repaid.

THE BULLY

The start of this was a common enough tale when new sections in a government department are created out of nothing. When this happens, it provides a section without structure. One where a bully can get a quick foothold. In this case too, there should have been a supervisor who could have seen what was happening and put a stop to it, but if it's the supervisor who is the problem, then no one knows who to go to or what to do. I've seen people like those who were involved in this come and go. This time it didn't end the way it usually does, and in the end, I kept silent on one thing. I could never have told that bit. What happened was bad enough.

It started three years back when my government department bought a new computer system. To match it, they began a help desk, and that was where the trouble started as well. I'd worked for the department for years, I had friends and my cousin was assistant director. I was moved into the office just as they got the help desk up and running. They'd employed people from all over other government departments, and it seemed to me the only criteria had been that they had to have a good security clearance and a knowledge of computers.

"How long am I supposed to stay in this office?" I asked.

"A year maybe. Until we have the new annex built."

I snorted in disbelief.

"I mean it, Diane. A year at the most. You aren't working on the help desk; you're just using a convenient corner in their office. You don't answer to anyone there. After a year the annex should be finished and you're gone."

I nodded. "A year. After that I'll be gone one way or another." I looked at him meaningfully to make sure he understood. My cousin was overseas on a year's exchange with government people in another country. He'd only just left, but once he was back, I could speak to him and I'd be moved to wherever I wanted. It was something I'd never used, but I could – and he knew it.

"One year, Diane. Next year a job's opening up in third level support that will be sited in the new annex. We'd want you there anyway."

I nodded, went to clear out my old desk, and settle into the nice new office where the help desk would be set up. I wasn't too happy with any of this, but after so many years in the department I'm used to the odd upheaval.

Next day my new colleagues started to arrive. The first was a big, smiling woman only a few years younger than I was, and named – most inconveniently – Diana. I was Diane, usually called Di, so almost the first thing I said to her concerned the possible confusion of our names. She agreed. From now on she would always be Diana, I would always be Di. We'd make that clear to everyone as soon as they settled in.

The next few months were a mess. Most government departments have built up over the years of their operations with just the occasional new employee arriving to fit into his or her designated slot. The other staff helps the new arrivals learn the job, and generally round off the edges of any square pegs. Here, though, everyone but me was new with different ways of doing things. Worse still, we had no continuity of supervisors to smooth out problems.

By the time the help desk was in full operation it was six months later. There were ten employees – no supervisor who'd stayed longer than a month, often less – and the section was in a lot of trouble. There was a permanent supervisor for the section finally. A woman named Mary Haslam. That day she was almost yelling, loud enough for the whole office to hear her. I often noticed what people said to Diana anyway. My attention tended to be caught by the name so similar to mine.

"You'll do the shifts I've allocated, Diana."

"But I've just finished doing…"

Mary's voice took on a note that felt as if it was etching into my eardrums. "We're starting from scratch. You'll be on the evening shift for the next week and don't argue. I'm your supervisor."

Diana subsided, still looking mutinous. I wondered about that. She was a team player and it was unusual for her not to be cooperative. So later on, I checked the new roster pinned on the board. Once I'd done that, I could see the problem at a glance. The last two temporary supervisors had made out elaborate work shift rosters and had also insisted on beginning from scratch.

The result was that Diana had done six weeks on the same shift, when we were supposed to change shifts each week so all had their turn on the unpopular ones. I considered mentioning this to Mary, then decided that saying nothing was the better option.

I'd summed Mary up quickly. She was a control freak; the sort who saw her rank as giving her absolute power. Anyone suggesting otherwise was challenging her. I suspected that she was also insecure, uncertain of her abilities, and unused to having authority.

In a quiet way, Diana was good at her job; and she knew the work inside out. I thought that Mary resented that, perhaps she even feared that if she couldn't be seen to control her staff properly it would be Diana who replaced her.

By now I didn't like the situation I saw developing in the office. Diana was a worker, but she seemed to be isolated in the midst of a busy section. Maybe because she was in her mid-forties, whereas the others were mostly in their twenties. She was cooperative, pleasant and friendly, but she rarely socialized with her younger colleagues.

I knew why that was. She came in to work from outside the immediate area, and had a mother hospitalized in a convalescent home after a severe stroke. Between the extra travel and wanting to spend as much time as she could with her mother, Diana didn't want to waste what spare time she did have outside her job on drinking with fellow staff members after work.

I didn't blame her. I looked at the younger lot with whom I worked and felt I too had something better to do with my evenings. The other staff members were pleasant enough, but we had nothing in common. Sometimes I saw Diana considering our work-mates with amused tolerance. If the look ever turned wistful it was more along the lines of an older dog watching a tumble of puppies and envying all that youth and energy.

Not that the puppies stayed. It was something I'd noticed after eight months sharing their office. I knew what was behind a number of the departures. Many of those employed had taken the job to be able to add it to a CV. An increasing number of employers for help desk and allied jobs were insisting on experience. Four to six months was sufficient to count as the required experience. Of those who went, some also left because they disliked Mary Haslam and her need to control and belittle anyone with whom she worked.

We had no union representative. I didn't want the job. I'd done it for six years in my previous section, quitting ten years back and I didn't want the hassle again now that I was older. If I *had* been the union representative I'd have complained to management about our environment first. Apart from what was intended to be in the big open-plan office, they'd also crammed in a fax machine and all its supplies, along with a whole bank of extra cabinets, plus my own workstation and my decoder in a corner.

Perhaps I should have done something about the developing situation – but the truth was, I'd had the effects of a really bad and lingering cold for weeks. We were short-handed at my job so I'd kept working, but I had no energy left over to waste on arguments with Mary Haslam. So, I let it slide.

It did occur to me after Mary's arrival as supervisor, that I seemed to be hearing Diana's name a lot lately. Mary had something to say to her on a daily basis, and all of it seemed to be unpleasant. Others had started to take their cue from that and Diana was becoming the office scapegoat. Perhaps that was because they feared that Mary would turn on them if they didn't. Finally, after a loud scene in which Diana was accused of changing the figures on a log-in sheet, I looked up to intervene.

"That isn't true. Ken Charles changed the record." I looked Mary very firmly in the eye. "Ken asked me to initial the alteration." I received a savage glare in response to that, but Mary couldn't say much. Diana and I had the same first initial. But I initialed changes as DJMc. Diana initialed as DF. No similarity. After that Mary started to abuse me verbally. I took her aside at once.

"I'd prefer you didn't speak to me like that." I cut off what was to be a heated reply. "I don't work for you, Mary. I answer to the A.D. O/S. My workstation is simply in the office until the new annex is completed after which I'll be moving into third level tech support decoding."

Mary stared angrily at me. "What grade are you?" she asked abruptly.

"Third, direct, with a level one clearance." I replied, seeing that hit home. Officially I was the same grade as Mary, but the next bit meant I answered to no one but upper management, and my clearance was top level, far higher than hers. I was someone it wouldn't be smart to antagonize.

Mary left me alone from that time onwards, concentrating instead on making Diana's life miserable. Soon after that episode, I caught another cold which immediately turned nastier than the last one. I had to go home and nurse myself this time; it was too bad for me to continue to work. I was ill for two weeks and when I returned, it was clear things in the office had gone from bad to much worse.

Mary seemed to have stopped yelling at Diana in front of everyone. Initially I thought this was a good thing, until I heard the rumors that someone had made a confidential complaint about all the yelling in the office – and Mary had been censured. So she had instead begun calling Diana into the supervisor's office where she could yell at her in some sort of privacy. I saw the glitter of an almost sensual pleasure in her eyes when she could find an excuse to do that.

The atmosphere in the office was winding ever more tightly. People snapped at each other, sometimes refusing to cooperate when asked, sending unpleasant e-mails around the office and apparently forgetting to pass on important messages to those staff members with whom they were temporarily feuding. It was as if people were always holding their breath, waiting for an explosion. More staff found positions in other offices or departments and left.

Mary would fling open her door, yell for Diana to join her, then slam the door after her once Diana had obeyed. I made it a habit to walk past the door slowly at such times. I was worried about the atmosphere and I had never seen Diana as less than professional at her work. However, I had now heard her accused of incompetence, laziness, refusal to obey orders, and disrespect.

The personal accusations were even more unpleasant. I'd heard her told that her work mates disliked and distrusted her – something I knew was mostly untrue, but did Diana know it for the lie it was? She was told her dress sense was a disgrace to the workplace – it wasn't, but again, how would Diana feel after hearing that? There were other, extremely personal accusations, brutal and distressing, and again, quite untrue.

When Diana exited the office lately her eyes were those of a tortured beast. Dazed, agonized and uncomprehending. This latest time it was only a few minutes before twelve o'clock. I turned to take her by the arm, as soon as she left Mary's room, sweeping her with me from the office and out of the main building. We were outside before she asked a question.

"Where are we going?"

"To eat downtown. I think you could use a decent meal and a break from that place. I'm paying."

I knew most of her money went on keeping her mother in the home. I had no mother to support, lived nearby, had a little family money, and my sideline of writing articles on various aspects of security for professional magazines in our field added to my income.

Diana said nothing until we were safely behind a table. The food was very good at the place I had chosen to bring her, and I ordered an ample amount. I watched her as she dug in almost savagely. She finished, then sat back looking at me.

"Why?"

I knew she meant a number of questions all rolled up in one word. Why hadn't I done anything before? Why did Mary hate her? Why did no one do anything? I'd have found any of them hard if not impossible to explain. I'd done nothing to intervene before because I, like many of the others with whom she worked, didn't want to rock the promotion boat, didn't want to gain a reputation as a troublemaker, and personally I loathe public scenes.

Nor did Mary hate her – exactly. I believed she saw Diana as a target to be destroyed. Once Diana left the department Mary would find a new victim. She was insecure, afraid Diana's ability and work-reputation threatened her own position and authority. To destroy a threat also fed her ego. I'd read some of that in articles about office bullies. Some of this knowledge was based on my almost thirty years of workplace observation. But try getting that across to someone when you can't put a lot of it clearly. So, I shrugged.

"You looked as if you needed a break," I repeated. "Maybe you should consider making it permanent."

"You mean get a job somewhere else?"

I nodded.

An obstinate look answered that. "I need this job, and anyhow, why should I?"

I said nothing. If she couldn't see she'd be better off away from Mary and the section, what was the use of talking further? We went back to work together and Mary, eyeing me doubtfully, left her victim alone for the remainder of the day.

I was off on shift-change break for the next four days. I took the opportunity to go over and talk to Patti Paiwai; she'd been an old friend of my mother and Patti was street smart. She understood people and the way they thought and I hoped she'd give me another perspective on what was happening.

She listened, then nodded. "You're right, and I don't like the sound of any of it. There's going to be trouble sooner or later, Di. Best you step back from the situation now. I don't see how you can do anything short of going to management, and if they don't know what's happening already then they aren't much use. Stay out of it, girl. Watch everything so as you can be a witness if there's a need for one, but otherwise keep your head down."

I agreed with that, so I settled into my own work when I returned, saying no more than that I'd had a pleasant break. From things I heard, Mary had been quieter these last four days and the staff all seemed to be happy about that. All was peaceful in the section that morning until about half-past ten. Diana, looking a little more relaxed from the lack of stress, had gone to morning tea – but just as she got back, Mary slammed out of her office.

I felt tension in the room rise to an almost unbearable pitch of anticipation. The feeling was that of a massive thunderstorm about to break. The period where the air itself is electric, all the hairs on your arms rising as you tense, knowing that in minutes thunder will crash out, and lightning will tear open the sky. Involuntarily, I shivered.

"Diana, come in here!" The yelling started at once with the door not quite shut. I – and everyone else – heard the accusation that Diana always spent too long away from her desk. She was taking advantage of the already generous time allowed for breaks. Then Mary's voice dropped to a mutter, I couldn't hear what she said, but her tone was utterly vicious.

Diana emerged about ten minutes later, a sick greenish tinge under the stark white of her face. She went to her desk near mine, began to work in silence and then everyone in the office jumped as Mary tore the door open again, hitting the wall with a crash. She took one pace past the doorway and yelled.

"Diana, get in here, I want to speak to you again!"

Everyone looked away from them both in embarrassment as the tension ratcheted up that final unbearable notch. Everyone but me. I looked at Diana and saw the sudden brief change in her expression. For a second it was as if shutters dropped from the back of her eyes and a terrible raw hatred stared out of them. My gaze snapped away as the noise began. A low eerie snarling deep in the throats of everyone present but for Mary, Diana, and me.

It escalated into a deep-throated harshness of sound that shrieked danger. I felt the hair on the back of my neck rise and I found I was crouching lower as if my desk were a barricade between what was coming and me. Diana, sitting motionless behind her workstation, had her eyes fixed on Mary, who stood paralyzed with indecision in her office doorway still. I was frozen in place.

Abruptly there was movement like a tidal surge as our workmates flowed forwards around their desks, and Mary was drowned in the flood. She went down under their hands and feet with a chopped-off angry cry. The sounds that followed were something else; terror, agony. They lasted only a few seconds.

The hearing that was held some weeks later lasted a lot longer. I gave evidence of the brutal emotional abuse Mary had meted out and how even I, who was not under her authority, found it agonizing to witness. When asked for an opinion I suggested perhaps the incident had been some form of mass hysteria. A proxy attack. Two psychiatrists could do no better.

Most of the events quietly were swept under the carpet. The last thing our rather secret department wanted was newspaper reports saying a government department's supervisor had been slaughtered bare-handed in an attack by most of her workmates.

Those responsible were remanded for psychiatric examination. They were pronounced sane and very quietly released again a few days. The records of their act were expunged and they were moved on to other government departments. They would survive, and in a few months, the event in which they had participated would be no more than a vague memory to them.

Fortunately, Mary had no family to make a fuss and the department paid for a plain – and unattended – funeral. Mary's superior, who'd missed all the signs of trouble, took hasty early retirement while Diana who had taken no part in the attack, was found a suitable job in another department – where she remains.

So far as I know she's happy there, or at least content in her work and with those with whom she works. I moved into my own office and the third level job I'd expected. I'd very wisely kept my mouth shut on the subject of Mary's death – for which the department was duly grateful. They'd have been far more grateful if they'd known the one thing I'd told no one but Patti – who'd counselled I say nothing to anyone else, certainly not to my superiors or to the inquiry.

It was why I was sure that Diana's new job and new workmates suited her. Why I was quite certain that no one was bullying her there. It was when Mary had fallen under those punishing hands and feet, I had been doing as Patti suggested, I was sitting very quietly in my corner watching closely what happened, the only neutral observer the inquiry would have.

And for a fleeting time, a period as brief perhaps as fifths of a second, I had seen something I would never be able to forget. For that moment, the face of everyone attacking Mary, the faces of all those who trampled, punched, and kicked the one who had become the hated tormentor of all of them, had shown only one clear likeness. In those fractions of a second of murderous activity – they had all looked exactly like Diana.

A DOOR IN THE SUBWAY

The year Mrs. Hika Morrison was eighty-seven, the city's transport department completed the new subway. It provided clean and tidy electric transport across the city, around the suburbs, and all without adding to the traffic congestion. In fact, after it was running, many people chose not to use cars to travel in the inner city and switched to using the new trains.

Hika disliked the subway but she had to use it for any journey of more than two or three blocks. She usually couldn't afford taxis on her pension, she wasn't permitted to drive, and the younger generation lived so much further from the city center.

But this house was the one in which she'd been born. On their marriage, her husband had joined her here; in this house too he had died so that now she lived alone except for her much-loved big black cat to whom she talked because, mostly, there was no one else. Unless her old friend Ngaire – known as Granny by a cheeky younger generation – called to visit for a while.

"You know," she said to Ngaire one day as they shared afternoon tea, "things have changed so much around here. I remember when there were trees all down this street. It was so nice in summer and quite safe for a girl to take a walk – even after dark."

She sighed, remembering last night's newspaper. There'd been a story about a child abducted from an ordinary street. What was worse, it was a street that Hika had walked down more than once on her way to buy groceries. The police had recovered the child unharmed, but everyone concerned was traumatized by the event. There was also the accident recently suffered by a neighbor when some young idiot had raced his car down the quiet street and nearly killed the old man who couldn't dodge in time.

There were other strange stories lately too. A local woman had apparently vanished somewhere in the city. A younger woman of course, a mere seventy, but she'd taken the new subway home from her daughter's house and never arrived – or so her neighbors said. At least there'd been no sign of her since and the newspaper said, "grave fears are held for her safety." Her daughter didn't seem to be much concerned, more annoyed at the fuss and inconvenience. Hika guessed that the woman was hoping to inherit her mother's house, and she wondered how her own grandchildren would feel if she vanished.

Mrs. Morrison shook her head. Life had changed so since she was a girl in this house. The trees in her street had been cut down when they widened the road in 1980. She still missed the cool green shade they'd provided. She missed the long strip of lawn that had surrounded them too, even though it had had to be mowed regularly. Most of her old neighbors had moved away over the years – those that hadn't died.

Ngaire nodded, her own thoughts following a similar trail. "I know, it's the same in my street. Everything changes and there are times when I just want to stand in the middle of the road and demand it stops. That nothing alters anymore." She sighed quietly. "But that's progress for you. I've even had offers to buy my house, and everyone knows I'd never sell."

Hika snorted. "I've had those too. Some young man who seemed to think that offering me half the amount my house is worth and talking about how I could retire to live peacefully in the country would make me keen to sell. Idiot! I was born in this house in this city, why would I want to go and live in the country? It's too quiet out there, I was on holiday once with my husband and we couldn't sleep for the quiet. I just wish this street stayed as unchanged as the inside of my house and I'd have no complaints."

Ngaire agreed with that as her gaze took in the furniture that had been new when Hika's mother was married, the curtains that were replaced regularly but always in the same material and style as the originals. She admired the neat lace doilies under ornaments, the lace runner along the sideboard, and the crocheted headrests on the armchairs.

"You're right. And I dislike the subway as much as you do, my dear. But I suppose there isn't much choice these days, you have to use it sometimes."

She went home that afternoon feeling sorry for her friend. Poor Hika. She was just far enough out from the city center that she needed to use that infernal subway for almost any trip she made. Granny Ngaire thanked heaven that she herself lived in the heart of the city and had no need to do more than walk to her destination and home again most times.

Hika Morrison put away the tea tray and its contents and settled onto her couch for the evening. In the morning, she rose reluctantly for breakfast, sighing as she cleared the table after her solitary meal, finished the dishes and reached for her coat and purse. She hated the subway certainly but she must go shopping. In two days her grandchildren would call to have lunch with her. She plodded to the subway entrance dragging her trundler and thinking that at least there was an escalator to save her the stairs. The train came silently into the platform and her shopping day started.

At last, wearily, she was returning, so tired that she no longer watched the subway walls as she trudged along – until she noticed that at a bend in the corridor there lay a small door marked with an exit sign. Hika paused and stared thoughtfully at it. That was odd, she hadn't used the escalator yet so she should still be underground. How could there be an exit door? She hoped she wasn't having a senior moment?

She glanced about her. It was well before the time when rush hour started and there was no one near her in the subway. Mrs. Morrison moved unobtrusively to the door, opened it and peered out. For a moment she stared in astonishment. Her mouth opened as if to exclaim – then slowly shut again.

She looked again at the incredible scene that met her fascinated gaze. Out there were the familiar trees, rooted deep in the tidy strip of curbside lawn on the quiet street of her childhood. Her house across the road from the doorway gleamed with fresh paint, the lawn had been neatly and recently mowed, with the flowers standing bright and proud around the house footings and along the white picket fence. Everything there was as it had been when she was a girl.

She had to be dreaming, yet so strong was the pull of what she saw that she would have stepped through the door and into the dream but for a sudden thought. If she was going mad and seeing things, who would look after Sooty? If she wasn't, then the same question applied. She couldn't let go and accept the dream. There was Ngaire too, what would her oldest friend say if Hika vanished or went mad? No, she'd walk home, have a nice cup of tea and think about this for a day or two.

Once she was home, Hika reached for the phone and summoned her friend. "I saw it Ngaire, my own street the way it used to be. The trees were there, the lawns, my house was – well, it looked as if it had been painted only the other day and all the flowers my mother used to plant were in bloom."

"What time of the year was it?"

Hika thought back. "Spring!" she said decidedly. "I'm sure it was spring. All the horse chestnuts along the street were flowering."

Ngaire sounded thoughtful. "It's almost winter now. I don't think it was a dream, dear. I think it may have been an opportunity, but I quite see that you'd want to take Sooty and say goodbye to me."

Hika Morrison looked at her old friend and saw she was serious. She nodded and changed the subject. She would think the whole thing over for a day or two as she'd intended. The day or two became a week, then a month. The stories in the newspaper seemed to be uniformly unpleasant, and fights in the street twice disturbed Mrs. Morrison. Her street. A place that up until now had been free of that sort of casual violence. The estate agent called again, she had an obscene phone call, and another neighbor sold his house and moved away to live with his daughter's family in a town to the north.

But then came the day when she must take Sooty in for his annual vaccination. She considered the journey carefully. Going in, she would meet many of the morning rush hour workers on the way to their hive-like offices. It would be hot, noisy and miserably crowded in the subway. She should take a taxi in. She could afford it one way and on the return trip she would be traveling outside the usual rush hour. She did so and emerged from the clinic with an indignant and vaccinated cat in the plastic and wire carrier.

Wearily she plodded to the escalator and leaned a little on the railing as she descended. The subway always seemed to be too hot, Sooty was heavy and she was so tired. At the foot of the escalator, she trudged down the passage that seemed to stretch out as she walked. A breath of cool, fresh air suddenly reached out to touch her wrinkled cheek. Sooty gave a small mew of interest. Mrs. Morrison's head came up in a jerky movement that was half hope, half fear.

Before her was the door again – small, painted a nondescript gray-green, set in a deep alcove in the concrete wall, with the exit sign glittering invitingly at her. She paused, then accepted the offer and opened the door.

Outside in the quiet street, the horse chestnut trees rustled in the soft invitation of spring, the warm air seemed to stroke her cheek again while her house gleamed before her in the sunlight of early afternoon. She looked down. Sooty was with her this time. If this were madness at least they'd go into it together.

Hika Morrison clutched the cat carrier and stepped quietly through the door. She paused to look behind her, up and down the subway tunnel. There was no one in sight. Hika turned to shut the door firmly behind her, denying a world in which no one cared for their neighbors any more, in which atrocities and terrorism happened and were regarded almost as parts of life instead of the terrible events they were. All around her the air carried the light, sweet scent of her mother's lilacs. She felt suddenly light, young again as all the sights, sounds and scents of spring poured over her.

She glanced down to find that the carrier was now a wicker basket although it still contained the same cat, but – hadn't she had Sooty when she was a young girl? She was sure she remembered him. The odd dual memory faded as Hika Rapata shrugged; why was she standing here by the brick wall of the old theater? Her parents were expecting her home. Laughing, she shook out her calf-length skirt to walk lightly across the quiet street. She opened the wicket gate, smiling up at the soft green of the trees. Her street was timeless; nothing would ever change here.

Nor did it.

LEAVING THE NEST

Tina sat miserably on the sofa listening to her parents argue. It looked as if she'd be off to her high school prize-giving without them again this evening. The third year in a row.

"It's your turn. I have work."

"And my work isn't important I suppose? I have to have this presentation done before tomorrow."

"You knew you were going with Tina tonight. You should have done the presentation before."

"I couldn't. It's an emergency and Mike gave it to me only today."

"Then you should have said he'd have to wait." His wife looked at him in silence and he backed up. "Well, no, maybe not. But I can't go; I have to leave here at seven for dinner with an important client. And I can't skip it. The appointment was made days ago and he'll already be on the way."

Her mother looked over to where Tina sat on the sofa trying to look as if she didn't care about being argued over like an unwanted parcel.

"You're fifteen, sweetie. You're more than old enough to go on your own. I'll talk to the taxi company. They'll send a nice woman driver to pick you up and take you to the prize-giving, and she can go back to bring you home. You can wait for her down in the lobby if you want to. That'd be okay, wouldn't it?"

Tina didn't say that being old enough to go on her own wasn't the point. It was prize-giving, the one evening in the year when she really wanted her parents there. The one evening when it would have been nice if, just for once, it was she who was central in their lives. She wondered, as she'd done before, why they'd bothered to have a daughter if they never had time for her – but under the hopeful gaze of two adults, she shrugged.

"It'll be fine. I can sit with Lyn and Janice and their parents." Their slightly anxious faces asked for further reassurance and automatically she provided it. "Don't worry. You have work to do and I'll be okay."

They turned identically relieved looks in her direction. "If you're sure, dear?" her mother said.

"Yeah, I'll see you when I get home."

"I'll be here," her mother said brightly. "I'll probably be up until midnight on this presentation anyway."

Yeah, Tina thought, as she headed for her bedroom to dress for the school event. *Of course you will. It's nothing to do with waiting up to hear how I did, I told you I've won a couple of prizes and that I was short-listed for the Melford Prize as well this year. It'll be another year before it's given out but if they announce tonight that I'm still in the running then I have a good chance.*

If I win it, I get five years' worth of study paid for from the time I'm eighteen. I can choose the university I attend. I can pick what courses I want to do – even if neither of you approve of them – and I can afford to take both my degrees without having to worry about taking out a loan or relying on you. It's a huge deal for me. I don't even know yet what courses I really want to do anyway.

"Tina, I've called the taxi, they'll be here at a quarter to seven."

"Thanks, Mum."

Her mind went on muttering angrily as she washed, dressed, and made up discreetly. She mostly loved her parents and she thought that they loved her. It wasn't that. She even knew that they'd have happily paid for her to take her degree when she left high school in another three years. It was the idea of being independent of their money that she liked. Being able to say she was taking this degree or that and knowing that she could, that they couldn't say they'd pay only for one they approved.

And more and more lately, while she didn't know what she wanted to study, she felt that whatever it was, it could be something that they wouldn't like. Something they'd consider a waste of time. Why was that? It was as if something in the back of her head was starting to gel, as if she already knew what she wanted to do but her subconscious wasn't ready to let her know yet.

"Tina? Taxi's here, dear."

Oh, it was early. She gave her parents absent-minded hugs, raced for the lift, and descended to the lobby, waving politely to the man who guarded the privacy of those who lived in the flats. Outside the big revolving glass doors, she climbed into the taxi and shut the door. She supposed it wasn't that bad having parents who both had important, well-paid jobs.

They could afford a big penthouse at the top of a new building in the heart of the city, and a housekeeper who came in at ten every morning and stayed until six in the evening. Tina had decent presents and if she could make out a good case for it, she could usually wheedle anything she really wanted from one parent or the other. But there were times when she saw Jan's or Lyn's mum paying her friends real attention and Tina felt sort of left out.

Her parents couldn't even manage one single evening in the year to come and see their daughter accept her prizes. And the only thing she'd ever wanted with all her heart they wouldn't give her. She'd asked a number of times over the years.

"I'd walk it, honestly, Mum?"

"We can't have a dog, dear. They're noisy and we go away too often – and besides, our lease says no pets."

That argument didn't make sense to Tina when she was two years younger. She could train the dog not to bark, and it could stay in boarding kennels when they were away; she was sure her parents could get the management to agree too, but her parents were adamant on the subject. No dog.

They had similar reasons for rejecting a kitten for her, and no, she couldn't have cage birds, or even fish. They were all good arguments and her parents didn't see – or didn't want to see – that Tina's main reason for wanting a pet was that she was lonely in the big penthouse when she was alone except for the housekeeper. That was not susceptible to reasoned arguments.

Tina stepped out of the taxi at the school and paused to admire the glittering lights that draped the old brick façade. It looked pretty good and she could see Jan's car just arriving. Tina turned to her taxi-driver.

"Thank you, did my mother say that I'd be ready to come home at any particular time."

"At ten o'clock, she said."

"That's fine. I'll be waiting for you then."

"Okay, dear. You enjoy yourself. Prize-giving is it?"

Tina looked at the taxi driver for the first time. She saw a pleasant-faced Maori woman in her mid-thirties. The woman's face had deep smile lines and Tina suddenly liked her on the spot.

"Yes, I'm up for two prizes and short-listed for another important one in a couple of years." She wanted to tell someone.

"That's wonderful." The tone was enthusiastic. "I think everyone should make the most of school. I wish I had."

Tina lingered. "Why didn't you?"

"I didn't know how important it would be. I messed about, didn't study much, then when I left, I got married."

"Do you have children?" Tina asked politely.

"No, my husband was killed in a crash after we'd been married five years. I'd have liked kids but it didn't happen. I was drifting for quite a few years, But I finally figured out what I wanted to do and now I drive a taxi. I meet a lot of interesting people and I'm saving to buy a second car and license. One day I may have my own company."

Her gaze went to something behind Tina. "I think your friends want you, I'll see you at ten. Have a great night."

Tina glanced over her shoulder and saw Janice and Lyn walking towards her. "I will. Thanks." She shut the door and turned to meet the questions.

"No, they couldn't come *again*, but it's okay. I can sit with you two, your parents won't mind, will they?"

"Of course not." Lyn was reassuring. "They like you." She grinned. "Mum says we're the three musketeers and there's times she expects to be tucking all of us into bed together at night and she's surprised to find it's just me."

Tina laughed. It was true she and Janice did spend a lot of

time at Lyn's house. There were sleepovers, dinners, study evenings, and now and then she'd stayed a weekend while the three of them were doing something special. Lyn's mum didn't go out to work. She always said she had enough to do at home and that it was important for Lyn to find her at home after school.

Tina thought wistfully that it would be nice to come home herself sometimes and find her own mother waiting for her daughter. A mother who wasn't always engrossed in government papers and too busy to listen, but someone who was eager to hear about Tina's day and interested in what her daughter had to tell her.

On the other hand, she thought as she followed her friends and their parents into the big auditorium to find their seats, there were benefits to having working parents. Pocket money was generous, she had all the latest computer stuff, and so long as she told Mrs. Wallington, the housekeeper, where she was going, her parents didn't hassle her about being at friends' places or out around the shops.

She knew Janice and Lyn were envious of the freedom her parents gave her, her ample allowance, and the fancy building where she lived. She'd never let on to them that she envied them just as much for other things, although she thought they suspected. She sat and waited eagerly as the lights dimmed, the school staff filed onto the platform, and the prize-giving started.

Fifth form prizes were being given out. "And the winner of the Perdue cup for highest total of marks in this year's exams goes to Tina Salton." Tina went up to collect the cup, a small, beautifully engraved and ornamented piece of silver given by a woman who'd left Melford private school thirty years earlier.

Tina accepted the cup, the certificate, and the book vouchers that came with it, turned and smiled out at the sea of faces, before walking back to her seat. About ten minutes later she was rising from her chair again along with her two friends.

"And the winners of this year's Johanson Award are Janice Murall, Tina Salton and Lyn Warne. This award is given to the pupil or pupils who completed a single outstanding project and this year. These three girls won it for their work which was entered in the science fair and which won a special award from the Department of Conservation..."

Tina wasn't listening as Ms. Harper rabbited on about their entry and how great it had been. It had been fun doing it, and it had been her suggestion that they studied the city's wild bird population. The Salton penthouse roof had been the perfect aerie from which to watch with their binoculars and list the birds and their carefully observed behavior. They'd taken some great photos to illustrate the project as well.

But the Johanson Award gave them only a cup to share and more book vouchers. It was the Melford results so far that she wanted to hear read out. That wouldn't be until the end of the prize-giving though. Right now, it was pleasant to have Janice and Lyn's parents congratulate the three of them and admire the silver cup they'd take turns to display at their homes.

The vouchers were a bigger deal to her friends – five hundred dollars' worth. She knew her friends' parents made sacrifices to have Janice and Lyn attend Melford. There wasn't a lot to spare for some of the more expensive books her friends wanted.

"Five hundred dollars' worth," Janice marveled. "How do we split them up?"

"You two split them," Tina offered. "I got the Perdue and there's a stack of book vouchers goes with that anyway."

"Are you sure?"

"Yeah." She didn't have to add what they all knew. That if she wanted books her parents would buy them for her. They'd be happy that she wanted something they could give her that didn't cost them in time. Money was less difficult to find. Her friends understood and anyhow, they knew Tina was right; the Perdue came with five hundred dollars' worth of book vouchers. She could easily afford to let Janice and Lyn share the Johanson prize.

"Okay. Want to go book shopping tomorrow?"

"Yeah, sure." It'd be more fun if they each had a lot of the vouchers, Tina thought. She enjoyed spending time with her friends in bookshops. They'd get such a kick out of being able to buy the more expensive books this time and the book shops would be open on a Saturday.

"See you at my place at ten?" Janice hissed. Tina and Lyn nodded. The prize-giving had continued as they whispered and Tina felt her stomach give a sudden lurch as she realized what the headmistress had said.

"And this is the announcement of the short-listing this year for the Melford Award. As some of you know, this award is given every five years to the girl we think is best able to make use of it to obtain her degree or degrees at university. The actual winner of the award is announced two years before she may take it up, when the winner is sixteen, in order to give her time to consider which studies she wishes to pursue in her seventh form year.

"Each year for the first four years we announce the continuing short-listed candidates. The last year before the scholarship is taken; there is additional money also set aside to help the winner take extra-mural or special courses towards her eventual goal. This year the candidates still in the running are Mary Anaru, Karen Wright, and Tina Salton."

Tina slumped back in her seat showing a blank face to the world, but inwardly rejoicing. She was still on the list. Next year she'd be sixteen and they'd announce who'd won the award. Then she had two years in the sixth and seventh form to decide which career she wanted to pursue.

She bit back a small sigh. Both of her parents had been trying to persuade her to follow one of their own career choices. But the idea of being a CEO or director of a government department didn't appeal. Both jobs paid good money of course. But somehow, she loathed the idea of being in a small office all day, of never having enough time to do what she wanted because there was always another important meeting, another presentation to do, another work-related person to meet for dinner while all you ever talked about was the job.

Everyone was getting up. Tina stood with her friends and allowed the others in her classes to admire her cup and the other cup that Janice was carrying. There was a cheerful babble of congratulations and jokes.

"Why do I have to drink my tea out of a saucer? Because this lot have all the cups – and the money to buy them." That was Karen Wright. On the words, it was just a joke, but there was a slight edge to the tone that told Tina that Karen wasn't as amused as she sounded.

"Oh, well, next year you'll probably win the Melford then you can buy yourself a whole new tea service," Tina responded, grinning to show goodwill. She saw the flash of dislike as Karen looked at her.

"I intend to."

Janice stepped in quietly. "Tina, are you coming back with us, we can drop you at your place as we go home, it's on our way."

Tina turned away and lowered her voice. Karen was still standing there and she didn't need a smart crack about rich kids and their limousines.

"I've got a taxi coming," she glanced at her watch, "in about ten minutes. I'll come outside with you though – to get away from *her* for a start."

Lyn snorted. "Yeah, she's got a thing about rich kids, but the weird bit is that her family's got money too. Neither of you really needs the Melford."

Janice looked at them and lowered her voice. "No, she doesn't but her father wants her to win it. He expects her to win everything. I heard him being nasty to her tonight because she didn't get the Perdue. He was saying that either she hadn't inherited the family brains or she hadn't worked hard enough."

"What's his problem?"

"Dunno."

Lyn was impatient. "Who cares?" She held up the cup. "We won the Johanson. We can buy heaps of books, and we'll have our names in the school magazine. My family thinks I'm brilliant. That'll do me."

Janice grinned. "I bet you didn't tell them the project was all Tina's idea?"

"What am I, an idiot? I said we thought it up together. We did our share of the work anyhow."

Tina smiled. "Yes, you did. And it was just something I thought of one day when I was up on the penthouse roof. It doesn't matter who thought of it, we all did the work together and we all won."

She remembered that moment when she'd sneaked up onto the roof as she often did. The building management didn't officially permit it, but so long as she didn't do anything silly and get hurt, no one would complain. There'd been a big downturn in renting for the more expensive city penthouses since their building had gone up. A lot of the really expensive apartments and penthouses were standing empty and management wouldn't want to irritate her parents into leaving.

Tina had stood on the roof watching the pigeons and seagulls circling. There were other birds up here too, some nested in sheltered hidden corners on building roofs and last year a pair of New Zealand hawks had actually nested on her own roof. That had been in September and the babies had been so cute. The parents had hunted in the hills past the Gorge and Tina hadn't told anyone what was on the roof. It wasn't really a nest anyway, just a couple of broken twigs tucked under the edge of the cornice, and three fluffy nestlings that didn't seem afraid of her when their parents were gone.

They'd flown eventually, and this year the hawks hadn't returned. She hoped the fledglings were okay, flying free somewhere. Nesting and rearing their own babies in turn and living as they were supposed to do. It was remembering them that had made her suggest the "wild birds in the city" project. The man from the Department of Conservation had been quite impressed by their statistics, written observations, and photographs. He'd even asked if any of them were considering a career in that sort of work. They'd all said that they didn't think so, but Tina had wondered about the idea since then. She wasn't sure and her parents would have a cow at the idea.

The taxi was already waiting as she said goodbye to her friends and their parents. She climbed into the front seat clutching her purse, the Perdue cup, her certificate and envelope of vouchers, and she was greeted with a warm smile.

"Looks as if you did okay for yourself."

The driver looked genuinely interested and Tina found herself telling her about the prize-giving as they weaved through the streets.

"Good job with the bird project. I know there's a lot of different ones in the city. I wouldn't mind seeing your stuff on them sometime?"

Tina remembered she'd be going to the bookshops tomorrow when they'd be open, but most schools would be shut. She'd said she meet Janice and Lyn at Janice's place. "Can you pick me up tomorrow about nine-thirty, I'm going into Kelburn?"

"Sure, I don't have classes on a Saturday."

"I'll bring a copy of the bird project for you to read. It doesn't matter if you don't give it back."

"Thanks. I bet my grandmother would like to see it too. She knows about the birds here. She's lived in the city her whole life."

"I don't mind if she sees it." Tina offered. The taxi came to a halt outside her building and she scrambled out holding her gear. "I'll be ready at nine-thirty tomorrow."

"Okay, see you then."

Tina plodded into the lobby of her apartment building feeling a bit let down. It had been a pretty good evening, but it would have been even better if one of her own family had been there to congratulate her. She traveled up in the lift, used her key and entered the lounge quietly. Her mother had papers spread all over the table and her greeting was absent-minded.

"How did you do, darling?"

"I won the Perdue. Janice, Lyn and I got the Johanson – and I'm still on the Melford short-list," Tina said concisely.

"That's nice, darling. Now you're home, make me a cup of coffee, will you? I should be finished with this in another hour and you can tell me about it."

Tina made a whole pot of coffee, brought a cup in and reported that there was more coffee staying hot in the percolator. Then she went quietly to bed. When she was younger, she'd have stayed up waiting, only to find that her mother would take longer than she'd said and would be too tired to listen to Tina once she was finished with the work. Her father must be still out with the client and Tina wasn't waiting up for him either.

The next morning was fun though, as she'd expected. Ms. Paiwai picked her up in the taxi and accepted the folder with the copy of the bird project with enthusiasm. "That's great, thanks. I told Granny Ngaire about it and she's dying to read it too."

Tina beamed at her. "Tell your grandmother if she really likes it, you're welcome to keep it."

She found she was talking again, about the birds she'd seen from her roof, about her parents who never seemed to have time for her, and about her friends' families who always had time not only for their own children, but for her as well. She shut herself up after a while. The poor woman didn't want to hear all that. She was silent then until she was dropped off at Janice's home near the university.

Janice met her inside, swept Tina into her bedroom where Lyn was waiting, and produced a list of the books they'd like to buy if they could stretch their vouchers that far. They carefully considered the long list before Janice asked.

"What are you going to buy with your Perdue vouchers?"

Tina shrugged. "Dunno. I'll probably see something once we get there."

"Then let's go."

They caught the cable car down the hill and wandered out onto the Quay. Once at the nearest bookshop Tina found her attention drawn to a new stack of books the shop assistant was just placing in a cardboard display unit. The unit had a sign saying "Discounted for damage." The books were beautiful and Tina couldn't see any damage. She looked over the top book, studying the title and the author before opening the copy to flip quickly through the pages.

"New Zealand's Extinct Birds," said the girl stacking more into the unit. "It's very good value. It's by some chap who knows what he's talking about and the pictures are great."

"How can they have pictures of extinct birds?" Tina asked – reasonably, as she thought. In reply she received a mildly disgusted look.

"They have drawings of the birds, and some of them haven't been extinct that long, so there's still stuffed ones around museums. Then there's water colors by artists who drew the live birds back in the eighteen hundreds."

"Oh. Yes. I guess." Tina was looking at the watercolor of a moa knee deep in ferns; it was all in browns and greens and looked stunning. That had to be the artist's imagination. She was sure moas hadn't been around even in the eighteen hundreds. Still, the drawings and stuff were great as the girl said and the price wasn't nearly as bad as she'd expected.

"I can't see any damage?"

The girl nodded. "It isn't obvious, but somehow they bound one section in the wrong place. The page numbering is okay in the index, but the book pages themselves go from one to fifty, then from a hundred to one-fifty and then back to pages fifty to one hundred. It happened with only thirty copies. The printer said someone there put a few of the book sections in the wrong bin."

"Why didn't they reprint the damaged ones?"

"I guess with only thirty copies wrong in the whole edition it wasn't worth it. Anyway, we're selling them on special, they are first edition and down the track the dud ones may be worth more than the ones which weren't printed up wrong. The book's going to be a classic and they'll print thousands and thousands in the next ten years. But only thirty will be like this." She laid a hand on the nearest copy. "Want to buy one?"

Tina looked at the book and spoke without thinking any further about it. "Yes, please."

She picked up the copy she'd looked at, closed it and headed for the counter to pay. It sort of pleased her that of all the copies that would eventually be printed over the years, she would have one that wasn't only a first edition, it was one that was different. She'd use that "investment" suggestion on her parents if they queried her buying the book. She handed over several of her book vouchers and went in search of her friends, discovering them in conversation at one of the other counters.

"What did you get?" That was Lyn.

"Book on extinct birds. You?"

"Horses." Lyn showed her a large book with a photograph of herd of wild horses racing over a plain across the cover and another with a horse and rider doing what appeared to be dressage. Janice displayed her own acquisitions, a book of Shakespeare's plays, and another on the art of stage dressing.

"Nice," Tina approved. "If we're done here, what about having lunch in town before we go back?"

"Back as in my place or are you going home?"

"Home sometime, I guess. I had breakfast really early and left before my parents were up. Today they'll want to see the stuff I won and talk about it – if they have time."

"Yeah. Oh, well, let's go and eat. See you Sunday too maybe? Mum's taking me to the beach and Jan's coming. Be nice if you came too?"

"Yeah, okay. When?"

"Be at my place at ten." Tina nodded agreement before they left the shop and strolled down the street to eat at a nearby café. She left them there an hour later and caught a bus home, her new book tucked securely into her shopping bag. Once she walked into the penthouse, she found her parents had eaten, completed their work, and had time in hand to admire her own achievements. Tina produced the Perdue cup and certificate, her certificate for the Johanson award, and her scroll to say she was short-listed for the Melford.

"That's very well done, darling. Isn't there a cup that goes with the Johanson award though?"

Tina nodded. "We're taking it in turns to have that. Four months each in alphabetical order, so Jan gets it first because she's M."

Her father spoke up. "Hang on, wasn't the original idea for that project yours? You shouldn't let other people take your credit."

"I'm not. We did all the work together and we share equally. That's fair."

The last two words made it clear to him that he should drop the subject and, wisely, Mr. Salton did. He disagreed in silence however. If you let other people steal your ideas you never got ahead, but then Tina had a few more years before that would become an issue. She'd have learned better by then – or at least he hoped so.

"I see you've been spending some of those book vouchers you won." He changed the subject. "Did you find anything interesting?"

"Yes. Look at this." She produced "New Zealand's Extinct Birds," and displayed it on the table. "Isn't it beautiful?" She flipped the pages to show them the painting of the moa in his ferns as her parents exchanged baffled looks.

"Very nice, dear, but – um – what use is it?"

As she'd thought. They couldn't see her using a book on birds as a study guide to the wildlife in offices and Government

Departments. Tina opened the book to the wrongly numbered pages and explained.

"It's an investment. The shop said that the initial printing was for five thousand copies, and so many have been ordered from overseas museums and libraries that they've already printed another edition. Only thirty copies in the first edition had this error. In twenty years, my copy could be really valuable, but I got it at a big discount."

The looks over her head this time were relieved. Their daughter was sensible. Investing the money she'd won in something which could make a good profit in time to come. They admired the book more honestly, giving Tina approving glances.

"You should have it properly covered with a clear plastic sleeve," her father suggested. "I could take it into work and have it done there for you, if you like?"

It would keep her book clean, Tina thought, and being able to do it for her would please her father. She thanked him graciously.

"I'll give you the book Monday morning."

"Don't forget."

"I won't." She wouldn't either. She took the book to her room and just sat on the bed thinking for a while. She'd won two prizes and bought a wonderful book. And all her parents thought about was that she should take credit for her friends' work as well as her own, and that her book – no matter how gorgeous and interesting – was still worth having only as an investment. She found she was crying silently and forced back the tears. It wasn't any good bawling, and her life and her parents could be a lot worse.

She remembered Karen Wright who'd worked really really hard all year to stay on the list for the Melford Award – and whose father didn't even praise her because he thought she should have done still better. Janice and Lyn's parents loved their daughters and they supported them in almost everything they did. But they didn't have the money for some things whereas Tina's mum and dad would buy her almost anything she asked for if she gave good reasons why she wanted it.

She cradled the book, thinking that her life and parents weren't so bad. If only they'd change – just a little bit. And if only she could decide what it was that she wanted to do with the rest of her life once she'd left school. And if only whatever she decided on was something her mum and dad approved. Or – if they didn't – if only she won the Melford and could afford to do what she wanted with her life anyway.

She grinned. Jan's mum used to say, "if wishes were horses, beggars would ride." Tina had a sudden mental image of a horde of the city's homeless thundering down Manners Street, the cops trying to stop them, the horses scaring car drivers into driving off the road and making people on the pavements jump aside. It cheered her up a lot. Life was okay really. She had friends and her book.

All that week she didn't have her book though. Her father took it into work to be covered and kept forgetting to bring it home until Tina was quite exasperated with him.

"I'm sorry." he kept saying. "I'll bring it back tomorrow." In the end Tina sneaked into her parents' bedroom on Friday before breakfast and stuck Post-it notes through the work in his briefcase, each saying the same thing. "Please bring my bird book home today!" Her father laughed when he found them during an office meeting and remembered this time.

Tina sat up late that Friday night reading the book. She loved the paintings, the drawings, and the bits of odd information that caught her attention. Here were the huia with their differently shaped beaks. It astounded Tina that birds should evolve to live as a pair in that way. Each with a different beak so they could supplement each other's hunting. She loved the moa, the huge ones that stood over two meters high and the tiny little ones the size of a chicken. She should go to the museum some time and see what they had there.

But the next school year started and she had work to do. Tina often asked for Nerida Paiwai to drive her now if she needed a taxi and they had become quite good friends. Once she'd asked Granny Ngaire to visit and she had. She was a strange old lady but Tina liked her. Over cups of tea Granny had told her something about the city.

"A city has its own life. Within the city are all the times and buildings that have ever been part of it. Sometimes, if you look at the city sideways you can see things that aren't there anymore."

Tina wasn't sure she believed that, but it was fun to think about when she had spare time, which wasn't very often just now. Her bird book lay on the shelf unopened for months as Tina went to classes, studied with her friends, and came back to the penthouse with homework sufficient to keep her occupied all evening.

Nerida had talked about the bird project. "Granny loved your project, she said I should remember to thank you for letting her read it. Are you going to do something else like that this year?"

"I guess not. I'm busier and there seems to be fewer birds about lately anyhow."

But in the early hours of one morning in September she heard odd sounds from her open window. They seemed to come from above her; cries, like a bird in distress or angry. Could the hawks have come back? Was one hurt? Tina scrambled into her dressing gown and went silently to investigate. There was a short ladder that could be pulled down in a corner of the passage outside the penthouse door. She hauled at it until it unfolded and the steps grounded and locked into position. Then she climbed up, her torch in one hand. The door onto the roof opened quietly and Tina stepped out.

It was a fine night, still and clear, with the stars showing like a million tiny eyes above her. In the corner where the hawks had nested, she could see something move. She stared. It was weeks since she'd been up here and the birds would have had time to nest, lay and hatch their usual three eggs in that time, but this wasn't three babies tumbled together. She moved her torch beam warily towards it, not wanting to blind the creature.

Then she stared as enough light shone on the moving body to show her what it looked like. It was huge. It must be almost ready to fly at that size, but there was blood on the concrete and along the railing, and the baby bird was making distressed sounds. Maybe the blood was something it had had to eat? And maybe not, a voice inside of her commented. Maybe the parents had been injured. There'd been a scraping sound going down the side of the wall by her window at the same time as the cries began.

Tina padded briefly back to her own room, grabbed her birding binoculars and peered down at the street below in the growing half-light. Just in time to see an oddly large bundle of feathers run over by a truck. What the heck *was* that thing? It looked to have been as big as an ostrich! It gave a dying squawk which carried upwards in the cool silence as it was flattened by the eighteen-wheeler. Somehow Tina knew it was the baby's mother; or perhaps the father – but a parent either way – and now the baby was probably an orphan. It was up to her to do something about that.

She returned to the roof to look at her new bird project. The project stared back, then opened its beak and produced a penetrating scream. Tina winced. If her parents heard that noise, the baby would be on the way to the SPCA in minutes. She raced back down the stairs and rummaged in the fridge.

Yes! A whole raw chicken her mother was thawing for dinner that evening. She fished another one out of the freezer and left it to thaw so that her action would not be noticed, then she rushed back up to the roof to offer the first chicken to the nestling. It eyed her and the offering doubtfully.

"Come on, it's food. Just eat it." It dawned on her that mother birds rarely offered their nestlings a plucked, still cold chicken, but that was what she had right now. Maybe after school she could find a shop that would sell her whole, unplucked raw chickens? She could give them a quick burst in the microwave to warm them into a semblance of just-killed prey.

Thc baby made up its mind and grabbed. Tina let go hastily. That beak looked sharp and really powerful. If the baby got her instead of the chicken, she'd have holes in her hand that would be just as hard to explain to her parents as the baby's screams would be if they were heard. She watched as the nestling tore its food apart and ate ravenously. One problem solved. On a full belly, her new project sank down, fluffed out, and appeared to fall into a coma.

After that, if Tina had thought she was busy this school year, she came to understand she'd been only coasting. Caring for her new friend took up time – lots of it. Money too. In a couple of weeks, the baby wanted either two chickens or a whole small turkey each time it fed. But he'd also come to know her. The small eager burbling sound he made when she appeared delighted her. The wicked beak was never used against her. Instead, he would draw strands of her hair though it, breaking off to nibble very gently along her bare arm.

Tina kept her mouth shut about "Icarus" as she'd named him. She was fairly sure her parents would have a cow if they saw the size of her friend, and they'd insist he went to some sanctuary where experts could care for him. Looking at Icarus one afternoon Tina wondered just what experts would be needed anyhow. It had been clear from the start that he wasn't a hawk. New Zealand didn't have eagles, although that was what he looked like, but maybe his parents had escaped from a zoo or wildlife park.

She read enough bird books since she'd discovered him to fill a small shop and all of them said that he was larger than anything she could find, except a South American Condor. If he was one of those, at his current size he should be flying by now anyhow, and he wasn't. She'd come to believe that he'd been just feathered when she found him, which meant he could grow bigger yet. She eyed Icarus and grinned. Maybe she'd found a dragon. If he kept growing, he was going to be big enough in a few months to match the descriptions of such mythical creatures.

"Are you coming to the movies tonight? It's Saturday tomorrow and we can sleep in."

Tina shook her head. "I have to get home. I've got homework to do and Ms. Webber will kill me if I don't get that essay in on Monday."

Janice looked at her. "Tina? We haven't done something, have we? I mean, you don't spend much time with Lyn or me lately and we were wondering if we'd upset you somehow?"

Tina dug out the excuse she'd prepared against this day. It had the benefit of being more or less true so Jan would believe her.

"I know, I'm sorry. It isn't you, not either of you." She looked from one concerned face to the other. "I guess I should have said something at the start of this year."

"Then what is it?" Lyn stared at her.

"It's the Melford Award. This is the last year. If I do really good work all year then I could win it and if I win, my parents can't make me go into some office."

"They want to?"

"They want me to be like them. They'll pay for me to go to university *if* I take the courses they want." She didn't know that for sure, Tina thought, but it wasn't unlikely and Jan and Lyn would believe her.

"Do you want to do something else?"

"Yes, I don't know what yet," she heard her own voice sounding exasperated. "I just know it isn't any job like theirs. If I get the Melford I can choose and they can't do anything to stop me because the award will pay."

Her friend nodded. "That's okay then. If we can help let us know."

"And we're okay?"

Janice grinned at her. "Sure, you work, girl. We'll be there to cheer when you win. That's what friends are for."

"Yeah!" Tina grinned back at them, picked up her case and headed for her small car. It wasn't new but her parents had thought that this year she needed her own transport and it was cool. The more so because it was a lot easier to buy dead poultry and take it home in her car than try to haul it home on the bus. And this afternoon she'd ordered several turkeys. She'd park around the back of the building, haul the sacked birds into the freight lift and sneak them up that way. She hadn't been caught – so far.

Once inside, she dodged the housekeeper, dumped her school bag, and got the sack to the roof undetected. Icarus was delighted to see her – and the sack's contents. She fed him, then spent some time just sitting with her friend. He was growing proper feathers now and his weight was continuing to increase too. She was sure of it. He had to be a condor, and what on earth a pair of those had been doing in Wellington – besides hatching Icarus - she had no idea. She'd scanned the papers, the Internet, magazines on birds, and nowhere had there been any mention of imported condors, or of a pair of them getting loose. Nor had there been any mention of a huge bird being killed on the road – but then that had been an eighteen-wheeler and possibly the remains had been too damaged for anyone to notice how unusual they'd been.

But it didn't matter to Tina. He was her friend. She loved him and one day soon he'd fly. At the thought, tears welled into her eyes. He couldn't stay once he was old enough to fly. He'd have to leave to find a home of his own, feed himself, and maybe – if someone had lost more of his kind – choose a mate.

The whole time, ever since that first early-morning discovery, she'd taken photos of him. One day she'd show them to someone who'd know what he was, but not for a long, long time. Just in case they wanted to catch him and put him into a cage like the one his parents must have escaped from.

"No cages for you, you beautiful bird. When you can fly, you can leave the nest and be free somewhere. Maybe you should go south. They say the bush is so thick in some places they've lost a whole herd of moose down there."

Icarus squawked at her softly and she handed him more turkey. "Yes, if you get much bigger you probably *could* hunt moose."

She grinned at him. He could just about hunt a calf now. She hoped he'd stay away from cattle though, or some farmer would shoot him. After another half-hour talking to Icarus and feeding him raw turkey drumsticks she stood up.

"Gotta go. I really do have homework to finish. I'll come back and see you before I go to bed."

Another week passed and Icarus appeared to have all his plumage. He was flapping his wings hard enough to lift just clear of the roof, and Tina could see that in another two or three days he would fly properly. Then he'd be gone. She'd miss him and every time she thought about being without him, she started to cry. So she'd mostly stopped thinking about it. The weekend came and she knew it was time. He'd fly and she'd lose something she really cared about.

She still didn't know what Icarus was, a condor or some sort of eagle, but none of the bird book descriptions or their pictures looked exactly like Icarus. Tina had decided that he must be either a rare species from the other side of the world, or perhaps some ornithologist had been experimenting with crossbreeding. But between caring for Icarus and trying to keep up with her increasing homework, she didn't have time to go hunting through any more books.

It was Saturday night when he flew. He'd been flapping

his wings all day, lifting just clear of the concrete before settling back again. A short rest, then more flapping. Finally, it dawned on Tina that his problem might be lifting higher than the concrete wall around the roof and beside which he had always nested. She could lift him to that, but she decided not to. The longer he exercised his wings before he could rise high enough, the better shape he'd be in to fly.

At nine o'clock on a fine moonlit night he managed that. He cleared the wall and fell towards the ground far below with what sounded like a scream of triumph. His wings spread, caught the air and a thermal and he came soaring back above her. Stooping and soaring again in delight, dancing on air, an heir come into his inheritance. But after half an hour he settled to the roof and stood staring at her.

Tina grinned at him, forcing back the tears of desolation. "Clever bird. You can fly now. Guess you can leave any time." He moved towards her, making the small throaty sounds that indicated affection. "Yes, I love you too. But you have to leave, go south, Icarus. Don't fly too high like your namesake. Just be free."

She gave him food, filled his water bucket and left the roof, to huddle, crying silently in her bedroom. All that week he refused to leave for good while she watched him fly, her heart breaking with pride in him and at her impending loss. But on the Friday night it was blowing hard, a strong wind that would carry him far south if he chose that direction. He'd landed on the wall top after a short flight. And as she watched, it seemed that he was making his choice.

"Go on then. You can't stay in a city, someone will see you and they'll want to put you in the zoo, cage you for good." He looked at her, turning his head to one side. "Yes, it's all right." She remembered something she'd heard once about letting the terminally ill go. She lowered her voice but concentrated on her words and him.

"I love you, Icarus. I always will, and I'll remember you all my life. But you were born and hatched to fly, that's why you have wings. Now fly away and live the way you're supposed to live. I set you free!"

For a moment more his yellow gaze pierced hers, then he raised his wings and swept them down in a powerful stroke as he left the wall top. His wings cupped the air and he spun back to float over her head and his beak opened in a scream that cut through all the sounds of the city. Tina was crying as Icarus swung to the south. Resting on the wind as it blew him across the city and away, his shape becoming smaller and smaller until she could no longer see his wings outstretched against the moonlit sky.

She went inside to her bedroom and knew that something wonderful had gone out of her life – but there was still homework and she'd be in trouble if it weren't turned in on Monday. Miserably she began to work, getting caught up in her essay until it was finished and she returned to the contemplation of her loss. She hid her broken heart quite well as the weeks passed. At least there'd been no stories about giant birds being shot or killed or even sighted or found starving. Wherever Icarus had gone, he seemed to have arrived safely and learned to hunt.

The school year had almost ended. The exams were hard but she attacked them with all her knowledge and study, and in the last weeks after exams she had more free time again. One night she tried a new program on her computer. It was a voice-activated search system and she described Icarus, using everything she had learned about him. She listed his weight, his wingspan, the sounds he made and the coloring of his feathers. Nothing showed, so she tried again, varying the different information she input.

The final attempt, with only his current age, general shape – eagle-like, his weight – almost twelve kilos, and his wingspan – just on three meters nowadays, gave her an answer. For long minutes she stared at the information that formed on the screen.

It was Icarus, it could only be him, but she was unable to guess how it had happened. How his parents had come into being above a modern city, and if there were more of his kind? Unless – somewhere in the city there was a mad scientist recreating long-extinct species – or unless Granny had been right. After that she wiped all obvious clues about her search and shut down the computer.

Prize-giving came, although one of the announcements that would be made was no surprise to Tina. She'd been informed in advance to ensure her own attendance and - with heroic efforts this time - she'd made sure her parents both attended as well.

"Do they know?" Jan asked very quietly as they all settled into their row of seats.

Tina shook her head. "No, I thought it would be a nice surprise for them."

"You mean you think they might not be pleased and they can't make a fuss in front of people?" Lyn said shrewdly.

"Maybe." Tina shrugged. "We'll see."

Both of her friends eyed her thoughtfully. They'd gone through eleven years of school together and they guessed there was something behind her attitude. In fact, Tina herself wasn't sure of what she'd do, she just had a feeling that tonight could be her turn to make a choice and fly. The moment of flight came soon after the last prize-giving announcement.

The Headmistress moved to the front of the platform. "And finally, we have the preliminary presentation of the Melford Award. The announcement is made a year before the award begins to allow the winner to make necessary decisions. The award covers five years' study at university or at a specialist school, if that is preferred because of the career chosen.

"Sometimes if the winner is only seventeen, she chooses to take a gap year before attending university. For this reason, and in any case, there is a minor amount of money that can be used this coming year or the next for brief courses, visits to relevant places or seminars that would contribute towards the winner's chosen career.

"If not used this or next year that money is added to the main award. I am happy to say that this year the award goes to a girl whose hard work over the past four years has fully justified her receipt of the Melford Award. Will Tina Salton please come forward now to accept her prize."

They were cheering her, Tina thought. It felt as if she was flying free, towards the life that would be hers, like Icarus. And she knew at last with complete certainty what her career choice would be. She walked up the steps to accept the scroll; her headmistress smiled at her, speaking into the microphone.

"You have a year now to make your decision, Tina. Unless you have decided already?"

Tina turned to the mike. "Yes. I have," she said clearly to all the interested faces that looked down at her standing on the platform. "I'm not quite sure how I go about it, but I want to study extinct birds, and if I can, I want to work to bring some of our lost New Zealand species back to life again."

She knew her parents wouldn't be pleased, although they'd probably let her do as she'd said. Jan and Lyn would be pleased for her, that she knew what she wanted to do. And as she walked back to join them, clutching her scroll, she wondered which of her guesses was right. Who had the scientist been? The one who'd tried to reach into the past to return the magnificent long-extinct Haast's Eagle to the country from which it had died out.

Then again if, as Granny Ngaire said, all times were one to the city maybe two of the eagles had looked sideways at the city one day, come through and laid an egg – which had hatched into the bird she loved – and they'd died before they could return. Maybe one day by one method or another, she could set free more of Icarus' breed so that the city's children would see the sight only she – and possibly that other – had ever seen.

She didn't know which possibility would lead to the result she wanted with all her heart, but she could see her dream quite plainly now. A vision of the great eagles soaring and swooping above the dense green forests of the south. Beautiful, majestic, and forever free again in the land that had borne them. Sons and daughters returned home.

SLIGHTLY POTTY

I was mildly surprised when Grandma took up pottery. She was over eighty and she'd never been very good with anything manual like crocheting, painting or sewing. From the gifts of pottery – along with generous cheques – that she gave us the next Christmas I could see things hadn't changed either. My cousins were horrified. The pots were badly made and not something you'd want to display for visitors – although they did.

No one who knew both them and Grandma would have wondered why. Grandma had money, not a huge amount depending on your standards, but she owned a good-sized house in a pleasant, long-established suburb, owned an almost new, expensive car and – quietly tucked away – she also had quite a lot of very valuable jewelry which her husband had given her during their marriage.

Grandpa was a man who'd sailed very close to the wind in his business dealings, so for years whenever he'd made a chunk of cash – often tax-free, well, so far as the Inland Revenue was advised – he invested some in jewelry for Grandma. The items were plain, nothing more than casings for the gems, but the stones were always of very fine quality. The idea was that if anything ever went wrong, Grandma could sell them and have something to fall back on – and his creditors couldn't grab them because they were officially hers.

In the end, Grandpa died in the middle of one of his affluent periods and Grandma ended up with the house – a very nice four bedroomed building with extensive grounds – cash in the bank and a lot more in short-term investments – and her jewelry. She never wore the very expensive pieces, saying that the items were far too valuable to risk, so that it was years since any of us had had a close look at them.

The investments brought in a steady stream of money on a quarterly basis. There was enough for Grandma to live on comfortably, pay a cleaner to come three mornings a week, and to hire a gardener who came one day each week to keep the gardens ablaze with color and the lawns neatly mowed. Grandma could afford to go to dinner when she wanted to eat out for a change, and in general she could afford to live a peaceful life uncomplicated by the financial problems of either too much or too little wealth.

She and her husband had never spoiled their children – my mother and the uncles – during the affluent periods. They'd been brought up to solid trades – just in case Grandpa's dealings went really bad – and they were all hard workers. But from what my mother told me, as children they'd often worried about what would happen to them if Grandpa died during a financial downturn, and as a result the uncles had brought up their own children to worry and care about money – quite a lot.

My mother didn't bother about finances so much. My father was a high-school teacher, very competent and popular with his students so that there would always be a job for him, while my mother had initially trained as a hairdresser, gained her certificate, and then – by way of a change – gone back to study at a technical institute and gained a community-nursing certificate as well.

They'd married, but being determined to own their own home first, they'd had me quite late in their lives and as my mother was the youngest of Grandma's four children, my cousins were a lot older than I was. I didn't like any of them very much – and maybe it was for that reason that I encouraged Grandma to continue with her pottery. Anyhow, I didn't see why she shouldn't. It was something she enjoyed and even if she wasn't much good at it, I understood why she potted once she'd discussed it with me one afternoon.

"For one thing it's fun, dear. The other women in our group are all about my age and we talk." She chuckled happily. "Heavens, how we talk! I hear all the local gossip, and we talk religion, politics, and," her smile became a grin, "sex."

I looked up in surprise, saw the twinkle and giggled. "I wouldn't tell my cousins that, they'd want to have you locked up."

She sobered abruptly. "Yes, my dear. I'm well aware of how they think of me. They consider I'm a nuisance, keeping them out of their inheritance. Such a pity." Her voice had become acid on the last words and I nodded understandingly.

Grandpa's will had been clear. He had angina and diabetes by the time he was in his late thirties and in the end, he'd died quite young. Grandma, on the other hand came from very long-lived stock. Her half-sister, known to many as "Granny Ngaire," was well into her eighties and showing no signs of dying – or even slowing down – any time soon. Their mother had made it to over a hundred thus far and was still going strong.

So Grandpa's will had skipped a generation to save death duties and he had left his estate to be divided amongst his grandchildren. Grandma had the lifetime use of everything but she must maintain a good car, keep up the house, and not devalue the investments.

For some years my cousins hadn't worried, but now I was in my twenties and they were into their forties they'd started to wonder just how long they'd have to wait. Grandma showed no signs of dropping off her twig, and they were beginning to hanker for life on a more lavish scale than they could normally afford.

I didn't care that much. I was the only child. My parents owned their own house and had modest investments; all of which I would eventually inherit. I had achieved qualifications and a job I loved – as junior vet in three-vet practice only a kilometer away from Grandma's house, so that I often went over to share her lunch and gossip about everything from my patients to her clubs.

Grandma had gone back to her original subject. "I love pottery. I like to feel the clay in my hands; pinching out a pot is creation, putting clay on the wheel and seeing it change under my hands as it spins is – almost Godlike." She smiled just a little sadly at me as she added. "Although I could never explain that feeling or use those words to my other grandchildren."

I nodded agreement. They'd see a comment like that as evidence of incipient megalomania. The next thing would be one of them arriving with a man in a white coat to ask if Grandma also believed she *was* God from time to time? And if so, perhaps she'd like a nice rest in a place where she'd be taken care of – oh, and did that mean they could share out the inheritance now?

"I know I'm not very good at potting, but I do enjoy it and it amuses me to see your cousins display my pots anyhow." Her smile became wicked. "And how uncomfortable they are, feeling they have to have them on display if others are there to see them as well when I'm expected to visit."

I gasped. "Gran, you awful woman! You've given those pots to them just to watch what they do."

"Of course, my dear. Or do you believe I don't know how they think of me?"

"My mother and the uncles like your pots." I offered.

"Yes." Her expression softened. "They love me and I love them – and you. But I'm sorry to say that I know my other grandchildren are not particularly fond of me and they are also greedy. Oh, well, I could be gone soon enough and then it'll be too late."

"Too late for what?"

"To finish the set of pots I'm working on. Margaret at the pottery center is showing me how to do opalescent glazing. I want to make a set of pots for a plant table. Five different sizes with bowls underneath them to make an interesting grouping."

I imagined them on the small table in the surgery's client waiting room. "If you do the set I'd like to have them for Christmas."

"Maybe. I have to be fair though, perhaps your cousins would like a set of pots for themselves?" I said nothing but our glances met. I rolled my eyes, and she twinkled at me again. "On the other hand, maybe they wouldn't."

Life continued busily over the next seven years. My cousins watched Grandma attentively for any signs of deterioration. My mother enjoyed herself working two nights a week as a relief nurse at our small hospital and two days a week at the local hairdressers. Dad taught school, and I looked after a varied list of animals while Grandma kept on potting.

But I was worrying lately about Grandma's health. She'd had several bad colds over the past winter and while she still went to her pottery meetings, she had gradually dropped membership in all of her other organizations. Which was why, I found out, I was hauled off to join in a meeting with my cousins that April. John started.

"The old woman is getting senile. We may need to take action. She's stopped going out and I've heard that she's started giving her things away to people."

His sister, my cousin Amanda, was horrified. "What?"

"Some of her paintings, some ornaments…"

"That's our inheritance!" That was Amanda again.

I snorted, fed up with their nonsense. "The things she's giving away are hers. They aren't part of our inheritance at all and what if they were? They're worth a few hundreds and who *is* getting them – and how do you know about it anyway?"

John gave me a pompous look. "I was told in confidence."

"Which you've promptly broken by telling us," I snapped. "So, who is getting these things of great value?" He listed names and I stood up, my eyes narrowing in outrage at their greed.

"Where are you going, we haven't decided what to do yet?" another cousin protested.

"I'm leaving. But let me point out a few things to you first. Grandma is giving some of her bits and pieces to old friends. Mrs. Marshall has been her cleaner for almost twenty years. Mr. Poanga has been her gardener for fifteen years. She'd given small items to her next-door neighbor's children whom she's known for most of their lives. No court is going to take any of that as evidence of senility. As for her staying home all the time. That's rubbish! She still visits friends and she goes to her pottery class every week."

"Pottery" John sneered. "The perfect occupation for an old fool who's going slightly potty."

I took one step forward, smacked him hard across the face, then turned on my heel and left. I didn't know what to do about their meeting though, I just couldn't tell Gran. It would hurt her even though she already knew what they thought of her. I thought about it and in the end, I had a quiet word with her lawyer. He considered carefully what I'd told him of both sides of the conversation, and then spoke even more cautiously in reply.

"You are right. The minor items Mrs. Olsen is giving away are her own property. They are not of huge value and they are being given to people she has known for many years. There is no legal reason why these gifts should be taken as anything but evidence that she is aware her time is finite."

My gaze jerked up to meet his at that. I didn't say anything in direct response, but it made my next words plainer than they might have been otherwise.

"I love my grandmother," I said flatly. "If my cousins try anything legal against her, I'm on her side. I'll do whatever is necessary to make sure she's left alone. If that takes a lot of money, I can take out a loan against my share of my practice."

He nodded, showed me out graciously, and I went back to work still steaming about how some people would do anything for money and to hell with family. I don't know what was decided at my cousins' meeting after I'd left, but maybe they'd realized that I was right and legally there wasn't much they could do. They took no further action, had no other meetings that I was aware of, and it was a further year before Grandma caught one cold too many.

She died peacefully at the start of spring and I knew very well that of all of my generation, I was the only one who was truly grieved at losing her. My cousins were much too busy walking about the now-uninhabited house and adding up what it and the contents would fetch at auction – in between squabbling about which of her possessions they'd take for themselves.

Grandma's own will turned out to be simple. The cash in her account and her own small investments were to be divided equally amongst my mother and the uncles. As for her possessions, we grandchildren were to choose those in turn, one item at a time in order of age, until they were all taken. This was to be done immediately and decisions were final. The choices made were to be regarded as her specific bequests with a clause that added if another challenged the choice of any of us then the challenger forfeited his or her own chosen share of her estate.

Of course, all eyes were on the jewel cases. As all of them were older than me my cousins grabbed eagerly, a jewel case at a time, and in the end all that was left for me of the glittering array was a green garnet set of necklace, bracelets, brooch, and ring which had been Grandpa's wedding gift. The set was Victorian in a fitted case and of some value, but nothing compared to that of the other jewelry. Not that I minded, they were the jewels Grandma had loved to wear and to me they spoke of her. I too would love and wear them as she had, remembering her when I did so.

After that came the furniture, ornaments, books, paintings, and oddments unearthed from cupboards. I opened a large grubby carton to find a set of five pots. They descended in size and each came with a shallow bowl beneath to hold any watering overflow. They were a little lop-sided, but the glaze was an undeniable opalescent and I took them as my next share. John looked at me scornfully, keeping his voice low so his parents didn't hear.

"Some of Grandma's potty productions I suppose."

I clasped the pots to me defiantly. Years ago, Gran had said she'd let me have a set of them if her glazing worked. Maybe she hadn't thought they were good enough to give me in the end, but I thought they were pretty. I'd do as I'd said to her at the time and plant ferns in them, placing them on the corner whatnot at the practice. I'd think of her every time I saw them.

I did, and for the next two years the pots sat in splendor in our waiting room. But being a vet means animals and sometimes they are boisterous. Chappy was a Great Dane puppy – the name is short for Happy Chappy – he's only a baby and still very clumsy so I wasn't surprised when his owner came out apologetically as I arrived at the waiting room to call for my next patient.

"I'm so sorry, I think Chappy knocked this plant over and he's broken the pot and the bowl it sits in. Tell me what they're worth and then add it to the bill."

"No need, they didn't cost me anything, and maybe I can glue them back together again." I recalled his words, and asked a further question. "You said you *think* he did?"

"There was an old lady waiting in the surgery. She seems

to have left, but Chappy went across the room to see her and she didn't seem to be scared of him. So I left him tied to the bench and went to the toilet, but when I came back the old lady was gone and this pot was on the floor – broken."

He gave me a clear description of the old lady that made my eyebrows rise in half-disbelieving interest. I took the broken pottery, placing it in my car before returning to give Chappy his vaccination. That night, I took the broken bits of pottery inside, fetched a glue-stick and laid the pottery on the table. Carefully I fitted it together – suddenly noticing as I did so something rather interesting.

I made a closer examination of the bits, then quietly drove back to our surgery waiting room and took away all the other opalescent pottery items. I stopped at The Warehouse and bought sufficient pots to replace them in fake terracotta plastic; it would be safer anyway. I repotted the ferns into the plastic pots and returned them to the waiting room, saying nothing to my colleagues. However, I made a quiet visit to Granny Ngaire, Grandma's half-sister after that, followed by productive visits to Grandma's lawyer and to my bank.

Six months later my cousins were almost bitter to receive polite invitations to the opening of a new surgery I'd had built in which I would be the practice head with two staff on salary. John was the one who seemed most irked by my apparent success.

"I suppose you're using the money you inherited from Grandpa's will after Gran died. It wasn't that much though. You'd have had to take out a huge loan to build your own surgery and pay staff." His voice became kindly sanctimonious, "I do hope you know what you're doing. You know that if you find yourself in financial trouble you can't expect any of us to bail you out."

"I won't," I told him – and I wouldn't. But I did wonder what my cousins would say when sooner or later one of them had the jewelry they had grabbed after the funeral valued – and found that the gemstones in the real settings were only good quality paste. The real stones had all been removed, carefully embedded and covered over again, in the hollow bases of the five opalescent pots that Grandma had known I would choose as a part of my share of her estate.

It might have been a silly thing to do. The pots and bowls could have broken in a way that didn't show me the hidden contents and I could have thrown them out. Or they could have lasted unbroken for my lifetime and some stranger would have benefited.

Or so I thought until I went to tell Granny Ngaire about it and discovered she had known and been watching the situation all along. So, I thought although I did not say so, had my grandmother. I'd been taking too long to find the gems and dead or not, she, or someone exactly like her, had paid a visit to the surgery and broken a pot to give me a strong hint.

Still, it was possible that the cousins were right and that in the end, Gran had been slightly potty, because things could have gone wrong anyhow, but – I smiled to myself as I cut the ribbon and declared my new surgery open – I would have the broken pot mended as best it could be, and I'd display the set in a case on a wall in my surgery. If anyone asked about the pots, I'd tell the inquirer that my Gran and I were both slightly potty about pottery. It would be no more than the truth.

FULL CIRCLE

His hands were around her throat. She couldn't breathe. Inside she was screaming, begging him to stop. She needed air. He'd asked her to pose for photos, nothing wrong, just cheesecake pictures of a pretty sixteen-year-old in shorts and a halter-top. She'd known him, liked and trusted him, how could he do this? She needed air, please God make him stop and let her breathe. Oh, God, *please!* Blackness reached for her, flowed over her like cool water in the desert. She fell into it, submerged, drowned, and then – she was gone.

* * *

I'm Margaret, but I'm known as "Meg" to everyone. At school I've heard some of the kids call me "Meg the cripple" to distinguish me from another Meg who plays hockey a lot. I don't mind that much. They don't mean it to hurt; it's just a handy tag so people know who they're talking about.

The kids at my school aren't mean, we don't have bullying or anything anyway, and there really isn't any of that on an organized basis. It's just that sometimes people say things without meaning them, but they hurt anyhow.

I'm not a real cripple with a wheelchair or crutches, I can't run because I was born with one leg shorter than the other and my hip's a bit of a problem too as a result, that's all. I can ride a bike all right though, and I can walk for a long way, so long as I do it at my own pace.

I study a fair bit and I do well in school, so I do get called "Teacher's Pet" now and then, and I don't have a best friend since Marjorie's family moved to Auckland. But none of that's mattered to me since Wendy arrived. I don't notice anyone much anymore, just her and how she makes me laugh. I don't go to school at the moment anyway and she keeps me company.

I'd been lonely before that so it was great to have a best friend again – even if she was almost three years older and wouldn't be able to come to school with me when I went back. It was Saturday, so there'd have been no school anyhow even if I was going, and we were together as we always seemed to be now.

"What should we do today?"

"Hang out by the river?"

"Okay, I have to get food first though."

"In the supermarket?"

"Yes. Sorry."

"That's all right, I'll wait outside for you."

I hurried. I could easily carry it and it didn't seem fair that Wendy couldn't come inside the big supermarket, but that was the way it was. Wendy always told me that she'd explain why she couldn't come into the supermarket one day, but not yet. I guess I don't mind. In a way it makes it fun, my best friend having this huge important secret that she'll tell me when the time is right. The man on the counter ignored me so I just dumped the cash on his counter and grabbed my food in the bag. Wendy was outside.

"Got everything?"

"Yes. I can make us lunch and we can stay out all day."

"That'd be good."

It would be too. Being with Wendy was always great. She has a sort of bubbling to her. It was at times as if she fizzed when she talked, ideas tumbling one over the other, so eager to come out that they trod on one another's heels. I loved her. Her beauty, her brightness, her friendship – and her secrets. I knew not to nag her about those. I may be only thirteen, but I'm not stupid. I get top marks in my classes and I know when to keep my mouth shut.

It was sunny today. It always was lately but it seemed extra bright when I woke up this morning. The river would be a great place to spend the day. I limped along the banks, Wendy saying outrageous things to make me laugh, and finally we got into one of those fits where no matter what you say, it seems funnier and funnier until you can't stop laughing. Tears run down your face, your stomach hurts, and you just keep on laughing.

We stopped in the end, and ate our lunch. I was stiff when we got up off the bench again and Wendy had to give me a hand up. That's my stupid leg. They plan to operate soon and fix the hip I think, but they have to wait for something or another. You know doctors? I had head injuries in a recent car crash too, but those are getting better on their own – I hope.

"See you tomorrow?"

"Of course you will." I grinned at her. "What would life be like without my best friend?" Her face clouded and I stared at her. "What did I say?"

"Don't say that, Meg, about what would life be like? I won't be here forever. People move away like Marjorie, they die, they just have to leave sometimes."

"Is that all? Don't be daft. We'll grow old together, and you don't ever have to leave."

"I could have to."

"Then you just say no, you won't. You're old enough to make that stick. You could get a job in town and stay here."

She shook her head. "Maybe, I don't know. When you're told you may have to leave and it's stronger, wiser people saying so, then sometimes you have to do it."

"No, you don't," I pointed out. "Even if they give you good reasons, you don't have to agree. And what's this stronger stuff? Is someone leaning on you?"

"A bit."

"Can I do anything to help?"

"You do already. You were the first person to notice me for a long time. So long as you really need me I guess I can stay."

I was puzzled by some of what she was saying – but at that I was relieved. "That's all right then, because I'll need you all my life. Now, what about tomorrow? There's a cat show in the town hall that'd be fun to go to?"

Wendy brightened. She loved cats. "Great, when does it open?"

"Ten o'clock to the public. But it's open to exhibitors from eight. We can probably go in any time. They won't mind our looking at the cats while they're getting things ready."

"That's okay. Let's go at ten, look at the cats, and have lunch at one of the cafes. After that we can go back to the show and see what cats got all the prizes." She giggled. "I'll bet you I can guess the ones that do?"

I laughed. "No bet. I've been tricked that way before. But if you do, you can have dinner at my place with me."

My parents and older brother wouldn't be there, but that was okay. I know where everything is and I can cook quite well.

So that's what we did on Sunday. The cats were lovely, so friendly, and of course Wendy won the bet. She knows cats. I love our own family breed but I don't know as much about what to look for in other breeds. But then Wendy's had more time to learn about things. In another three years I'll probably know a lot more too.

I do have my own cat though. Thunder's an Ocicat, Mum breeds them under the Shadowlands kennel name and I adore him. I knew he was mine from the day he was born and he agreed because he hates me to go anywhere without him. In some ways Ocicats are a bit like dogs, they can be harness-trained, and taught to retrieve, and most of them love people.

A couple of times I spoke to the cats' owners too, but they ignored me. Of course, the hall was very noisy and all of the exhibitors were busy. I didn't take offence. Dad says that before you do that you should be certain that offence was intended.

Wendy came back to have dinner with me, and Thunder made a fuss of her. Wendy loves him too and I like to watch them together. I went to bed early that night, right after Wendy left at eight o'clock, Thunder slept on the bed with me, as he always does, and the rest of my family must have come in late and gone to bed quietly because I never heard anything. I got up early before they woke up and grabbed something to eat before I plodded off to find Wendy. She was standing outside the supermarket.

"What are you doing?"

"Thinking."

"What about?"

"Why I'm not allowed inside."

I managed to say nothing for a minute. This was on the fringe of the stuff we don't talk about and I wasn't sure if I should ask questions or even say anything at all. I nodded when she looked at me just to show I'd heard, but I waited to see if she wanted to talk to me about it. She did – a little bit.

"I don't really understand the ban. It's there, I'm not allowed inside, but no one's ever made it clear why." She shrugged. "I think it's some sort of rule. Oh, well. Who cares? It's a lovely day again and you don't have to be in school. Let's go and window-shop?"

We did. It was fun looking at everything and discussing what clothes we'd buy if we had all the money in the world, and arguing if diamonds or colored stones were prettier. Afterwards we bought KFC and took that to eat in the little park opposite.

It was a good summer that year, months of fine clear weather, not too hot, but bright and sunny. The perfect summer if you didn't have to swelter in a classroom and I didn't. Wendy and I went everywhere, we laughed all the time, and while I never seemed to see my family I didn't mind somehow. It was so good just hanging out with Wendy, feeling the sun on my arms, and doing whatever I wanted. There were times when things were cloudier, mostly when she had something on her mind and it spilled over onto me.

"Want to go to the river tomorrow?"

"I'm sick of the river." Her face twisted up as if she was going to cry. "I'm sick of being here, waiting for something to happen. I'm sick of – oh – everything."

I was terrified. "Of me?"

Wendy turned, saw the real panic on my face and hugged me hard. "Not you, Meg. Not ever you. I'm just in a bad mood, you know everyone has one of those now and again. Ignore me, I'm talking through a hole in my head. Let's go look at your school for a change? I'd like to walk around it and see your classrooms."

That was something new. We'd never done that before and I liked the idea. "Yes, pick me up at eight in the morning and we'll go before anyone's there."

Wendy's always on time. My watch had barely ticked over onto eight when she was knocking at the door. I shushed her. My parents must have had a late night last night, they weren't down for breakfast yet and I didn't want them woken up and grumpy about it.

"Come on, or do you think you should change into school uniform first?"

I sneered. "I do go to the school, they'll let me in. Maybe it's you that should borrow one of my uniforms in case."

"Oh, I can go almost anywhere. They'll let me in there all right."

We didn't have to worry. The school gates were open and there was no one about. We walked into the nearest classroom, which happened to be my homeroom, and I showed Wendy around.

"This is my desk." I checked the books inside. "Josie Willingham's sitting there at the moment. "I'll make her move when I have that operation and can come back." I looked up at the walls above me. "Look, they still have my illustrated poem up here. I painted that last term after I'd seen a new book on illustrated medieval manuscripts in the library."

Wendy moved up under the sheet of paper and read it. "Hey, that poem's not bad and the illustration's lovely. What book was it?"

"One about how the monks in the Middle Ages decorated prayer books and bibles. They had a bunch of color plates showing stuff that had survived and I thought it'd be fun to see if I could do something like that."

"You think the monks were right?

"What about?"

"Well, death and heaven and all that."

I shrugged. "I dunno. I like to think that when I die, I'm not gone. That maybe dying is a doorway into a different place, but if that's heaven I don't know." I giggled. "Not the sort of heaven Josie Willingham talks about anyway. I don't want to sit on a white cloud, wearing a nightdress and a halo and playing a harp. For one thing, I like pajamas, and for another I can't play a note."

"Maybe they'll teach you?" That idea gave both of us the giggles.

"Yeah. And maybe I can negotiate and get pajamas too."

"What about the halo?"

"Thunder can wear that as a collar."

"They might not let cats in?"

"Then I'm not going. Anyhow, you know cats, there's no place they can't get into if they're really determined to be there."

"Great. An anarchist angel in heaven, wearing pajamas, playing the harp all wrong and with her cat chasing angel toes and wearing a halo around his neck. That should liven the place up a bit."

I considered the idea and grinned. "Yeah? I'm not sure Josie would agree."

"Too bad, I'm sure lots more people would prefer your heaven to hers." They probably would, but as I wasn't planning on going to heaven any time soon, they'd have to settle for Josie's version.

I led the way through more of the school classrooms. It was fun showing Wendy my school, and while I thought now and again that it was strange no one was around, I guessed that I'd lost track of some holiday or another. Probably one of the kind teachers give themselves, something to do with the union, or a staff meeting where for the first couple of hours they've off somewhere and the kids are all told to come in later. What did it matter?

We left the school mid-morning and wandered off to buy something to eat. We ate that on a bench in the center of Lower Hutt before we went off to spend time at my place. My family was out again and I have to say I was getting a bit sick of never seeing them. Rob, my older brother, was apparently getting all the attention these days and I was a bit fed up with that. Next time I saw them I'd say something to them about it, not being nasty, but just getting my point across.

I said that to Wendy. I guess I went on about it rather and she got this odd look on her face. I shut up. One of the easiest ways of staying friends with someone is to know when to do that. She changed the subject.

"Now we've seen your school, what about we go window-shopping again for a while?"

I agreed. Somehow the school wasn't the same as it had been before my accident. It was nice to see the old place. I mean, I quite enjoy being at school. I'm not always top of the class, I share that in turn with Josie, and one of the boys. But

I'm usually in the top three in every class but Algebra. My dad says that you either have the sort of mind that's right for that or you don't. I do try, but my exam marks at the end of last year weren't even a pass. I said some of this to Wendy as we walked back to my place after we'd spent hours at the shopping center.

"I know," she agreed. "I didn't like it much either. Hey, why don't we do something really different in the morning?"

"What?"

"Didn't you say you've got a bicycle? If there's a spare one, we could cycle out to the reservoir?"

She has gorgeous ideas. I couldn't think of anything better than cycling slowly out to sit and eat lunch by the still water; if only there was a little bit of a breeze wiping out some of the hot sun. My bike has a big flat-bottomed basket on the front too so I could put Thunder's cat carrier in that and once we were at the reservoir he could run about and share our lunch.

My parents were still out when I got back with Wendy. I thought they must have left me a note somewhere but I couldn't be bothered to look for it. I just fed Thunder, who was yelling to say he was starving, made us dinner, and after we'd eaten we checked the garage. Sure enough, my bike was there and so was the larger one Rob had used until my dad bought him a small secondhand car last year.

"You can use this one."

Wendy wheeled it out of the garage, checked the tires competently, and reached for the pump. "The back tire's flat, but it should be okay unless there's a puncture."

"It won't matter if there is," I told her. "There's a repair kit on the shelf and I've fixed punctures heaps of times."

"Miss Efficiency."

"That's right. Anything else I can do for you, just ask."

"Meg, there could be one thing one day soon. It's really important to me."

I could see by the almost desperate look on her face as she looked at me that this was the truth. It terrified me. What could I do to help her with anything that meant that much? But that's what friends are for – as the song goes that my mum often sings. I nodded, letting her know I was listening and I'd help if I could.

"It could be something that looks bad, though it really isn't? You'd have to do it in secret and it could be a bit dangerous for you too." She was starting to look worried. "I'm not sure I should have said anything."

"It's all right." I closed my fingers around her hand where it curled over the bike handlebars. "We're friends. If there's something I can do, I will. All you have to do is tell me what it is and I'd do my best."

"You're sure?"

"Yes." I was suddenly certain. Wendy had principles; she wouldn't ask me to do anything that was really wrong. Hadn't she said that it only looked bad?

"You don't have to do anything for a while yet. We have summer. It's after that I'll need your help."

"Then when you do, you tell me." I was firm. "Right now, we'll finish checking the bikes, we can make lunch to take with us, and put that in the fridge for the night. What would you like in your sandwiches?"

"I fancy salmon."

I checked the cupboard over the bench and found a couple of small tins of salmon, for myself I wanted chicken, and Mum often had a cold roast one in the fridge. That was there too, so I made sandwiches for us both, added a big crisp apple to each lunch, a packet of chocolate biscuits, and put bottles of water in the freezer compartment. By the time we left they'd be solid ice, but over our ride to the reservoir they'd start to thaw. That way we'd have lovely ice-cold water to drink for most of the trip.

It was the most perfect day right from the beginning – apart from one small worry that I forgot almost at once. Mum, Dad, and Rob must have been out late last night again because they were still in bed when I got up and after Wendy arrived. I left them a note. I wasn't going to let their neglect spoil another wonderful day.

Wendy laughed as Thunder stuck his paw out through the wire of his carrier. "Hey, fella, you having fun too?" Thunder purred at her and she reached in to scratch behind his ears. I'd included his leash and harness with my gear and I had a favorite ball of his as well. It has a bell inside and he loves chasing it, bringing it back to us, and shaking it so that the bell rings.

The ride wasn't that tiring and once we were at the reservoir it was great. Thunder chased his ball everywhere and when he was tired, he came and lay beside us like one of the cenotaph lions and shared bits of salmon and chicken from our sandwiches. The water was deliciously cold and I poured some into Wendy's hands so Thunder could drink. I'd forgotten to bring his bowl, but I don't think he minded. We lay back looking at the sky and talking for an hour or so then Wendy sat up abruptly.

"Meg, put Thunder in the carrier, there's some people arriving with a dog."

She was looking down the hill to where a big white car had pulled up. Two adults had climbed out and there was a big dog with them that they didn't have on a lead. Thunder doesn't mind friendly dogs at all, but this was a big dog and it mightn't be used to cats. I looked around. Thunder had wandered down to the edge of the water and was lapping. I called him – but he's a cat, they don't do obedience very well. He likes retrieving his ball but that's more his having me throw it obediently for him so far as he's concerned.

The dog was bounding towards us. Thunder saw it and crouched. I started to limp towards him as fast as I could before Wendy went past me at an all-out run towards my cat. She reached him, stood in front of his small furry body, and faced the dog. Until then it had been bouncing forward with the attitude of "look at the cat, see what I can do to the stupid cat."

Thunder had realized that he was in trouble and the fighting ridge had come up across his shoulders while he was making his fighting howl that sounds like an off-key violinist tuning up. He doesn't fight often, but he's a big powerful cat. He weighs just over seven kilos and he's very fast. When he does fight, he can make mincemeat of any other cat. But this wasn't another cat. The dog looked like a cross between a Staffordshire and some even bigger breed with longer hair, and you should have seen its teeth! If it got a grip on my cat, it would be Thunder who was mincemeat.

I kept limping forward. If I was bitten instead of Thunder, that would be okay and maybe the owners would call the dog off before it could bite me. The dog had been charging forward, but Wendy had a shorter distance to cover. She was facing it long before I arrived so I saw everything that happened and it was weird. The dog stopped dead, looked up at Wendy, down at Thunder, and back at Wendy. She took a pace forward.

"Go home!" she said very softly.

The dog stared at her. Slowly a white rim appeared around his eyes, he gave a whimper that escalated into a moaning howl, and he fled – full tilt to his owners where he tried to hide behind them, all the time staring back at us as he moaned and whimpered. His owners were glaring towards us. Wendy scooped up Thunder.

"Let's get out of here."

I was only too happy to agree. We tucked Thunder back into his carrier, scooped up the remains of our lunch and our half-emptied water bottles, and dived for our bikes. Wendy led the way past the dog and his owners. The dog went mad as we passed, winding the leash they'd just put him around their legs and yelping like a smacked puppy. Wendy waved to them as we raced by but they completely ignored us, some people are like that. They don't care to admit they should have had their dog on a leash all along.

Thunder had settled in his carrier and was washing a paw with the sort of look that indicated he hadn't needed rescuing. If that dog had been silly enough to start something, Thunder would have enjoyed finishing it for him. But I knew that he could have been killed and I was grateful. Once we were home again, I said so while we put the bikes away.

"I owe you one."

"Don't be daft. All I did was speak to the brute and scare him off."

"Yeah, so well that he was still crying like a puppy when we went past. Bet the owners wonder what we did to him?"

"Yes." Her tone was oddly neutral. I opened my mouth to ask what that was about and shut it again. Wendy often told me things but she liked to do it in her own time. She always knows what's on my mind and she looked at me.

"I can tell you soon, Meg. Very soon now. The time's coming." I nodded. That was good enough for me. This had been the most perfect summer of my life so far and I wasn't dumb enough to do anything to wreck it.

The truth was that it hadn't started out so well. Marjorie's family had moved and all the other girls in our class had best friends already. Then it had been a wet day at the start of the summer term and Rob had agreed to give me a lift to school in his car. Some idiot had come flying out of a side street and hit my side of it. I remember looking out of the window and seeing the SUV getting bigger and bigger as it rocketed towards me and then it was lights out for a bit. So I've been recovering ever since, but making friends with Wendy made up for a lot of it.

The summer got better and better, now and again, I was bothered about not seeing my family – but then I'd forget about it. Until I noticed that it was almost autumn, I couldn't remember when I'd seen them last and Wendy told me that we had to talk. It was then that I started to get worried.

"What about?"

"I don't like to ask you, Meg, but you said you'd help me if you could."

"I will. What do you want me to do?"

She was looking more serious than I'd ever seen her before. "I swear it'll be the right thing to do, but it doesn't look it at first."

"That's okay. I trust you. What should I do?"

"I'll tell you a step at a time. You may not be able to help anyhow, so I won't tell you all of it. Just do each thing as I work it out and you can stop any time. Okay?" I nodded. "Right. You'll have to sneak out to meet me after midnight." So far, I thought, that isn't anything I can't do.

"It's probably best if you meet me at two this morning. Do your family keep petrol for the lawn-mower?"

"Yes, and Rob always has some spare for his car."

"Okay. You'll need your bike. But Meg, the petrol will feel really heavy. It'll be almost impossible to lift. You'll need to put it in the bike basket and once you have it, I'll meet you outside at the end of your road."

That last bit wasn't confusing. I live in a cul-de-sac and there is only one end I could ride out of. I considered everything so far. No problem being out at that hour. I'm not nervous and Wendy would meet me before I'd gone far. I didn't know what she wanted to do with the petrol and what was this stuff about it being impossibly heavy? I'd lifted the five-liter can Rob had before. But I didn't argue. If I was finally getting in on some of my best friend's secrets, I wasn't going to spoil that.

"And if your father's got a candle or two and matches, bring those."

Okay, that was odd, but I said I trusted her and I did. I was surprised when I lifted Rob's petrol can though. Wendy had been right. I heaved it up, sweating and straining my arm muscles until I thought I'd never get the darned thing high enough to put it in the bike basket. I did it in stages in the end, hefted it up and rested it on the pedal, then up onto the bike frame, the seat, and up again, a step along and into the basket. I stood and panted for a minute after that.

Now – a couple of candles from Mum's emergency kit, matches ditto, and I had everything. The candles and matches seemed far more heavy than usual too, almost as if they were made of lead – but I had no time to think of that, Wendy should be waiting for me by now.

I pedaled down our road with only the streetlight to show me the way. I didn't think it would be a good idea to be all lit up in case someone looked out of the window just then. I could do without the neighbors ringing Mum or Dad to ask them why I was cycling down the street at this hour of the night.

Wendy was waiting for me. "Did you manage everything?"

"Petrol." I pointed at the can. "It's full. And I took two candles and a box of matches from Mum's civil defense box. Which way do we go?"

"This way." She walked while I cycled slowly beside her. I knew where we were going before we got there and I looked at her. It all came together in my mind with a click. Petrol, candles, matches – we were going to burn down the supermarket that wouldn't allow her in.

"Wendy?"

She turned to face me. "I swear, Meg. I swear. This isn't a wicked thing. There's no one working there tonight, no one will be hurt. I wouldn't do that no matter how much it meant to me. But it has to be destroyed. It's the only way I can be..." she hesitated, "It has a hold on me." She took my cold hand in hers. "Please, Meg. I promise doing this will be a good thing in the end. You'll know why soon. Just do it for me if you can."

In the streetlight I saw that she was crying and I couldn't say no to her. She was my best friend. I loved her and I probably owed her Thunder's life. If no one would be hurt, it wasn't that bad. And the owners of the building would be insured, wouldn't they? I started pedaling towards the supermarket again and saw her sigh of relief as she followed me. Wendy led the way around the back and we looked at the doors.

"How do we get in?" I asked.

"Well, by a coincidence the staff door didn't catch when the last person left." I knew she must have done something to fix it that way but I didn't ask. "Get the petrol can onto that little trolley, wheel it into the middle of the store, and come back."

I won't say the rest of what I did at her direction. It was bad enough I did it. I don't need to give anyone else ideas. I had to do it all too. Wendy couldn't set foot inside the door. It seemed weird, I mean, so they'd banned her or something, but we were burning the place down, that was as bad as it gets. So how come she still wouldn't set foot inside the building?

When the fire started, it caught hold fast. I shut the door so that the catch caught and Wendy gave me a sort of half-smile.

"They don't have anything to stop that. Not with the other things you did. Grab that petrol can and let's go back to your place where we can talk." Great! I was finally going to get some answers. But I didn't. Not really.

"We have to talk about you, Meg." She wanted to talk about me, why? "What you did tonight may have – well – done something for me that I needed to be done. I couldn't do it myself and no one else would do it for me before."

I felt hurt. "You asked other people?"

"No. I saw at once that they wouldn't help me, so I never even tried to ask. You were the first person, Meg. The only one I could rely on." She seemed to hear something and she stopped to listen. "There isn't much time left. Come upstairs to your bedroom." I followed her to the small bedroom that had been mine all my life. "Lie down on the bed. Here's Thunder to join you." I lay down obediently. Thunder jumped up to lie snuggled, purring beside me.

"Okay, now what?"

"Now you make me a promise, Meg, as we're best friends." She took my hands in hers. "Don't talk about me to your parents or to Rob. Don't say my name or talk about me at all. Just wait. If what we did tonight works, I'll see you again, I swear it."

I could feel a huge wave of sleepiness pulling me under. "I mustn't tell anyone about you or tell your name, but I'll see you again?" Her hands tightened on mine.

"That's it. Trust me, Meg. You're the best friend I've ever had."

My lips curved into a tiny smile. "You're mine too. Don't worry." Then sleep dragged me down and I was gone for a while. I woke up to find Mum, Dad, and Rob staring at me. They all had tears in their eyes and Mum was holding my hand.

"Oh darling, can you hear me?"

I peered up at her. "Course I can, why is everyone crying? What happened?"

"The doctor said you probably wouldn't remember it but there was a car accident. An SUV ran into Rob's car on the passenger side. He had a few bruises and a broken arm but you had serious head injuries. They had to operate and they put you into an artificial coma for about ten days after that to heal. They've only just allowed you to wake up."

I opened my mouth to protest. That was all nonsense. The accident had been at the start of summer and I remembered it perfectly. I'd had a concussion and slightly blurred vision for a while, that was why I hadn't been at school. The doctor said my eyes needed rest – and that was all. I'd met Wendy immediately after the accident and we'd had months of fine weather, shared laughter, and – I'd burned down the supermarket. Wendy had said not to mention her name or anything about her to my parents. The police could be after me too. I should be careful. I smiled up at my family.

"I sort of remember the accident. I saw the other car coming towards me. Then there was this huge bang and I can't remember anything more. Have I been here long?" That was the trick. I'd ask questions, let them tell me all about whatever they thought had been going on. I was already getting the impression that it wouldn't match anything that I remembered.

"The ambulance took you straight into hospital, sweetheart," That was Dad. "They operated that night. You've been unconscious ever since, exactly ten days."

That was interesting. I'd lost the summer I'd lived, apparently while I was unconscious – and a best friend. I closed my eyes and remembered Wendy's face. No, she'd said she'd see me again. I shut my eyes and resigned myself to hospital and recovering as quickly as I could. A week went by, and another. I still hadn't a clue if the events I recalled clearly had happened or if they were dreams or some sort of delirium while I'd been in the coma.

I was getting well rapidly, and at the same time, my number came up for the hip operation. They decided I was well enough for that and since I was already in hospital my opinion was asked. I agreed, so they did it right then and there. Next term I'd be back at school and once I'd had all the right therapy and treatment, I might even be known before I left school as "Meg, the one who plays hockey."

"Mum, could I have the newspapers to read, the ones that came out after the accident and before I woke up?"

"Of course, darling."

She brought in a big stack of them the next day and I started reading. On the front page of the one dated the day I woke up I found what I was looking for. The pictures and an article on the supermarket fire. It was definitely arson they said, but the police were baffled as to how or who. There were no suspicious fingerprints, the petrol container had been taken away by the perpetrators, and there had been no signs of forced entry.

But the building had been over fifty years old. It had been built in the early 1960s, and the owners had decided not to rebuild. Instead, the building was to be demolished, the whole site cleared, and a multi-level car park would be built there instead. Apparently, the car park was something that the council had wanted for ages and they moved quickly once the decision had been made.

By the time I was almost ready to leave hospital all the necessary permits had been obtained and plans were in place. On the day my parents and Rob guided me in my wheelchair out of the hospital and into the family car, a start was made at breaking up the huge slab of reinforced concrete that had been the supermarket's original foundations. I'd been home three days when what they found in the slab became a nine days' wonder. I was watching the news on TV One when I heard about it.

"And workers breaking up the supermarket slab in the center of Lower Hutt today downed tools in a hurry when it was found that the slab contained a body. Police were immediately called to the scene and have announced that they are investigating what they have labeled as a 'suspicious death.'"

Dad made a disgusted sound in the back of his throat. "A glimpse of the obvious. Suicides don't rush out and bury themselves in concrete foundations after they've died."

I sat mutely through the rest of the news hearing nothing. I was putting all the clues together, everything I remembered from my lost summer, and I was understanding at last some of what had been going on. I hadn't been dead, so I was able to do things. Suspended between life and death I could hear someone who desperately needed me to listen and help her.

I didn't know the mechanics of most of what had happened, how Mum, Dad and Rob weren't ever there but some shopkeepers seemed able to sell me things. How Thunder was there the whole time, but no one was at my school. None of that mattered to me. I knew who'd been buried in that huge slab of concrete, who'd needed to be found and who – maybe once she had been found – could now be buried properly.

It took a year. But five weeks after I turned fifteen, I stood alone – on two legs of the same length. I stood at the back of a huge crowd come to listen to the memorial service for the girl who, unbeknownst to anyone else, had been my best friend through a long summer that had existed nowhere but with us.

Her killer had been known but it hadn't been his conviction she wanted. It would have been impossible anyhow. He'd been found dead only days after she vanished. No, she'd wanted what I'd given her. Her mum was standing to speak.

"One last thing I want to say. The police never found who burned down the building that my Wendy's body was buried under. But if it hadn't been for that person she'd never have been found and we'd never have been able to give her a proper grave. Our family can rest now, knowing that Wendy's at peace. And while the police probably wouldn't like me to say this – I thank who ever set that fire from the bottom of my heart. We owe you Wendy's being returned to us and wherever she is, I'm sure she thanks you too."

I felt a hand slide into mine. I turned and looked into my best friend's eyes, and a voice that only I could hear spoke to me.

"I said I'd see you again, Meg."

I moved away from the people nearest me and asked very quietly. "And *do* you thank me for what I did?"

"For all eternity, Meg. I have to go now but I'll see you again. It may be a long time before I do, but in the end, you know I'll be there."

"I know." I said as she hugged me and was gone, sliding sideways through a door that I couldn't see. And in my heart, I did know. After all, best friends are forever and Wendy and I – we're best friends.

THE DOMEN

Seven. All that remained of a once-proud race. Seven, who fled a de-populated world; six adults, and one cub – the last of his kind. Or he would be if they didn't find another world upon which to feast.

Their ship hurtled through the void as the Domen slept in stasis, until the computers announced that they had found a suitable world. The ship edged into a crevasse, switched on the camouflage units, and had the abused systems been human they would have sighed in relief as they shut down.

The landing site was just above a small flat-bottomed valley. The land was cultivated, landscaped, and inhabited by 'food,' all that could be wished for. The ship's systems followed procedure, they woke the Domen cub, tossed him out, and left him to survive – or die – as scout for the adults. His life or death would prove the viability of this new world. His fangs and claws would taste the flesh and blood of the inhabitants, while his mind would feed on their agonized emotions. If that was tasty and life-sustaining, if those who lived here could not overcome him, then his seniors would emerge to feast.

While the method had always worked before, on the last world the people had been more civilized, they'd realized what was occurring before they were completely overrun. They'd fought back – too effectively – and the seven Domen who'd fled were the only survivors. Now it came down to a cub, crouched shivering under a rosebush by a neatly raked gravel path. He was too young to be sent out, but computer systems have only protocol. He was the youngest. Therefore, he was cast out as the forerunner, sacrifice, and the last hope of his people. He whimpered under a bush until someone heard.

Miss Karen was old, her eyesight had never been good and now, in her seventies, it had almost failed. That did not matter though because she knew every inch of her cottage and every foot of the grounds. She loved walking through the gardens and only had one regret about moving in so many years ago. This retirement home, wonderful though it was, had no resident cat and she missed the brush of fur against her cheek, the touch of a gentle paw. She had been owned and loved by cats all her life until she moved into the valley several miles outside of the city, so when she heard the whimpering, she could not resist. She knelt, guided by the small crying and scooped up the bundle of shivering fur.

"Poor little kitten, poor baby, have you lost your mother? Don't worry, it'll be all right. I'll look after you."

Her sight was too blurred to distinguish the formidable claws and fangs that even a Domen cub possessed. And instinctively, once picked up, the cub had retracted claws and fangs until it knew if it must fight. The brush of its fur against her face was enough, the way its small whimper stopped in her cradling hands, she did not need to see.

The cub was startled, this did not fit what it knew, this being was unafraid, it did not threaten or flee; there was also no paralyzing fear on which it might feed. It was still trying to make up its mind whether to attack when Miss Karen carried it into her home, warmed milk, added a little honey, and fed it.

The cub drank and was comforted by the sweetness and warmth. It nestled into gentle hands and fed again – on the affection flowing from the one who nursed it in her lap. It savored the stroking hands, the warm body against which it was cradled. And, soothed, fed twice, full, it slept. Miss Karen sat, holding the small warm body and missing all over again the presence of the cats she'd always known.

The retirement home in which she lived was a community. Cottages lined the winding paths, reserved for those who could manage on their own. The main house – a long, low building complex – was reserved for those whose infirmities needed nursing assistance and full-time care. It was entirely staffed by women, catering to women who were alone. It paid for itself since it accepted only women who could afford its amenities, but there was a sufficiency of lonely solo women who had money. Those who were contentious, or with disruptive family who visited too often, those who hoped still to find another man, or who did not appreciate the quiet isolation of the home in a valley far from any city, left – or were encouraged to leave. While the home, and those who lived within its shelter, prospered.

Miss Karen fed the kitten again when it woke. Each time it cried, she comforted it, not only with warmed milk, but unknown to her, by the love that flowed from her to be absorbed by the Domen cub, who had never known such a food. It reveled in the outpouring of affection. It was a food that never ran dry, that nourished, sustained, was sweeter than anything ever tasted before and, if that was unknown to Miss Karen, what was unknown to the cub was what the food it absorbed was doing to it.

It grew slowly and as it grew it altered to fit the shape she projected from her long memory of the cats who had shared her life. Once when it caught a claw on her fragile skin, it felt her broadcast the bright little pain, and then the reassuring hands, the love that never faltered brought it back from any discovery of a different form of feeding.

Initially Miss Karen kept quiet the knowledge that she had a kitten, just in case the staff objected. However, after six months she allowed her favorite staff member to discover the kit's existence.

Janice smiled at the young creature. She too loved cats, and she knelt to drag a piece of ribbon for the now lanky youngster to pounce on, stroking it when it came and nudged her hand. The Domen cub savored the outpouring of affection from this new being. Food, there was so much food here in this place, a flood of it that never ceased, never ran dry.

Janice shared the secret of the kitten's existence with other staff members, who held a meeting.

"A kitten? How long has she had it?"

"About six months she said. She found it starving. She thinks the mother may have been feral, perhaps a bobcat domestic mix. It's larger than an ordinary feral, but so gentle."

"I've always wondered why we don't have a cat or two."

The administrator frowned slightly. "The owners considered that, but cats don't live much past twenty at most.

They were afraid that the ladies would become too attached and then be upset when it died."

"I think they miss having a cat about, though," Janice dared to say. "Miss Karen's had this one for months. If she has to get rid of it, she'll be far more upset."

"Oh, well, we can let it stay and see."

Miss Karen named the Domen cub Valentine, because she said he was her love these days. Valentine knew his name, and while he was always willing to be loved by others, it was to Miss Karen that he never failed to return. In three years, he was adult – and magnificent. He made certain that no one who did not live in the valley ever saw him. Increasingly he worried. His own kind, the last of his race, slept on and should he not wake them? But he dimly recalled how it had been on that other world, and he feared for his friends here. He was five when he risked an awakening at last; the two Domen who'd sired and birthed him, and them, once awake and ravenous, tottering weakly from their long sleep, he led to Miss Karen.

They crouched to attack, just as her eyes dimly saw that Valentine had brought friends. She laughed, stooping to stroke the furry crouched bodies.

"Valentine, you've brought friends to me. How nice. And aren't they beautiful?"

Her hands where they touched poured out warmth, kindness, love – the starving Domen drank and were filled. Sated, they communed with Valentine.

Are there more of these beings?

Valentine nodded.

Are they all fools to feed and love those who would slaughter them without hesitation?

Valentine led the way into the bushes outside, some distance up the nearest hill and faced them. In the Domen's silent language, he laid down the law. **They feed without stint. I came to my being starving. She held me without fear and fed me. She has never failed me. She is to me as another Domen. She is not-food. Touch a single one of them, lay a fang, a claw, on any, and that one who does so I will kill. Here we have no need to be afraid that one day we will be known for what we are and hunted down.**

His sire, once leader of all Domen, snorted. **Because here you are a pet, and besides I touched her mind and yours while she* *stroked me. You have been taking away the pain she would feel in her joints. You feed on pain as much as any Domen.**

Valentine rejected that. **No, I take away her pain because it hurts her, because she is my friend. If I wanted, I could leave her in pain and with that pain growing, she would fear too. You fed on pain and fear, with each sparking growth in the other until you found the food as rich as you desired. I have no need; the food she gives me is richer, sweeter than any I found before. You tasted it; you know.**

I know that you would destroy our way of life and all that makes us Domen. I know that it is better I destroy you first.

The struggle was fierce – and short.

Fed full for almost all of his five years, in the flower of his youth, Valentine was larger and stronger than his sire, and when it was over his dam, who remained aside from the fight, rolled in submission before him.

Well, will you leave the beings alone? Will you accept only the food that they choose to give freely?

As you order, Leader of the Domen.

* * *

Over the years they woke the other four one by one. Taught them human ways, assigned them each to their first human – always those who were dim of sight or mind and the love that flowed between Domen and humans was food and catalyst both. There were no new cubs; that required a different diet, but only the old Leader had known the full truth and specifics of that. The valley was isolated. They made sure that few from the outside ever saw them.

Staff, carefully encouraged, never noticed that the Domen lived on and on, and that for the old ladies of the valley, while their eyesight might fade, their brains dim, and their organs fail, pain did not touch them. Miss Karen died at last, a very old lady, first in Domen hearts, the only one to be permitted a Domen likeness, and never to be forgotten so long as any of Valentine's kind lived.

There were still six of them when Miss Karen's great-great-nephew stepped onto a new world, and learned the legend of the Domen. He studied the pictures, the carvings and engravings and, once back with his friends, he chuckled.

"Amazing how some legends grow."

"So, what do the dreaded Domen look like?"

John Anson laughed. "Like cats. In fact, they look rather like an old sketch I have of a cat that belonged to my great-great-aunt Karen. He was a magnificent animal. She called him Valentine and they adored each other. The sketch was done by a friend of hers who lived in the same place as Aunt Karen and who was a good artist. But family history says that for all Valentine's size he was incredibly gentle. I just can't imagine him as a ravening beast slaughtering whole populations, or," he chuckled again, "piloting a space ship."

He was right in that last. In the crevasse above and beyond the valley the ship in which the Domen had arrived was quietly moldering into rust and ruin. The Domen would fly it no more. And in the valley the 'ravening beasts' of the tales of many worlds, lived in peace. Reshaped, disarmed, and forever tamed – by love.

ENDLESSFREEDOM.COM

There were always three of us, right from the beginning: me, and Tina, and Jan. We started in primary school together, went on to Melford Private School for Girls when we were twelve and graduated from there at seventeen or eighteen. It didn't hurt our prospects that we'd won a major science prize and impressed a Government Department in our fifth form year either.

Tina went off to do a year as an assistant at a bird project down in the South Island – funded by the government department that had been impressed by our "Wild birds in the City" project two years earlier. Jan went off to reside with family in England and I went to visit with my aunt up in Whangarei. It felt like an endless summer up there and I made the most of it for the December/January/February that I stayed.

After that, my parents wanted me home. Dad had arranged a job for me so I could start to save for textbooks for university the next year. I packed up all my gear into my backpack, said goodbye to my aunt and my cousins – I'd had a great time with them all – and caught the bus to Auckland. At which point I was meeting a friend of my aunt's who was driving through to Wellington and had said she'd be happy to take me. My aunt had taken the phone call on her speakerphone with me beside her two days earlier. Her friend was talking.

"Of course, Jean. I leave Auckland at ten o'clock tomorrow morning. Your niece could catch the bus to Auckland tonight, stay in a motel, and I'll pick her up outside the Britomart at ten. I may not be in to Wellington until almost midnight; I'm not in a big hurry. But if that will suit her?"

She left the question hanging and my aunt looked at me. I nodded eagerly. Getting a lift most of the way would save the fare, which I could put towards textbooks and have to save that much less for them.

"Yes, that's fine, Moira. She's very grateful and she'll be waiting for you."

"What does she look like?"

I spoke into the speakerphone. "I'm seventeen, I've got black hair and blue eyes, and I'll be wearing black jeans, a black top, and a bright red parka. I have a black backpack with a couple of red stripes, oh, and…" I hastily translated my height into old measurement, Aunt Jean's friend was in her sixties, and "I'm about five foot four inches in height. Okay?"

There was a chuckle from the phone. "Thank you, Lyn, I have the picture." Aunt Jean flipped off the speaker part of the phone, listened a minute and then laughed.

"Yes, she is a nice considerate girl. Just deliver her to her parents safely and I'll see you next time you're up this way."

I flushed as she rang off. "I just thought – well – for some older people they still think in those measurements."

Aunt Jean smiled. "They do and Moira thought that it was considerate of you to think of it. You haven't met her but she's an old friend of mine and you've heard me speak of her. You'll be in safe hands. She's an excellent driver and always keeps her car in good condition. Now. Do you have everything you brought with you? Because you'd better start packing and make sure. Phone your parents tonight and let them know when to expect you, and since it's your last night here we're having a special dinner at six o'clock."

I thought that was great and said so. "I've had a wonderful time. I almost wish I didn't have to go home – but Dad's got a job lined up for me for most of this year from now until next Christmas and it should pay enough for me to buy all the textbooks on my list."

"Then you have to go, dear, but we've loved having you and you're welcome back any time."

The dinner was fun. We all did a lot of laughing, talking, telling old family jokes and stories – and eating – Aunt Jean's a great cook. I got up the next morning, caught the bus, spent the night in Auckland at the Bayside Motel in Takapuna and then took a bus to the Britomart – the big railway station – in the morning. I found the main entrance, put my pack at my feet and waited until an almost new red car pulled up in front of me.

"Lyn Warne?" I nodded hopefully. I liked the look of the driver. She might be in her sixties, but she had the sort of face meant for smiling a lot, and she was nicely, if casually, dressed. "I'm Moira Cowan. Hop in, dear. I want to get out of central Auckland as soon as I can."

I stowed my pack in the boot and myself in the front seat. Then I shut up and let Ms. Cowan drive. I know from my dad that it's irritating to have someone chattering on when you're trying to concentrate on driving. I did notice that Moira was a very good driver as Aunt Jean had said. Moira slipped through the traffic with no jerkiness, seeming to anticipate every opening. Once we were onto the motorway and purring along, she spoke again.

"Now we're on our way." She grinned cheerfully at me. "I usually break my trips at Taupo and Palmerston North. How does that sound to you?"

"It sounds fine, Ms. Cowan."

"Moira, please."

"It sounds fine, Moira. Aunt Jean said we'd be late into Wellington?"

"Not necessarily. I said close to midnight but that's the worst case. If we get clear roads, no problems, and don't take breaks that are too long, we could be into the city as early as eight or nine o'clock. "You have a cellphone?" I shook my head. "Okay, I have one in the glove box. You'll see if we've going to be earlier into Wellington via Palmerston North. You can ring your parents after that to let them know if it's quicker and what time we may arrive."

"Thanks."

She grinned at me. "No trouble. Now, tell me about yourself, Lyn. And no, I'm not being polite, I'm interested. Jean is an old friend of mine, but this was the first time you and I had been up that way at the same time."

"Yes, Aunt Jean's talked about you. You work for a big racing stables, don't you?"

"I do. I'm in charge of all the horses' transporting around New Zealand and sometimes overseas as well. It's very interesting work and I enjoy it. What about you, what are you doing now you've left school?"

"I start university next year. The three of us – that's my friends, Jan and Tina and me, are all taking a year off beforehand. Tina's down in the South Island with a small group that's doing studies on weka for the Department of Conservation. She's going to study extinct bird species at university and the job will be useful for her on her CV. Jan's grandmother was French and Jan's gone over for the year to stay with family in England. She's working in the business they own."

"Will that be useful for her too?"

"Jan thinks so. The English business is a branch of the French one and they can use Jan because she speaks both languages. In between that, she'll go over to France to stay with her grandparents. Her mum says that if she does well there, comes back and gets her degree in business studies, the French side of the family is considering offering her a position as their representative in a linked firm here."

Moira twinkled at me. "So that's both of your friends settled. What about you? What do you want to do with your life?"

"That's it." I groaned. "I'm still trying to decide. It's one of the reasons I took this year off."

"And you haven't decided yet?"

"No."

"Don't worry about it. You still have most of the year to go. Something will happen and you'll know. Or it may be that you'll fall into a job that's right for you. I did."

I asked questions about her job and Moira talked. She loved her job, liked living alone, and seemed to have stacks of friends.

"I must think about getting another cat soon. My old Tiger died last month and I really do miss having a cat around."

"You could get an Ocicat. A girl at school has one and I've met him. He's gorgeous, just like a little snow leopard. They can be trained and everything and they really love people. There's a breeder in Lower Hutt I heard about, but the girl at school got hers from a breeder in Palmerston North." I added, stressing the city name.

Moira smiled. "And we'll be there in a few hours. Maybe it's fate? I could stop and talk to them if we're good for time. Maybe get a card and their website address and have a quick look at whatever cats they have there."

I was pleased. She'd looked really sad for a moment when she thought about her dead cat, and she was saving me a lot of money with this lift that I was getting for free. I was glad that I might have been able to do something for her in return.

We stopped at Taupo for a toilet break, grabbed something to eat and kept going after half an hour's rest. The weather was fine but not too hot and the car was comfortable. It was early afternoon in mid-week so the roads stayed fairly empty and we were making good time. Past Taupo it was a straight run to Palmerston North on main roads or motorway the whole time and by four o'clock we were nearing that city.

That was when it happened. We came over the brow of a hill to find a car coming towards us with a big truck passing it. They were heading for us and taking up the whole of our side. They had no right to risk passing there, but as Dad says, "right of way is something somebody gives you – and if they don't give it to you, you haven't got it." In that few seconds that I had to see what was coming for us, I understood his saying.

The road was quite narrow at that point and there was no place for us to go. Moira yelled at me to hold on and braked as hard as she could to lessen the combined impact. I hit my seat belt while bracing my feet against the car floor and holding on to the door handle for dear life. Moira spun the steering wheel, the car turned, sliding sideways, the truck hit us like a bomb going off – and it was "lights out everyone."

I'm always glad that I don't remember any more. The truck hit Moira's side of the car as it turned and she was killed instantly. Later on, Aunt Jean said that was Moira. She was a very good, very experienced driver and in the seconds she had, she'd have known if the impact was head-on we'd both die and she'd tried to save me. They didn't tell me that at first, but I kept asking and Aunt Jean came to see me on her own. She told me and I cried.

"I liked her."

"So did I. She was a good-hearted woman and a very old friend. I loved her. She always said she was selfish, that she lived alone because she liked it that way, and it was true. But she'd do whatever she could to help a friend and I never knew her to do a mean thing."

"We were going to look at Ocicats in Palmerston North." I sniveled. "She said her old Tiger died last month and she missed him so much."

Aunt Jean patted me. "Then she'll be with him and they'll both be happy. Don't cry, sweetheart. She had a wonderful life doing what she enjoyed and now they're together. I knew Tiger, he was almost eighteen when he died and he adored her as much as she adored him."

I cried harder at that. It all seemed so sad and my emotions were all over the place since the accident anyhow. Aunt Jean hugged me until I finally stopped crying.

"Just get better, Lynnie, that's what Moira would have wanted. She'd had her life. She'd been a lot of places, done so many things, and this last year she'd been talking of retiring." She took my hand. "It wasn't a bad way to go, dear. No long-drawn out illness and no pain, she'd have been dead before she had time to know it."

"Are you sure?"

"Yes. I am. I came down on the plane to the hospital immediately I heard. I met the ambulance officers while I was waiting to see you and they told me her death was instantaneous. She'd have just felt a hard blow and that would have been it. Don't grieve for her too much, Lynnie. I knew Moira for years and it's the way she wanted to go. Her mother died of cancer when Moira was in her twenties. Moira watched her mother die slowly and miserably over months. She often told me that she never wanted to die like that. And she was fussy about her will, kept it up to date along with all her financial affairs. There shouldn't be any problems with her estate."

I felt better about Moira after that, but being happier didn't last. I had myself to worry about once I had time to think about me. At first, I think I'd been so weak that I didn't realize that not being able to move wasn't normal. My arms were so heavy that I couldn't seem to lift them and my legs wouldn't move when I got to where I wanted to turn over in bed. When all of that sank in, I was terrified. For weeks I didn't ask, didn't dare say a word about it, I did all the arm exercises over and over that the physiotherapists gave me and waited for someone to tell me something.

No one mentioned it. I found out later that even with what Moira did to save me I'd almost died, and the doctors had said that it would be a good idea to say nothing of my long-term chances of ever walking again until I asked. That was to give me a chance to get some strength back before I had to face the truth. But after four weeks they didn't have to tell me at all. I just knew – and the knowledge devastated me. My arms were improving. I could write a sentence or two at a time and I could turn the book pages as I read. But my legs were still immovable.

I'd always been active. I played hockey, did athletics, swam, bicycled, and walked for miles in the city. Now I guessed that I'd be spending the rest of my life in a wheelchair and what about a job? I knew people in wheelchairs had problems finding someone to hire them. I couldn't even use my arms properly. If that didn't improve, what sort of a job could I get? What about university? Could I still go? I'd lost the job that would have paid for my textbooks so how could I pay for them now?

And it hurt, not a physical pain, but the deep destructive understanding that I'd never run again, never ride my bike, never even walk the kilometers home from my friends' places on a cool quiet night. The pain of that knowledge was always there, stabbing whenever I remembered what I'd lost, aching when I forgot and tried to move my legs.

Around two or three a.m. most nights I stuck my head under the bedclothes and cried for a couple of hours. It was in those hours when everything was quiet that I thought most about what had happened and I couldn't bear it. The hospital transferred me to Wellington after a month. I had to face seeing my family and friends all the time after that, smiling and talking to them and not letting them know how I felt.

I stopped eating, not completely, but I left most of my meals, I kept crying at nights, and I was losing weight. I guess the doctors knew the symptoms because one of them started trying to get me to talk about it. I couldn't do that either. If I said the words, it would be as if I were ensuring that it happened. They got a counselor in to try to talk to me after I'd been depressed and quiet for two months and I went hysterical. At least the quiet stopped – although they didn't seem to appreciate it.

"Get out, get out, go away!"

"Lyn, you have to talk about it. You haven't asked but we know you've worked out what's happened."

"Go away. I won't talk to you."

"Lyn, you really need to..."

"What I don't need," I snarled at her. "Is some do-gooder trying to tell me how I feel, what I think about it, and how I should just cheer up because worse things have happened to other people."

"I wasn't going to say..."

"I don't *care!* Just leave me alone."

"I can't do that. You need to talk..."

"What would you bloody know?" My voice was going up to a shrill edge that must have had everyone who could hear me wondering about my sanity. "When you come in to see me in a wheelchair maybe I'll listen. Until then you can just fuck off to hell and stay there!"

I went right back to being a two-year-old at that point, stuck my fingers in my ears and stayed that way until she gave up and left me alone as I demanded. They actually found a counselor in a wheelchair after that, wheeled him in and he tried. But he was an old man, he must have been forty if he was a day and what would he know about being a seventeen-year-old girl who'd just found out that she was crippled for life? I said that and quite a lot more, and he left too.

Then Aunt Jean had a bright idea. She got me a new computer. A small powerful top-of-the-line laptop, with a broadband Internet connection and an account that allowed me to surf the net as long and as often as I liked. I was so miserable at the time that I never asked how she afforded it, but I found out later that Moira had left a large insurance policy to my aunt. That had come with a small one-bedroom flat in Kelburn in Wellington, and some good jewelry Moira had inherited from her own mother. Aunt Jean felt that investing some of the money in cheering me up was worth it.

It worked. The motor control for my fingers, hands, and arms improved quickly and I spent endless hours on the net; in chat rooms, talking to people overseas, and finding others like me. People who'd had their whole lives cut to ribbons by some idiot. What Aunt Jean didn't realize was that I've always been good with computers. I accessed sites – well – hacked into them to be truthful – and when I had the time and privacy, I found out about the man who'd killed Moira and ruined my life. The police were charging him with a list of things and he'd been hurt too. I didn't care, I hoped they'd throw the book at him and he'd spend his life in jail. I'd spend mine imprisoned in a wheelchair so that was only right.

But my computer was taking up more and more of my time. It soothed me when I was upset, cheered me up when I was down, and there was always someone out there to talk to at any hour. Jan and Tina came to see me as soon as they were back in the city.

"For God's sake, you two." I said after half an hour of halting, stilted conversation about the weather and how pleasant the newly painted ward looked. "Talk to me. My brain's still in one piece. What was France like? How are the wekas? I want to hear about your adventures. There's a window right by my bed here so I know too much about the ward and the weather already."

They looked at me, saw I meant it and started talking. In minutes we were back to our old selves. I heard about Jan's overseas trip, Tina's research on the wekas and all about their cute tricks, and the latest gossip Jan got from her little sister about our school.

"Oh, and Nerida Paiwai would like to drop in sometime if you'd be okay with that? Tina said.

I smiled. "Yeah, sure, tell her she's welcome. She can bring Granny Ngaire as well if she'll come?"

I'd met them both through Tina originally. Tina's family has money and her parents do love her, but they both have high-powered jobs so they never have much time to spend with her. To compensate they buy her stuff. Having her go everywhere in an approved taxi before they gave her a small car when she graduated high school was one of the things. Nerida Paiwai was the taxi driver Tina always used and we all liked her and we'd become friends. Nerida introduced us to her great-aunt whom everyone called "Granny Ngaire," and we absolutely adored *her.*

Granny had wonderful stories to tell about the city, and if we didn't really believe them – I mean we weren't kids to swallow fairy-stories – the truth was that it didn't matter. We loved the stories anyway and we loved Granny who was never shocked by anything we said and had a great sense of humor as well. I could remember conversations where we girls laughed until it hurt and Granny sat there po-faced making out she didn't see anything funny – which made us laugh even harder.

"Yeah, if you see them, Tina, say I'd really like to see either of them at any time."

"Okay."

She must have seen or phoned them that evening because Nerida turned up the next afternoon. We chatted for ages before she left and I hoped Granny would come and see me too sometime. It's weird, but talking to a friend who's twenty years older than you, but talks as if you were her age, makes you think differently.

Granny did come to see me as well, and talking with her always made me less miserable. She noticed that whenever she arrived, I was always on the computer and commented.

"That can give you freedom."

I was surprised. "Yeah. How did you know? That's exactly it. When I'm talking to friends or accessing sites, I forget that I'm crippled."

"That's because you aren't when you're on-line."

I couldn't believe how well she understood. I mean, Granny must be in her eighties and she doesn't use a computer – or I didn't think she did. I asked.

"Yes, dear, I have a computer and I surf the net quite often."

"Wow!"

Granny eyed me and smiled one of her patented great wicked-old-lady smiles. "As you say, wow! Stands for worlds of wonder. You'd be surprised at what you can find on-line."

I grinned back. "No, I wouldn't. I've been deep into computers ever since Tina gave me her old one when we were ten. My computer studies teacher at Melford said that I'm a natural on them."

Granny looked at me and lowered her voice slightly. "And it's never occurred to you that if you're very good at something, then perhaps it's what you're meant to do?"

It was as if she'd stuck a spike of electricity in my brain. My mind lit up with a blaze of so many thoughts at once that I couldn't say a word. I had to be an idiot, a real non-compos. For the last two years I'd been wondering what I wanted to do at university and computers had never occurred to me. That is, they had, but only in the context of doing Information Technology, help desk stuff or inputting.

"A natural," Granny added quietly, "could do original programs. She could create, not copy. Investigate, learn, expand, and grow herself into someone new and effective."

I went into a trance, I think. I thought of how I could do some of that already, I'm not a bad hacker now as it is. I could work for a private detective or a government outfit like Abby on NCIS. Or maybe I could write original programs for major companies. I could earn a good salary and do an interesting job and I wouldn't have to be dependent on my mum and dad who couldn't really afford to support me. After a long time, I looked up to find Granny sitting patiently in the visitor's chair still.

"Thanks," I said briefly.

"All you needed was the reminder. Too many trees there for you to notice the wood." Granny smiled at me. "See what you can do, and if life starts getting too bad again, call me and I'll come and see you at once. Not that I'll be staying away as it is."

She leaned over to hug me and I hugged her back, holding her small lean figure against me as if to steal some of her own strength. That must have worked for a long time because at six that evening when they visited, I talked to my parents for the first time about my being crippled and what I could do to earn a living.

"I want to go to university still but I lost the job Dad got me. How do I afford the textbooks?"

Mum was crying. "Darling, you don't have to worry about that."

"Yes, I do. You can't afford them and I don't want you to try. I have to earn the money." Dad stood up and walked nervously to the ward door and back again. That's his way when he has something he needs to say and knows that the person who hears may not like it. I knew him.

"Dad? What did you do?"

"We sued the trucking firm." I stared at them, stunned. My mum and dad aren't the sort of people to think of doing something like that. I tilted my head at him and he continued.

"It was your Aunt Jean's idea. With ACC you can't ordinarily sue for an accident, but Jean talked to Moira's employer. He was an old friend of Moira's as well as her employer and he was furious about the accident. He made a few inquiries and found out that the firm runs its trucks on a schedule so tight that the drivers *have* to speed to keep to it. He managed to get a copy of the schedule for that day and then he and Jean and your mum and I went to the company. We said we were bringing a lawsuit for punitive damages on your behalf."

"And they settled?" I asked.

Dad's face crinkled into a scowl. "They tried to wriggle out of it, so Moira's employer filed the papers. Their lawyers were on the doorstep the next day making a bigger offer. We sat tight and they upped it. You don't have to worry about your textbooks, love. And you don't have to worry about taking out a loan to get your degree either. What they paid has gone into a special account for you."

I didn't want to ask him how much the actual amount was and he saw that. "No numbers, Lynnie, all right? Let me just say that it'll pay for everything you need to get your degree. It'll buy you a small flat as soon as you're okay to be alone and you can afford to have that place converted to suit you." I said nothing for a while; taking it in that I didn't have to worry so much, and Mum and Dad stared at me anxiously.

"That's good." I said in the end. "That's really good. Did they like having to give us all that money?"

Dad's scowl became a rather grim smile. "No. They did not. But we had them over a barrel, and if it had gone to court, they'd have probably had the police after them as well. The truck driver's due to appear soon and I think they decided that it was better no one was asking too loudly why he was speeding that way. They'll have him primed with some story and without our case, that's what the jury will hear."

I came home soon after that, settled into my own bedroom that Dad had fixed up for my wheelchair and me, and gave evidence at the driver's trial. It was all hideously unpleasant and I could hardly bear to look at him. He'd murdered Moira, crippled me, and he had to be a monster. Except that he was just an ordinary looking man in his fifties, with a wife who cried for most of the trial, and two children who couldn't look me in the eye. He got three years and he was removed while his wife cried harder and his kids looked as if they'd been unexpectedly shot and it hurt really badly.

My arms improved over the next few months until I could use them as much as I wanted, but my legs remained useless. I started university but went on living at home. I used some of the money the company had paid to buy Moira's flat from Aunt Jean and left it just as it was. When I was strong enough, I'd move in there. I finished the first year at university and found, when the results appeared, that I'd done far better than I'd expected. I had an offer from an American firm with a branch in the city and said, "No, thank you."

I aced my exams at the end of my second year and the American firm made another – even better – offer. I still said no. I had my degree at the end of the third year and what Granny may have foreseen in the hospital, happened. I slumped. I'd been so busy the last three years that I hadn't had time to keep going over and over on all the things I missed. Now my studying was done for a while, it was summer, and I was remembering again. I was offered several jobs and asked for time to consider them.

But my loss was a continual bitter gnawing ache. I wanted to go for long walks in the cool evening. I could wheel my ordinary wheelchair along the streets or use the electric chair I had, but it wasn't walking. I wanted to ride my bike up to the Karori wildlife place but I couldn't do that. I wanted to jog, to feel the wind in my face, all my leg muscles pumping and the blood fizzing in my veins, the air clean and cool in my lungs – and I couldn't do any of that either.

I went into a depression that I managed to hide from everyone for a long time. I wasn't hungry and the weight dropped off me again. I hid that with another layer of clothing. I found excuses for not going out with Tina and Jan, and I stayed home, locked in my bedroom, claiming that I was working on my computer. I don't know how long my family and friends believed me, but I'd been in that depression for over three months when Granny marched into my bedroom, shut the door behind her and looked at me.

"You've quit, haven't you? You don't want to live."

I looked up and nodded dumbly. It was true – and I didn't care. I'd stopped wanting to live. I hadn't known it until that minute when she said the words and faced me with it, but I knew now. Half of my life had been lost, and quite simply I couldn't live without it. I didn't want to kill myself exactly, but I couldn't survive like this, and I suppose I was doing the next best thing. Allowing death to look until it found me.

I'd met people in my position in the various hospitals I'd been in. Some seemed to be able to get on with their lives. One had become a writer, although she'd been as active as I was. She'd already sold several books and while she missed what she'd had, she'd told me that now she put the action she couldn't do any more into her books instead and it helped her a lot. It seemed that I wasn't like that. Living crippled was pain for me, escalating since I'd finished my degree, into a constant tearing emotional agony, the constant inconvenience and the indignity, the misery of not to be able to walk, to run, and to *move* the way I'd used to! It was who and what I was and no compensation either in money or in new and interesting work would give me the strength to continue.

"Your parents will grieve for you."

I knew. But it didn't matter. I looked at her mutely. She took my hands in hers, and looked into my eyes, searching for something; the truth, I think. Was I merely self-pitying, or was the loss of my mobility killing me as I would have died if I'd lost enough blood, a part of my brain.

"I see," Granny said very gently. "Yes, I see. You have lost what you need to be who you are and you must find yourself again or die. I will give you a signpost on the road. Listen carefully. In your computer there is endless freedom. Look for that and if you find it, remember that a person is three things. The body, the mind, and the spirit. Neglect any of them and pay the price. Now go and find your road."

She added a Maori proverb I knew; we'd heard it from Nerida. "He moana pukepuke e ekengia e te waka." A choppy sea can be navigated. Or – and in short – persevere.

Granny fixed me with her gaze and shook me a little by my shoulders. "Remember what I've said. Now go and look, may you find what you need. And if you do, tell no one, the gift is for you. If others need it, it will be offered but that gift isn't yours to give."

She let herself out of the bedroom and I went back to sitting and looking at the wall, thinking of nothing. I woke up the next morning though with some of what she'd said running about in my mind. The most obvious place to look was on the Internet. I tried mindbodyspirit.com, then signpost.com. Nothing. I checked up on her proverb's spelling and input that. The computer seemed to hesitate and for a couple of seconds I was hopeful. Then it came back as no site and I slumped again.

It was almost a week of frustration and discovering nothing no matter what I input, before I dreamed of Granny's visit and in that dream, I heard her say again "In your computer there is endless freedom." I woke up, grabbed for my laptop and input the words endlessfreedom.com. The computer flickered; the screen came up with soft music and a glowing background. I tapped on the site and it cleared so that I saw my city on screen – as if it were spread out below me. I could hear the wind blowing, birds calling, and the rush of my need to be there, to move within it, overwhelmed me.

I leaned forward, yearning. I could see the streets I used to walk, the roads where I'd ridden my cycle, the school grounds where I'd often run. I wanted to run there again, I had to! The pain of my inability tore and savaged. If I couldn't be free, I'd rather be dead. I leaned closer, gave a small yelp of fright as I found I was falling – and landed on a surface I couldn't see wrapped in mist. I hadn't been crippled long enough, and I still walked and ran in my dreams. Without thinking about it I stood up on the invisible surface and looked down to check I wasn't hurt by the fall. Then I froze.

The surface seemed to engulf me. It upheld me, swept me into itself like a river in flood. And suddenly I didn't care. I allowed it to take me where it would while I surfed the stream's roiling substance. I bathed in motion, in light and the shifting flickering of my being. I rolled like a dolphin, leaping out of the river that held me and submerging again. Feeling the play and pull of my muscles and screaming in a delight that was so great

I felt crazed with rapture. I was tossed up on a shore after an endless time and found I was lying on my bed, the laptop open beside me, but the screen dark and switched off.

My computer wouldn't open the site for the next twenty-four hours but when it did, I dived into the river and flew again, buoyed up in the light, able to move as I never had been, even when I was whole. I didn't tell my parents, they couldn't have believed me and I didn't want them thinking I was crazy. I told Tina and Jan of course. They couldn't open the site and neither could I if they were present. As granny had said. It was a gift to me and I couldn't give someone else's gift away. But it worked for me, oh God, it works for me and I am free when I need to be.

I took the job I was offered with the American firm's office here and I enjoy it. I make very good money and I have the flat that the truck company's money bought me. I have all my friends and I'm happy. But whenever that terrible longing to be free finds me again, I can open the site and access the freedom I have to have.

Once I rode a bicycle. Now I ride the computer's power, soaring and diving in the great river of wild electrons – I go wherever they flow. And if I always have to return and allow gravity to claim me, then that's all right too. I have two lives, one spent surfing the river, and one spent in my wheelchair with friends and a family who love me – and both halves of my life are necessary to me. One holds me to the earth and reality, and the other allows me the freedom I can't live without.

Granny says that the city can hold all of the times and all of the places it has ever been, and that if you look sideways in just the right way, sometimes you can see those other times and places. She never said that sometimes, if you need to do it badly enough, you can see a time and a place that is yet to come. Or maybe one that is only a possibility. I don't know. I don't need to know. I swim and surf in my wild river of cascading electrons – and I am content.

JUST A POOR OLD LADY

"She's a nuisance. We need that last house vacant so the whole block can be torn down. Costelman plans to put up a block of fifty new apartments. They'll each have a carport for off-street parking and there'll be landscaped areas. The development will provide more revenue for the city and with that street looking over the bay, apartments in a new block of that quality will attract full occupancy. In fact, half of them are already sold."

Stephanie snorted. "Give me a break, will you. Mrs. Frater has lived in that house for the whole of her life. It was her parents' house before her and she loves it."

"What's to love? The place is a dump and it's about ready to fall down. Costelman is offering her fair compensation and an apartment in a new council block in a suburb that doesn't have so much crime."

"Maybe she'd like to still own her own home and stay in it?" Stephanie's voice was slightly edged. "She's just a poor old lady who doesn't want to move away from where she's lived her entire life. If you were ninety and you'd lived all your life in one place you might want to stay there too."

Robert Paratini snorted. "Not me. I know what's good for me. Catch me living in some old dump. Look, Stephanie, she likes you, convince the old girl to move, it'll be easier on everyone if she decides to do it of her own free will. You know we'll win in the end."

Stephanie considered. There were times when being a social worker wasn't very pleasant. Then again, there were times when it *really* wasn't.

"I'll talk to her, but I can't promise anything. She's had a hard life, Rob. Her parents had three children; the other two were older and left home. Apparently, they never came back, not even to visit, and when her parents died, the lawyers couldn't trace the siblings."

"What's hard about that? Rob Paratini said cynically. "The old lady inherited the lot, didn't she?"

"She misses her family," Stephanie said simply.

"I bet she'd have missed their share of the house even more."

"You're a cynic, Rob. She was married during the war too – one of those quickie marriages that didn't last. He left her and went off one day, deserted the army and her and never came back. She went back to her maiden name but kept the Mrs."

Robert shrugged. "From what my granddad told me that sort of 'marry and vanish' stuff went on during most of the war. The guy was probably married to someone else first and went back to her as soon as he'd had enough wedded bliss with this one. Just explain to Mrs. Frater that she moves out voluntarily and takes the nice new council apartment, and the compensation offered, or we make a compulsory purchase order and she goes anyhow."

A week later Stephanie was trying to explain the situation to a fluffy white-haired old lady – and failing.

"No, dear. I'm not selling no matter how much they offer me. I've lived here my whole life. Everyone else goes away but me, and I'm staying right here." Her eyes wandered away from Stephanie to stare at the line of silver-framed photos on the mantelpiece. "My family would have wanted me to stay. Ian and Bernie, and Sylvia and Margery and all of the others too."

Stephanie frowned. Surely Mrs. Frater's two older brothers had been called Mark and Luke – from the Bible as their sister had told her a number of times.

"Who are Ian and Bernie and the others?" she asked, suddenly curious.

"The foster children my parents took in during the war and afterwards. My parents always believed that you should share what you had with others. So sometimes we took in orphans to foster."

"Oh," that explained why these others hadn't been involved in the Frater parents' will, they weren't actual siblings.

But from the sound of it, she'd have thought they would have been younger than the old lady she faced. Hadn't any of them stayed in touch? If they had, it was rather mean of them not to have called to see if they could help – or maybe she was wrong and they'd all been older than their foster sibling or more sickly, and all of them were long since gone too? She didn't ask. It could have upset the old dear.

Mrs. Frater was still murmuring gently to herself. "After my parents died, I did take in boarders for a while to help with the upkeep. Nice young people, some of them, others weren't but I managed. But then it got too difficult for me, all that work. I wasn't strong enough to continue so it's just been me for the last twenty years, my dear." Her voice turned gently obstinate. "And I'm staying right here."

Stephanie gave up. She reported to Robert and the worried council that if they wanted to shift that poor old lady and demolish her house, they'd have to use a compulsory purchase order and remove her themselves, possibly by force – then weather the resultant storm of bad publicity that would cause if any reporters heard about it.

This thought wasn't something that enthused the council at all – but the plans for the new development had all been approved, complete with the necessary permits. Mr. Costelman, the developer/contractor, was threatening legal action if he wasn't given clearance to start the work, and half the potential units were already sold. After long discussions during which Mrs. Frater remained adamant, the council bit the bullet and called in the police – who weren't happy about any of it either.

"What? We have to drag a ninety-year-old woman out of her own home?"

His police superior sighed. "The council obtained a compulsory purchase order and it's all legal. The woman's known she'll have to move out for almost a year and she's made no attempt to relocate. The council has offered her a nice ground floor flat in the new apartment block over by the Basin and the rent has been discounted as a further incentive. She gets fair compensation, help with the removal, and a number of other perks including – for all I know – a free bus-pass for life.

"It seems none of that is good enough for her and she's sitting tight. The contractor has to start tearing down that house of hers this week to finish the work on time, so the council have called us in. Get over there and do your job, but for heaven's sake try to be unobtrusive. I don't want headlines about how the police were rough with a poor old lady." He glared.

His subordinate glowered back. "How do I manage that if she won't cooperate? If she stages a sit-down strike in the lounge, am I supposed to drag her out by the heels?"

"I have no idea, pick a junior and give him those instructions."

His own junior marched out of the room, made aware that as it had been done to him so it would be useful to pass that order on. He did, and it was Constable Bob Olsen who got the unpleasant job once the instruction had been passed right down the line to where it – if not the buck – stopped.

Bob considered what he knew of old ladies – which was quite a lot since he came of a long-lived family. Both his great-grandmothers were still alive. He could get advice from Granny Ngaire as well – which he did, and he acted promptly. At eight a.m. he arrived on foot at the Frater house with Stephanie. Bob explained the situation gently but clearly to the old lady and received the expected refusal.

He immediately gave quiet orders to Stephanie, scooped up Mrs. Frater, and carried her out of the back door as Stephanie opened it. He placed the old lady in the police car he'd parked unobtrusively and conveniently beforehand in the street that dead-ended behind the house and drove Mrs. Frater to her new apartment. There he tucked her into an armchair, switched on the wall-heater, and made her a good strong cup of tea before leaving for her old home to oversee her packing.

There was a considerable amount of that. The attic floor was covered by a layer of ancient trunks and suitcases, the downstairs rooms were filled with furniture and a host of knickknacks, and everything had to be carefully packed in case of damage. If her possessions were broken, she'd have cause to complain and probably to sue.

The removal men were embittered about the amount of

work that the house was generating for them. "For God's sake, what is she – one of these flaming hoarders?"

Stephanie was severe. "No, she's just a poor old lady who's lived in this house her whole life and her family lived here before her. Please be very careful with everything as you pack it. The council is paying for this job and if she makes a complaint about breakage or anything else they'll be speaking to your boss."

The removal men scowled at her but complied. It was a full day's work before everything was packed and removed, and the ancient house left echoing and empty. The furniture was carefully unpacked at the new flat and the old lady was surrounded with her own belongings again.

Of course, the contents of a three bedroom two-storied house don't fit into a flat half that size. Mrs. Frater's second bedroom was piled to the ceiling with the contents of the attic, but she could sort that out at her leisure. It wasn't as if there was anyone who wanted to come and stay in the spare bedroom. The job was done. The way was cleared for a fine new development and everyone – baring one poor old lady – was happy with the outcome.

"How did you manage to move her, Olsen?"

"Quite simply, sir. I know old ladies and a relative of mine gave me some good advice as well. They'll do almost anything rather than make a public scene. As soon as I picked her up, she surrendered. I came and went from the back door of the house and apart from that I went in at eight in the morning. Old ladies mostly get up early but the media don't, not if they aren't expecting anything to happen as yet. Stephanie – Ms. Woodly – told me that some of the reporters started arriving around nine, but by then Mrs. Frater was long gone and no one else was talking to them."

"I suppose she can't claim that it was an assault when you picked her up?"

"I shouldn't think so, sir. I was very gentle and she can't have been too upset. She made me a cup of tea in the afternoon while the men unpacked for her, and she said that I was a nice boy."

"Oh, well, in that case we'll hope for the best."

"I think we can, sir. She seemed quite resigned once she found she couldn't do anything."

Stephanie visited Mrs. Frater every day as the old house was being demolished. She brought biscuits for the old lady, and a regular progress report on the work.

"They've got all the framing down now, tomorrow they start on the foundations. After that, in a week or two, they'll start the real digging."

"Digging, dear?"

"Yes, they need good foundations for the apartment block and they're planning to have the carports in a basement. The main part of the new building will be right on your land. I think they'll dig down about fifteen or twenty meters at least."

The old lady sighed quietly. "We had a vegetable garden along the back fence. Wonderful it was, we grew huge cabbages and cauliflowers during the war, and there were fruit trees down both sides of the property. They're gone now but they bore excellent crops."

"You could start a window box here." Stephanie said brightly. "You could plant herbs, things like parsley and chives."

"It wouldn't be the same, dear, a garden needs deep-trenching and a good, rich fertilizer, you can't do that in a window box."

"No, I suppose not."

On the street where an old lady had been the last holdout a house vanished hour by hour, the framing, the foundations, every trace of the building that had once stood there. Almost four weeks after the old lady left, the contractors started final leveling of the whole twelve-house site. Stephanie called on Mrs. Frater to enjoy a cup of tea and pass on the latest progress report. She found the old lady looking very shaky.

"Are you all right, Mrs. Frater?"

"I'm afraid not, my dear. I don't want to be a nuisance but I really do feel rather faint. Perhaps a cup of tea would help?"

Stephanie made a pot of strong tea, quietly calling the old lady's doctor once she was out of earshot in the kitchen. He spoke thoughtfully from the other end of the phone.

"Her heart isn't good. I'd better come now. All that moving to a new place didn't help either." Stephanie winced and protested. "No, not your fault I know, I understand you've been kind to her. She likes you."

"I like her too."

The doctor arrived, examined his patient, looked worried and together they put the old lady to bed. She accepted a pill and the tea to wash it down, and drifted off to sleep as they watched her. In a low voice the doctor continued with what he had been saying after they had tiptoed from Mrs. Frater's bedroom into the lounge.

"Not much I can do for her now, she's ninety and just wearing out." Stephanie nodded.

"I'm sorry she had to move, but this is a nice place. I only hope she sorts out some of those old trunks and things she brought with her. Her family must have traveled a lot over the years. It's a pity there's no one left to keep her company."

"She's been unlucky in that." the doctor said knowledgeably. "I know something about her because my father was her doctor before me. I started treating her only when he retired. He said there were three children in the family but her older brothers left home and never even came back to visit. Her parents forbade their names to be mentioned. My father suspected there'd been some sort of scandal. There were a lot of people who boarded at the house in later years. Some of those stayed a few months but she always seemed to end up on her own after a while. A pity, everyone's always liked her. Did you know I witnessed her latest will the other day?"

"No?"

"I brought my nurse with me so she'd have two witnesses. I probably shouldn't say this, Ms. Woodly, but you may need to know about it in the near future. She's left everything she has to you. She told me that there was no one else remaining in her family and you'd always been very kind to her. She understood that you'd done your best to see that she stayed in her house. She doesn't blame you that she had to leave."

Stephanie sat down abruptly and gaped at him. "Well, that's very good of her, but I suppose it won't be much."

"I wouldn't bet on that, my dear. I know she has some lovely jewelry, and old ladies like her often have more valuables tucked away than people think. But I must be going." He went, only to phone Stephanie the following morning with the news; Mrs. Frater had died in her sleep during the night.

A lawyer rang Stephanie three days later to say that as sole executor and beneficiary she should sort out the estate. Stephanie went to the flat and began. She looked at Mrs. Frater's jewelry and admired it. The doctor had been right, there was more – and of a far better quality – than she'd expected. She decided to start her sorting out with the items stacked to the roof in the spare room. She opened a number of the ancient trunks and suitcases and glared at the contents in exasperation.

It looked as if the Frater family had kept everything they'd ever owned. Nothing of value, but frocks, shoes, even faded underwear, hairbrushes, and old combs, bent hairpins – it was ridiculous. She'd have a garage sale and rid herself and the flat of the whole lot. Anything that couldn't be sold could go to the dump. Some of the clothing might be useful to a theater group. It looked as if some of that dated back to the Second World War. All different sizes and – there was an energetic knocking at the door.

She opened it to find Constable Olsen looking agitated. "Ms. Woodly, can you come down to the building site at once please? Since you've inherited Mrs. Frater's estate my superintendent thinks you should be there in case we need any sort of permission from you."

Puzzled but compliant, Stephanie took her seat in a police car and was sped to the site where it seemed that building had stopped – but the number of people involved had dramatically increased.

"What's going on?" A man she identified as a senior policeman answered her. There was something in the attitude.

"Ms. Woodly?" Stephanie nodded. "The social worker for Mrs. Frater?" Stephanie nodded again. "The contractors found something when they began excavating." His face creased wryly, "Or rather, I should say they found a number of things." There was something in his manner that alarmed her.

"What?"

"Bodies, Ms. Woodly. Ten so far, all ages, all neatly buried in a line along what was probably the back fence area originally."

Stephanie stared at him, then in a way that made it clear she was quoting, she spoke in a small, horrified voice. "'We had a vegetable garden along the back fence. Wonderful it was, we grew huge cabbages and cauliflowers during the war, and the fruit trees down both sides of the property, they're gone now but they bore excellent crops for so long.'

"That's what she said to me, and I said that she could start a window box in her new place. I said that she could always grow herbs, things like parsley and chives."

"What did she say?"

"That it wouldn't be the same, because a garden needs deep-trenching and a good rich fertilizer." Stephanie shivered, thrusting down nausea. "I've been looking through her stuff at her council flat. She has nine engagement rings, over a dozen wedding rings, and there's a whole room filled with old trunks and cases. They came out of the Fraters' attic originally. I've been opening some of the trunks, the contents look as if they belonged to people who walked away and left everything they owned behind them, and the Fraters just packed up the lot and put it away." Her gaze on him was appalled.

"Ten trunks or suitcases I suppose?" the Superintendent said quietly.

"No, I'd say there's at least twice that, maybe a lot more, and I found all those wedding rings too."

There was a long silence while they stared at each other in wild and horrified surmise. Then Stephanie spoke again, her sadly cynical tone that of one who is finally disillusioned. "And I thought she was just a poor old lady."

ONE OF OUR OWN

Okay, I'll be honest with you – a joke, geddit? I'm a crook from a long line of them. Ma says that there were Howland's in Lowton when it was a village and not a suburb in London. Doesn't mean we aren't educated these days. I've got a degree in business management. It's logical; I have a business to run. I was running it peacefully when Beth came home to Lowton.

"Jimmy?" I'd glanced up when the skinny woman came in through my door and for a minute, I didn't recognize her. Then I did.

"Beth? Dear God, it's you."

We fell into each other's arms and hugged as if she were a sister come home to the brother she hadn't seen for too long – which in a way was true.

"Damn, it's good to see you."

"You too, Jimmy. And you'll be seeing a lot more of me. I'm coming back to live in Lowton as soon as I can find a suitable place."

I grinned at her. "I can find one for you, girl. But why would you want to live here?"

"My work can be anywhere so it may as well be here."

There was something in her voice and I decided not to ask. She'd tell me when she was ready. It didn't matter, if she was coming home, I'd be happy, and so would ma.

Beth smiled once she saw I wasn't going to nag her with questions. "How's ma, Jimmy?"

"She'd be all the better for seeing you. Have you been home yet?"

"Not yet."

"Wanna go now?"

Ma was delighted to see Beth and it wasn't long before they were engrossed in woman talk while I sat quietly, watching as the stress fell away and Beth relaxed. And that was interesting. Until she let go, I hadn't realized just how strained she'd been looking.

* * *

I'd first met Beth when her dad got into financial strife, downsized into one of a row of houses around the corner from our place, and started to work his way back up again. Beth had been seven, and I'd been eight, she'd been nothing at all to look at, and she still wasn't that much, but under that thin frame, the mousy hair, hazel eyes, and roundish face, there beat a heart of gold, a brain that fired on all cylinders, and very good reflexes.

She started at my school and when my pup followed me one day and was caught in the traffic, it was Beth who darted between cars, scooped him up and arrived panting back on the pavement. I'd seen it and thirty years later, I still couldn't believe it. She'd danced between the heavy traffic like a matador, picked up Morse on the fly, and got him and her back without a scratch. After that I stopped anyone teasing her about her accent, and discovered that she had brains.

"Damned if I can understand all that stuff." We'd been told to do an essay on themes in Hamlet. Our teacher was one of those people who believed that you should always aim high. In my case, he was aiming so far above my head he'd lost me in the stratosphere.

Beth giggled. "It's simple."

"Really, then suppose you explain it to me?"

She did, using ma and da, and my uncle Len as examples. I wrote my essay and got an "A," which stunned me – and delighted ma. I told her about Beth and ma invited her to dinner. Her parents weren't that happy about the friendship but Beth was obstinate. She liked me, my ma and da, Morse, and my little brother Billy. So, for the next eleven years we were mates and she was in and out of our place like it was her own.

The year Beth turned eighteen, her dad had worked his way up again, and he bought a house in a better suburb, while

Beth's mum couldn't wait to shake the Lowton dust off her shoes. Beth wasn't like that. She came back every weekend, spending a day with ma and all of us, catching us up on her news – she'd got a job with a small publisher – and us catching her up with ours – da had come up with a new profitable angle on the long con.

* * *

I tuned back into the conversation.

"Yes, it's gone into another edition and my agent thinks he may have a movie deal."

Ma chuckled. "Did you ever think you'd be a famous author, lovie?"

"No. It's great that so many people like my mystery books, but I could do without all the other stuff that comes with it."

I came alert. I knew that note in her voice. Ma had worked her around to where Beth might tell us what was really bothering her.

"Someone giving you a hard time?" Ma asked softly.

Beth slumped in the big old sagging armchair. "It's bad, ma. I can't go anywhere without them after me. Taking photos, making up stories, chasing my car and crowding me off the road so they can claim I was drunk and crashed."

Her voice was unsteady. "One of them offered dad a thousand pounds to give him a quote about how I liked men too much. He wouldn't so they claimed he'd said it anyway. And Mum forgot to get more milk for the cake she was making, she rushed out to buy some and a photographer got that photo of her in her old doing-the-housework clothing and they ran an article about how my mother was an alcoholic. Oh, that isn't what it *said*, but anyone could figure out what they meant and Mum cried for ages."

Ma's gaze met mine over Beth's bowed head. I got out of my chair and hauled her skinny body into my arms. She let go then and wept silently, her whole body shaking. After a few minutes she got hold of herself again and sat up. I let her go.

"Sorry, ma, Jimmy."

"Don't worry about it, nothing to a few tears among friends," ma assured her. "Who's doing this? Is it a bunch of them or mostly one fella?"

"It's all of them doing it, but one in particular."

"Who is he?"

"His name's Jerico, or that's his byline. He takes photos and writes his own articles to go with them. He's paparazzi and main rat for *Popular Voice*." I could see that now she was talking to us more of the strain was easing. "Most of them are there to get photos of you doing something stupid – he's the one that gets them because he pushed you into it."

"How does he manage that?" Ma was honestly interested but I knew her well enough to see that she was outraged on Beth's behalf as well.

"You've heard about Diane Hallivan?" We both nodded. The lady was a film star who'd recently had a baby, before that she'd lit up the TV screen in a long-running series about the Romans in Britain. "She came out of hospital. A man came running up to her and pushed something like a taser towards the baby. She jumped back. Her husband hit the man. Diane lost her balance, fell over and someone was taking photos."

She looked at us. "You've seen them. What did you think?"

I had to agree. "That photo was bad, the one with her skirt up to her hips so her pants showed, and the baby looking as if his head had just hit the pavement. The paper suggested her husband made her leave hospital too early and she was risking the baby."

Ma nodded. "I see, and that's the sort of thing they're doing to you?"

"Hacking my voice mails. Trying to hack my computer. They're out of luck there. The one I do my writing on isn't on-line. But that's mostly just business." She glanced at me. "You'd know." I did. Any smart businessman takes precautions and if your business isn't all that legal – or the product is as valuable as hers is – you take more care still.

"It's Jerico. That photo he got of me snarling at him and with my hand up looking as if I was going to hit him? Well, there was a good reason for that." Her face reddened. "I'd just come out of a restaurant with Paul." I knew the Paul she meant. He was a nice little man, an old pal of hers – and as gay as a Robin in spring. His partner, Marty, was an ex-wrestler, and now a club owner. "Jerico sidled up to me where no one else could hear and said something utterly filthy about me and Paul and Marty, and I..."

"Lost it." I said flatly.

"Yes. I shouldn't have, but you didn't hear him. If he'd said that to ma she'd have bounced him all the way down the street."

Ma chuckled. "Or repeated what he'd said at the top of my voice and asked him if *he* was up for it," she informed us both. "Dirty little sod."

There was more, but it all added up to this Jerico not being a man who waited for something to happen, he went out and made it happen and then collected his blood money for the photos, and the article he wrote – steeped in spite, innuendo, and with snide questions that got around the libel laws.

"So, you think he can't get at you in Lowton?"

"I think he'll find it harder."

He would if ma and I had anything to say about it. I'd had a brother, Billy. He'd been three years younger than Beth. He'd adored her and she'd loved him as a little brother. He'd got really sick at eighteen, about the time Beth sold her first book and unexpectedly it went onto the best-seller list. She'd been going to buy a small house, until the doctor told us what was wrong with Billy, then she used every penny to get him into a private hospital. She couldn't save him, but that operation gave him another ten years before the cancer came back. He had time to fall in love, marry, and have a son that was the apple of ma's eye. We'd have owed Beth even if we hadn't loved her.

So, Beth came back to Lowton and I dropped the word around. Beth Olson was a friend of mine. Anything happened to her and I'd take it personally. I found her a house in our street, and with work from the team of carpenters and painters I'd hired, it was a showplace in weeks. Ma put out the word on her own network too, and when Beth moved into her new home there was a housekeeper for her, and a lad who'd do the heavier work, drive her if that was needed, and keep an eye out for intruders.

The lad was my da's cousin Mickey, so I knew she'd be in good hands. He had a Black Belt from a local gym, training as a boxer, and could hold a sweet smile all day while he tuned you up for looking at him the wrong way. Best of all he was average-looking, nothing for anyone to remember.

"Don't start anything unless there's a real opportunity," I told him. "We don't want to see any photos in the paper."

Beth had started on her next mystery, and she was hot property, not the least because her mysteries were dark, with a wicked edge, and they weren't the sort of thing you'd expect from a female writer who looked younger than she was and naive besides. All the paparazzi were dead keen to get a shot of her doing something she shouldn't, but her living in Lowton was giving them fits. It's an old suburb, all narrow streets, rows of terrace houses, a population that's known for generations how to keep their mouths shut, and Beth was one of our own.

They did their best. Jerico did a story that managed to simultaneously leer and sneer about Beth returning to live in Lowton because she had some "rough trade" lover, that she was a gutter-bred girl returning to her roots, and suggesting that she'd lost all her money in some sleazy business and had to retrench.

He tried to bribe her housekeeper, who spoke in a foreign language, and finally shut the door in his face – Alyson, ma's old friend and distant relative, whose father was from the Hebrides and spoke Erse, which she'd learned from him. Jerico must have taped it. He found someone who could speak Erse and returned. Alyson switched to upper class tones and rang the local police station, complained that she was being harassed by two men who'd made indecent suggestions to her – and Jerico and his comrade found themselves trying to explain that.

The police were not amused. Jerico was unwise enough to threaten them that they'd regret hassling him, and he'd have been charged but that the paper paid Alyson off – with our agreement she should take the money – and Jerico tried another angle.

* * *

"Boss, someone wants me to set my house on fire at night. Says he'll pay high, and if I'm smart, I can start a fire that'll look bad, get everyone out of their houses, bring the fire brigade and cops, but without doing much."

"Who's the guy?"

"Dunno, but he's offering good money."

"Tell him you'll do it, and have a meet in *The Mucky Duck*. Half the cash up-front."

I tracked the guy back to Jerico and saw the idea. Reg's house was in the street that backed on to Beth's. If the wind was a westerly, the fire brigade would evacuate everyone in the nearby houses, including Beth. The paper would have great photos of her, out in the street in her nightgown. If she *was* dressed, they could make a big deal of the danger she'd been in and rehash why she was living in Lowton – where things like this happened to the feckless inhabitants.

Reg lit the fire two hours after midnight. The fire brigade – and uncle Len who runs that watch – turned up before the fire did more than flare once and put it out. They grilled Reg, who stood there looking innocent and sounding outraged. Alyson piped up.

"I saw a man sneaking around here. Maybe he started it."

"Where did you see him?"

"Over there," said Alyson, pointing to where Jerico and his pal were waiting to get a good shot of Beth being evacuated.

Jerico was faster on his feet than his photographer. The police were *really* not amused. The paper hired a high-priced lawyer. Reg said nothing, and in due course was paid off. The lawyer persuaded the judge that photographers can lurk anywhere they like when there's no evidence they've committed a crime. And I heard that the paper was thinking of telling Jerico to find another job since he seemed to have lost his touch.

In the spirit of that, I took Beth out for an evening. A nice restaurant, friends around, and in the middle of it, a man drifted up to me and whispered something. I felt a sudden burst of fury that surprised me, until I looked across the table and finally understood something I should have seen a long time ago. I excused myself, walked to the side where no one was near enough to overhear and listened.

"First up, she didn't do nothing. I swear. He give his game away too soon an' she dumped him. I liked her, and truth to tell, I'm getting out. Bin offered a job with a man that travels, an' if I had a bit o' cash to get a good suit or two before I join him, I'll make a better impression."

I paid him. In cash, where no one saw the transaction, and I made it very clear that this was a one-off deal.

"I know. Got family in Lowton. S'why I brought it to you. Word is that bastard's reporter been trying to get something on her for years and that's why she come back."

"She never let him touch her?"

He grinned cheerfully. "No way. He come back the night she dumped him, effing and blinding. Said she had to be frigid. She wouldn't let him get his hands on her an' if he couldn't, no one could. But that isn't what he'll say for this Jerico, see?"

I saw. I knew the little man's employer, a man who lived off women – one way or another. And a year back I'd heard some of it from Beth – and more about the man from people who knew him.

* * *

"You look a bit down in the mouth, girl?"

"I think I almost made a fool of myself, Jimmy."

"How so?"

"I met a man at a party my publishers gave. He seemed nice. He asked me out to a restaurant and I went, then to the movies, and on a picnic with friends. It was all innocent, I was between books, it was fun, but he started getting too keen, suggesting he could move in with me, that we'd go away on holiday. I had to tell him I was too busy. I wanted to start the next book and I didn't want to live with him. Once he saw I meant it, he got nasty. He said after the money he'd spent on me, he expected more."

I'd smiled at her. "He felt short-changed?"

"I guess so. But I didn't like him that way."

I bit back a wider grin. "You said so?"

"He didn't take it well. He said I was either frigid or a lesbian. He said I'd led him on to get taken to expensive places and then I wouldn't come across. I think if we hadn't been in a fairly public place, he'd have tried to rape me."

I knew the "gentleman" and he'd have done more than tried. "You won't be seeing him again?"

"Ugh." she shivered. "No."

* * *

That'd been twelve months ago, but Major Burlan would have made certain that he had people who could honestly say she'd gone out with him, maybe he had a photo or two that could be taken out of context. That was one of the ways in which he worked his blackmail. I went back to Beth – I could think of someone who'd have his own ways of dealing with the Major if he knew what I knew.

We had a great evening. Beth kissed me at her door, and I went home to make a phone call. A week after that Beth phoned me.

"Did you hear about Major Burlan?"

"I've been at my desk since seven a.m. I wouldn't have heard Armageddon, why?"

"One of Sheik Ahmed bin Hassan's men stabbed the major to death last night."

"Why did he do it?"

"No one knows. The man's disappeared. Gossip is that the sheik got him out of the country."

I made small talk for a while, invited her to dinner again and hung up, satisfied. After Beth's episode with the major, I'd had him checked out – and one of the things I'd uncovered had been the probable reason the sheik's daughter had committed suicide four years ago. All it had taken was an anonymous phone call to the sheik – while Mickey watched the major and I lurked, mobile in hand, by the major's residence. Mickey phoned to say what happened. I went in and tossed the place, found his nasty little stash of stuff on Beth, and got out of there. There wasn't anything bad, but if he'd been there to talk about what they'd done together – to hint and suggest – it could have looked damning on the front page.

Jerico must have been furious to lose his scoop. I heard that he'd tried to get into the major's apartment, failed, tried to bribe the little man's replacement, and received a punch in the face. He tried to get an injunction, claiming public interest in any papers, and failed there too.

Unlike his affairs, my courting of Beth was moving along very nicely. We were well past kissing – she wasn't nearly as skinny as I'd always thought – and when I suggested that marriage would be a good idea and that it would make ma's day if Beth agreed? She did. It would be a real Lowton wedding. The reception afterwards would be in our street and everyone would be welcome. Beth was happy. So was I, and ma wept when Beth told her that we'd name our first son, Billy.

"I loved him too," Beth said.

"I know, love, and he thought the world of you. If only he was here to see the day."

* * *

I left ma and Beth to the planning and tended to business that doesn't take care of itself, and just now, I had something coming in.

"He'll arrive a week tonight. Have you got everything ready?"

I nodded.

"Good. Once he's been fixed up, we'll be moving him to Northumberland. We've got a job there to slot him into. Where's he staying?"

I allowed my lips to curve very slightly and the man from MI6 stared. "Not in her house? You cheeky sod. He'll need someone to live in. Alyson, I suppose?"

"Yes, and Mickey'll stay in the house while he's there, just in case."

"Right, he's a good man, Mickey. I'll see you again in seven days."

He was gone without even the sound of a closing door and I allowed a very broad grin to surface. Yes, I come from a very long line of criminals, but my great-grandda found that it paid to be on the right side of the law now and again. The relationship flourished and these days about half my business came from certain agencies. We're good at our job, deniable at need, and oddly perhaps to anyone outside the circle, we're patriots.

I married Beth while our friends and family celebrated the day.

As Alyson said while we were leaving the church, "Now she's legally one of ours."

We honeymooned with friends in Wales and the obnoxious Jerico left us alone. That puzzled Beth.

"I would have thought that me getting married would have been a real opportunity to make headlines. He'd know about you and think what he could have said?"

She didn't know he'd intended a different coup even his paper hadn't known about. Jerico, having managed a sight of Beth's latest manuscript when it first arrived with the publisher, had sat up day and night writing something similar then got it sealed and time-stamped, so that when she returned from our honeymoon it would be to a lawsuit claiming she'd plagiarized someone else's book. Jerico was just searching for a hungry and crooked writer who'd be willing to stand up in court and lie if the money was right – and I'd had enough of the man.

I swept Beth over our threshold. The agent who'd been safe-housed there was gone. The photographers and reporters, even the tabloid ones had been – almost – reasonable. I was happy. Ma was happy. Beth was very happy – and already working hard on her next mystery. As for Jerico, people did look for him, but only the small hungry creatures that inhabit the lower portion of the Oaze Deep, ever knew exactly where he ended up – and they don't talk.

It's as Alyson said, Beth was one of our own – and Jerico who claimed to be a good reporter, should have known me – and known better. Too bad he hadn't.

WAITING TABLES AND TIME

Mary had always thought she was as ordinary as her name. She had medium brown hair, medium brown eyes, she was of medium height, weight and looks, and being middle-class, her clothes tended to the medium as well. Nothing about her had ever stood out at school, and now that she worked in a coffee café while she decided if she wanted to go on to university next year, well – that was pretty much medium too.

Even her relationships were medium she thought as she carried a tray of toasted sandwiches to the group sitting near the café door. She'd just broken up with Billy Cross; she'd liked him, but it was a comfortable, placid liking, nothing to make the heart race or the pulse accelerate – and wasn't that supposed to happen?

She hadn't got the impression that she'd broken Billy's heart either, so probably he'd felt the same way. Absently she distributed the toasted sandwiches, returned to gather the next tray full of food and continued to worry at the problem of being medium when you were expected to stand out. Maybe she could cut her hair and dye it green or something? The mental picture of her parents' faces if she returned home one day with short green hair made her stifle a giggle.

Oh, well, maybe she wasn't the green hair type either. But that was her trouble in a nutshell. She didn't seem to be any type but blandly average – medium, boring. She wanted passion and excitement, something magical in her life, but at eighteen she supposed very few people her age got those things. Once she was on lunch-break she sat chewing her sandwiches and staring into space, her mind nibbling all around the edges of her worry.

"Something on your mind?"

She turned. "Thanks, Liz, nothing really. It's just, I was thinking that I'm sort of unnoticeable. I wish I stood out more."

Liz Turner, the thirty-something owner of the coffee café and Mary's cousin, looked at her. "I see, you mean you want to look and be more like them?" She pointed at the other three staff where they stood laughing over some story Debbie was telling them.

"They're nice girls," Mary said, on a slightly protesting note.

"They are." Liz confirmed. "But they're not going anywhere. They're quite satisfied with a reasonably paid, secure job with perks, and time to party most nights. They drink too much, smoke too much, and one day they'll wake up and find either that they're in a marriage that they don't want with kids they didn't plan for. Or that they're living alone, getting old, and that the doctor has just been sent medical tests saying they have lung cancer or cirrhosis of the liver."

Mary looked at her. Liz stared blandly back, and then they both collapsed giggling.

"Heaven forbid that fate await me." Mary said dramatically.

"So, what fate *do* you want?"

"That's the problem, I haven't a clue. I just know I'd like to be a bit less medium. I'd like some excitement in my life."

"Is this something to do with Billy?"

"Not him exactly." Mary's fingers twisted together as she tried to explain. "The problem was more that I didn't *mind* breaking up with him. I mean, I liked him, he liked me, but there weren't any sparks. There wasn't any magic. It kind of felt like I was settling for him because he was there."

"And you wanted something more? There's nothing wrong with that."

"No, but what if I never find more? What if it's me? What if I'm so average no guy will love me the way I want?"

Liz looked at her watch and stood up. "It's time I got back to the kitchen. We'll leave the rest of this discussion for after work. Why don't you stick around when we shut and we can go out for a meal we haven't had to cook and talk over your problem then?"

"Okay." Mary went back to her job while Liz returned to the kitchen and contemplation of her young friend's worries. In a way it would be pleasant to have only that one, Liz thought. The coffee café did well, but Liz had always to keep an eye on the finances, the staff, the supplies coming in – sometimes deliberately or accidentally not what was ordered – and her personal life wasn't any better than Mary's. When a woman had her own business, she worked long hours. So when did Liz discover new or more interesting men either?

She smiled over at her young relative. Mary was a good kid, hardworking and bright, if she yearned for a few sparks in her life, a little romance, maybe someone could provide them. She'd heard that they were re-opening the Picasso coffee bar in Willis Street. It had burned down almost twenty years ago now – when Liz was a teenager.

Their cousin Linda had been hurt in the fire and Liz remembered how protective her own parents had been of Liz for months after that. She'd gone to the Picasso a number of times herself. In the old days it had been wild, and the kids who went there were known to be the wildest in the city – and the best dancers.

The owner's son had inherited the land and recently he'd decided to rebuild. She'd heard that the new place would open this weekend and it might be fun to take some time off and renew old memories. She'd take Mary to the opening; it'd be fun. Once the café shut for the night Liz went in search of the flyer she had received announcing the Picasso's opening.

"Mary? Look at this." Liz held out the flyer.

"What is it? Oh, a new coffee bar." She read aloud from the leaflet. "Come to the Picasso, relive the sixties when the Picasso first opened. Immerse yourself in the times, the music and the dancing. Twist the night away, rock around the clock, and dream, dream, dream. Prizes for the best sixties outfit, the best male or female dancer. Grand opening at eight p.m. Saturday."

Mary studied the address at the bottom of the flyer. "Hey, isn't this just up the road from the café?"

"Yes, so would you like to come with me? It'll be fun. You might even find someone who gives off sparks."

"Not likely, but yes, I'll come. Now, are we going out for that meal or sitting about here talking all night?"

"Food, then talk. I thought we could go to the Majestic."

The food wasn't bad and the talk was pretty interesting, Mary thought later as she stretched out in bed. She'd never known that the Picasso had always had an early sixties' theme and that in opening with that again it was only staying with its roots. Kind of nice. She wondered if she could find something to wear that suited the era, it was still three days before the opening. Liz might have something tucked away, she had a dim memory that sixties gear had always been "in" at the Picasso and didn't Liz used to go there sometimes?

She fell asleep to dream that she was dancing with Elvis to the loud music of a jukebox. He swept her around, swung her in a froth of her petticoats and set her lightly on her feet again while asking, "An' does that keep you awake, little lady? Awake? Awake?"

Her mother's voice sounded exasperated, "Mary, I said are you awake yet? It's almost eight o'clock, your breakfast is on the table."

Mary scrambled for the bathroom. Elvis? What on earth had brought that on? Oh, of course, the coffee bar opening on Saturday. She'd gone to sleep thinking about it and debating finding sixties gear to wear. She'd ask Liz about that at lunchtime.

When asked, Liz was helpful. "There's the shop up at the far end of Cuba Street, they sell retro gear. You could try them, and I still have a few things in the back of my wardrobe too. Maybe we could both go to the shop tomorrow and see what we can find? Then we can dig out any of my old stuff and mix and match with it."

The next lunch-hour they found the shop and were soon almost helpless with laughter.

"I can't believe people wore this sort of thing!" Mary whooped surveying herself in the full-length mirror. She had donned a skin-tight cheongsam in scarlet with gold and silver embroidery. "There's no way you could rock and roll in this surely?"

Liz grinned at her. "You'd be surprised, why do you think it splits right up both of the sides?"

"I thought the seams had just given way?"

"No, it's meant to be like that. What do you think of me?"

She pirouetted, showing off the huge flared skirt of the green dress with the half a dozen stiffened petticoats making it stand out in a bell from her waist."

"It looks great," Mary told her. "Are you buying it?"

"I think so. You should get the cheongsam. It suits you and you can wear a matching Alice band with it."

"A what?"

The assistant reached past them into a box on the counter. "We have some of the old plastic ones if you'd like one?" She produced a curved strip of white plastic with gilt edges and showed Mary how it fitted over her head, holding back her hair.

"Oh, yes, that's fun. I'll take it, and this dress too please."

The price made her blink but it wasn't as if she bought clothes all the time. She could afford it. Liz and she were the same size. They could swap outfits and mix what they bought here with the stuff Liz already had in the back of her wardrobe.

Mary ran her hand down the rack of clothing and it parted to show an old poster propped against the wall. On it, a girl sang into a floor microphone, her body snugly cased in sleeveless top, tight black jeans with only a belt made from silver plaques linked by chains to relieve the stark black of her clothing. She had silver earrings and a medallion on a long silver chain. It was dramatic, interesting, and Mary found herself wanting to look like that. So casual, comfortable in her own skin, sleek and arrogantly catlike – and somehow very slightly familiar.

She rummaged through the accessories and found a silver belt like the one in the poster. There was a top on the rack too, made from some sort of thin stretchy material, it had a high polo neck and the arm-holes were cut high, not just no sleeves, but making it clear the top had never been meant to have them. She could find similar jeans in one of the charity shops, Mary was sure. She'd be all in black and silver, for once in her life she'd stand out.

She found the jeans the next lunchtime, with them she also found a pair of boots, only ankle high, but the jeans tucked into them neatly. They had five-centimeter heels to make her sleekly jeans-clad legs look even longer, and yes! From the tangled metal in the charity shop's jewelry box, she pulled long silver-colored earrings and a medallion on a silver-tone chain. Mary looked at her plunder and smiled. She wouldn't look medium in this outfit.

Mary stuffed everything into a bag on the Saturday afternoon and hauled it to Liz's place. There they helped each other dress and looked at the results in the mirror. Liz looked almost ten years younger than her age in the green dress. The petticoats frothed around her knees, the green brought out the green in her eyes, and her face was softly flushed with excitement as she considered her reflection.

She looked at Mary and held back a gasp. Her young cousin was gone, in her place a stranger looked back from both reality and mirror. This person was cat-like, the long lean lines of her body showed as muscular in the thin black top and jeans. The silver of the belt, earrings and the medallion with its chain accentuated the blackness until Liz felt as if Mary were a piece of the night cut out and sewn into her shape. She reminded Liz of someone from the past, maybe a folk singer or someone.

"Wow," she said softly. "That's really something!"

Mary stretched, admiring herself in the mirror. "Not exactly medium, is it?"

"It certainly isn't. Where did you get the idea?"

"There was an old poster in the sixties shop. I think it was some 60s rock or folk singer. Anyway, I thought she looked great and it'd be good if I could copy the effect."

"You did. Have you been working out or something? In that top you look as if you've got real muscles."

"I swim all summer," Mary said, looking surprised. "And I do aerobics two evenings a week too. I suppose I'm fairly fit but yes," she turned, watching her reflection. "I do look pretty good, don't I?"

"What's on the medallion?"

"Dunno. It was the effect I was after. Are you ready?"

"Yes. Let's get going."

Mary strode down the street beside Liz, feeling good about tonight. Ahead she could see the garish lights of the rebuilt coffee bar and hear the music. In the night, her costume almost vanished with only the silver items catching the moonlight. She liked the way it made her feel different; stronger and more assertive, as if people would notice her. Liz had spent their spare time over the past two days in teaching her some of the rock and roll moves and Mary was looking forward to trying them out.

The coffee bar was a fascination of light and movement. They entered through a door at pavement level, climbed a long steep flight of stairs and came out into the main part of the building. Overhead a glittering mirror-ball revolved, throwing off blazes of flickering lights, while in one corner a jukebox played and on the small dance floor people spun and circled.

Before Mary could do more than glimpse a portion of all that was going on, she was swept into the next dance by a man dressed in a suit made from dark blue lame. She hopped, swung, and bounced in time to the driving beat of the music, laughed at her partner's silly jokes, and found brief spaces in time in which to look about her.

She guessed that the service rooms must all be downstairs below this one. They'd have to be; here she could see the whole of the room and there was no place completely hidden. In the corner by the stairs, there was a small bar dispensing soft drinks, beer and light wine along with casual food.

Along the back and down one side of the room there were booths, each would hold two people a side, three perhaps if they were very good friends. The ends of the seats in each booth came right up, so that once you sat down you were almost hidden from the general view. But then you wouldn't be able to watch the dancers either.

"Wanna sit down an' have a Coke?"

Mary nodded to her partner. "Okay, thanks."

He led her to one of the booths and she saw how wrong she'd been in assuming someone in a booth wouldn't be able to see out. Gently she touched the heavy glass that comprised the outer side of the booth. It was that one-way glass people said was used in police interview rooms. It had appeared plain black and opaque from the dance-floor side. Sitting inside the booth as she was now, she could see out quite well. That had to be modern, they wouldn't have had such a thing in the sixties.

Her gaze fixed on a young man as he spun. His gear was the same color-scheme as hers, black and silver – a thin black sweater covered him from wrists to the high neck, the sweater hem tucked into black trousers held up by a wide leather belt with a large silver buckle. On one wrist over the sweater sleeve he wore a heavy silver bracelet, while on his chest a square silver medallion on a long chain swayed to the shift of his body.

He was a terrific dancer too, Mary noticed. He knew all the rock and roll moves and almost floated as he flicked his partner around him. She wasn't so good. Her outfit wasn't authentic and she seemed clumsy. At the end of the dance, they vanished behind several other couples and Mary saw the girl emerge on her own looking disappointed.

"Here's your Coke." The man in the blue lame had returned.

She raised it slowly, following one pair of dancers with her gaze until her back was to the booth entrance before she was abruptly aware of another presence at her shoulder. The Coke was carefully lifted from her fingers.

"I don't think she should drink that, do you?"

She jerked around to find the man wearing the similar costume to hers holding her glass and looking very hard at her dance partner.

"What..." His voice overrode the beginning of her question.

"I saw you drop something in that after it was poured." He was speaking to the man who'd brought her the drink. "I think perhaps the lady should make her own decisions about what she does and who she does it with tonight."

The reply was so obscene Mary's eyes widened then narrowed in rage as that was followed by the snarled question – "Whyn't you mind your own business, mate?"

"Why don't I just call the police and have them test this?" was the reply. Mary's blue-suited dance partner sneered.

"Got nothing better to do with your time? I have. Not as if there aren't plenty more fish in this sea. I'll just hook another one."

He found his arm taken in a firm grip and a voice spoke softly, the tone holding a dangerous edge.

"There may be plenty of fish, but this is a private pool. Go do your angling somewhere else. The owner's a relative of mine and he'll back me. You're barred. Now get out."

The blue-clad man gave them both a vicious look. Mary glared at him and whatever he saw in the other pair of eyes that watched him was still more convincing. He barged his way through the crowd and vanished down the stairs. Mary turned to look up into dark eyes.

"Thanks. I do know to be more careful. I guess it was being here and feeling as if I really am in the sixties. They didn't have that sort of thing then."

The young man grinned at her. "Who told you that? They certainly did, the stuff they used was cruder and more dangerous. People could die, but it was around now and then and girls were smart to be careful the same as they are now. He won't be back though." He eyed her. "Care to dance?"

Mary eyed him back. He wasn't particularly good-looking. It was the dramatic costume that made him appear that way. But she liked the laughter in his eyes, and the way his lips curved up. She got the impression that he usually smiled a lot although he looked too as if he hadn't smiled much lately. His face was a little aquiline and the dark hair flopped untidily over his forehead. She remembered his dancing with the other girl. He could really dance and that was all he was asking of her right now.

"Yes, I'd like that."

He swept her onto the small dance floor and they danced. It was as if her hope for the perfect partner had been given expression in him. Nothing he did she couldn't follow, and when she tried out some of the moves Liz had taught her, he followed her in turn, meshing so smoothly it was as if he took the knowledge from her mind.

"What's your name?"

"Mary, Mary Brynn. What's yours?"

"Ian Gilles."

"I like your medallion." She grinned and showed it to him. He laughed.

"Where did you get that?"

"From a charity shop. I think they can't have looked at it before they put it out for sale." Ian studied the medallion's picture that showed a shepherdess apparently involved with a sheep and guffawed again.

"I'd guess not."

"What's the picture on yours?"

He held it up to the flickering lights. "An oak tree. A friend made it for me." Mary squinted and could just make out two sets of initials carved into the tiny trunk. Ian saw her looking and let the medallion fall down on the chain.

"Hey, they're playing "Wake Up, Little Suzie," let's dance!"

They danced again and again that night. Now and again, they separated, dancing with other partners, but always they made their way back together again. Around three the next morning the music stopped amid laughing protests from the dancers.

The big man who had halted it held up his hands. "License only runs until three, people. After that we have to shut down. We're open again at eight tomorrow night."

Ian took her hands. "Are you coming back?"

"Wouldn't miss it."

"See you tomorrow night then."

She smiled at him, her face alight with the pleasure she'd found in the dancing." Yes, you will and thanks for – you know."

"No trouble. I have to go now, but I'll be watching for you." He slipped through the crowd and Mary went in search of Liz. It had been a great night. She was already looking forward to tomorrow.

Saturday – she slept in, read for a while over a late breakfast and once the dishes were cleared she considered possible outfits to wear to the Picasso that evening. She'd really liked the effect of the black and silver. Ian had looked good in it too. Maybe she'd leave well enough alone and wear the same gear again? Yes, why not? She could vary the silver part of it, or even the black clothing, but stick with black and silver as her theme.

As soon as he came through the crowd towards her, she saw that Ian had made the same decision. He took her hand in silence, although his smile as he saw her said quite a bit she thought. They danced, sat talking in one of the booths while they drank Coke and ate toasted sandwiches, danced some more and parted once the music stopped for the night.

Liz came with Mary only once more after that. She'd met a man at the library; he preferred ballroom dancing and more often than not Liz spent her evenings waltzing. Mary didn't mind. It was nice that her cousin had found a man. As for her, she was happy. Ian didn't pressure her. They danced, talked about all sorts of things, and laughed a lot. They kissed now and then and it never mattered to her that when they did it was just friendship. Somehow there was a connection despite that, and she was content for things between them to develop at their own pace – if they ever did.

They met most evenings and it was almost six months before she realized that she only ever saw him at the Picasso.

"Come to the pictures, they're showing the new SF movie."

He hesitated. "I prefer dancing. I'm not much on movies."

"Oh, okay."

A month later she suggested they go out for a meal.

"We can eat here. Don't you like the food?"

"Yeah, sure, but I meant a proper meal, you know, three courses and sit down with knives and forks." She saw the hesitation again and wondered if he couldn't afford it. "It's okay, I'll pay. It'd just be nice for a change."

"I'm not really crazy about restaurants." Ian said slowly. "I like being here, it's all right if you want to go with someone else."

"I don't. I would have liked to go out with you, that's all."

She saw the quick look of sadness on his face and said nothing more – but it made her aware of the things she did not know about him. Who exactly was he? All she knew was his name and that he was supposed to be some relation to the Picasso's owner. She had no idea where Ian worked, no idea of his address or even exactly how old he was, although she guessed he'd be close to her own age, no more than three or four years older. She'd assumed he had a job, but maybe he was unemployed and lived on the streets? Maybe he came here to dance and eat because, for him, the entrance and the food were free?

The following night she was afraid he wouldn't be there. She went anyway and, to her interest, she found him setting up a tiny stage.

"What's that for?" He grinned at her and Mary relaxed. All was well between them still.

"It's for the singing competition. The Picasso always had one each year and they're starting it up again. The winner gets free entry here and free food and Cokes for the year. Why don't you enter, I've heard you singing to the juke-box sometimes, you aren't bad."

Mary laughed. "I'm strictly a bathroom singer."

"Most of the people who enter won't be any better." In the next half-hour he convinced her until she wrote her name on the entry list.

Five nights later it was Mary's turn to sing. She all but slunk onto the tiny stage. Behind her, the band, hired for the ten nights of the contest, awaited her signal. She gave it and the first ringing guitar notes slashed into a suddenly silent coffee bar. Mary's oldest cousin had written the song in the sixties. It had been the theme for a story Linda Rosen had written and sold. Years later a friend of Linda's had put music to the words just for fun and as a child Mary had heard it sung many times and loved it.

She'd decided that it fit the period, and at least it wasn't a song she'd have to worry about someone else singing before her. Those here would hear this song for the first time, and unless she was in the finals, that would be the first and only time it would be sung. Linda had given her the rights as a tenth birthday present. It was hers and tonight she'd share.

The band moved into the song's introduction and Mary was energized, pulled out of her nerves and into the music. Her voice soared up, unexpectedly wild and powerful.

"Rock and roll is my life,
Gives me a heart and a soul,
Gives me a dream and a vision,
True rockers never grow old!"

The music soared and she flew on the wings it gave her. She'd never sung so well, never felt so truly one with the sound that raised her up. When the song ended, there was a tiny moment of appreciative silence before the applause crashed out. Ian reached her first, swinging her around.

"That was brilliant! Bathroom singer my foot! You were great!"

The audience agreed. When the votes for that night were tallied there was no question that she'd won the night's contest. Mary listened with Ian to the singers after that. At least two she thought to be far better than she had been, but if she sang as well on the final night she wouldn't be disgraced. Liz promised to come to that one.

"I'll wear my green dress with the starched petticoats. You just do your best. I haven't heard that song for ages. It'll be great if it wins," she told Mary.

"Oi, I'm singing it. Don't I get some of the credit?"

"If you win you do." She looked at her young cousin. "Linda would have liked it that you're singing that song. She wrote it for someone."

Mary stared. "Someone? I always thought that the song was just written to go with that story she did. It sold, didn't it? Wasn't that what the song was for?"

Liz took her hand, drawing her to sit in an empty booth. "No, the song came first. It fitted the story she wrote later so she used it in that. But the song was written years earlier for Linda's boyfriend. They used to go dancing together. It's funny, but it wasn't until recently I remembered that it was here they often used to come to dance."

"What was his name?"

"John, I think. I never met him but I heard the story from Linda's mum, our Aunt Julie."

"What happened to him?"

"Linda never talked about him afterwards. But Aunt Julie told me most of it over the years. You know this place burned down?" Mary nodded. "Well, Linda was hurt in the fire. She had internal injuries from where a falling beam hit her, her heart was damaged and her health was very poor after that. The doctor said she shouldn't marry or have children. Her father had her in a private hospital under another name to keep people from upsetting her. I don't know the whole story, but I think she wrote to John as soon as she knew her injuries were permanent to tell him that with the fire and everything that had happened. She didn't want to see him again."

"What did he say?"

Liz gazed out across the crowded room seeing none of it.

"He never replied. I think Linda assumed he'd heard what had happened to her and agreed with her decision."

"What a loser."

"She accepted it. After that she stayed home and wrote. Her work started selling and that made her happy."

"And then last year she died."

"The doctor was right. She lived as long as she did only because she took life so quietly. She wouldn't have been able to do a normal job again and marriage would have been really impossible. John's not trying to persuade her to stick with him may have been all for the best."

Ian's voice broke into that comment. "What was all for the best?"

Liz slipped away leaving them together while Mary launched into her aunt's story. She finished with, "Linda wrote the song I sang. The one I'm singing again tomorrow night in the finals. Liz says it was written for Linda's boyfriend." Her eyes filled with tears.

"I think it's so sad. She loved him so she let him go – and he just went. He never even wrote to her or anything."

Ian nodded. "Perhaps he didn't understand her letter. It could have been that he was scarred too and thought that was what she was talking about. He could have been unconscious for a few days. No one would want to tell him she'd been hurt. Perhaps the first he heard about any of it was getting that letter from her."

Mary's imagination and sympathy were caught. "Oh, yes. Oh, that'd be awful! He'd wake up, look in the mirror and then read her letter. If it'd been me, I'd have just wanted to curl up and die after that."

"Yes." Ian's voice was somber. He forced brightness into his tones. "But forget all that. Tomorrow night's your night."

"Wish me luck."

"I do. I always will. Now, what about a dance?"

It was almost four o'clock when Mary returned home. She was tired but excited at the prospect of winning the song contest, and the songs she'd heard that evening were still playing in her mind. Tomorrow night she'd sing Linda's song again, and when she did, she'd think of her cousin and the sad story Liz had told her.

She was almost ready to go to the Picasso when her Aunt Julie arrived. "I hear you're singing my Linda's song tonight. I just wanted to give you this for luck. It was Linda's." Mary accepted the silver scarf and tied it as an Alice band.

"Thanks, Aunt Julie. I'll think about her when I sing." She paused. Would it be too sad to ask? Aunt Julie had given her the scarf and didn't seem to mind her using the song, maybe she wouldn't mind talking about it either. It had all been ages ago after all.

"Aunt Julie, did you ever hear what happened to Linda's boyfriend?"

Julie Brynn nodded. "Yes, we never told Linda and I suppose it doesn't matter who knows about it now. He was hit in the face with a length of burning wood and knocked unconscious for eight days. He was left scarred all across his face but he wasn't that badly hurt. He went home from the hospital almost as soon as he was conscious again – and killed himself three nights later. We kept that edition of the paper away from her and she never knew. We all thought it was best to let her think he'd just not replied."

Mary spoke slowly, thinking about the sequence of events. "John had to have had her letter saying she never wanted to see him again. He didn't know she was so badly hurt. He thought it was because he was scarred. If she'd known that, she'd never have forgiven herself."

"That's right, dear. Her father and I thought that it was best that she never knew what had happened."

Mary shook her head. "So she died believing that he didn't love her at all, and all the time he'd probably killed himself because he thought the same. It's like Romeo and Juliet."

Aunt Julie smiled. "Not really. There couldn't have been any kind of a happy ending even if he'd lived. She was very frail after the fire. She could never have been with him. If he'd stayed and insisted on being with her, she'd have died that much sooner, leaving him alone and probably blaming himself. It really was all for the best in the end."

"Aunt Julie?" Mary spoke impulsively, "Why don't you come with Liz and me. It would be great to have you there if I win."

He aunt peered doubtfully at her. "In a coffee bar, dear? I'm a bit old to be running around places like that."

"Oh, come on, please!"

Her aunt permitted herself to be persuaded and to Liz's amusement they arrived at the Picasso together. Aunt Julie was happy to be tucked into a booth, provided with a cup of quite good coffee, a ham sandwich, and Liz to keep her company while Mary waited her turn to sing.

The time came and she stepped out onto the small stage, noticing vaguely as she heard the band strike up the introduction, that for some reason the crowd was moving off the dance floor. It was as if they were moving because they wanted to. No one was giving any orders, but somehow as Mary began to sing the floor had cleared completely. She was swept up in the song and realized only during the second verse that two dancers had taken to the floor.

Through the song she'd been remembering Linda's story. Her oldest cousin had rarely smiled, never laughed, and had always been out of breath. She died quietly in her sleep one afternoon and Mary had cried when she'd heard. She wanted to cry again as she sang, letting the music carry her, feeling the passion in her cousin's song flow out across the dance floor. It came back to her like rapture as she started the third verse and focused on the faces of the two who danced in front of her.

They were both in black and silver, their steps and movements matching as even hers and Ian's had not. But – that was Ian who danced, looking up at her, a wild gratitude and loving affection on his face as her gaze met his. She looked at the other dancer and somehow she was not surprised to see her cousin, dancing as Linda must have danced before the fire. The music screamed up into the final lines and Mary held their gaze with hers as she sang, pouring all her friendship and love into that look.

He'd never been able to join her at the movies or come with her to a restaurant. He'd waited here, waited for love and closure, and she'd been able to give it to him – to them both. A last glint from Linda's belt, Ian's medallion, and they faded. Once they were gone the crowd thrust back unseeing to fill the dance-floor. Applause boomed out for the winner, Mary Brynn. Her Aunt Julie and Liz congratulating her as Mary accepted the prize, smiled politely for the cameras, and left with her family.

She would return the prize the next night and suggest the

owner give something to charity instead. The Picasso wouldn't be the same without Ian and she didn't think she'd want to dance there anymore.

"Oh, and we got the name wrong," Liz said as they waited for the taxi. "Aunt Julie remembered when we were talking last night, she says Linda's boyfriend was Ian, not John. He was the youngest son of the owner's brother, that means he must have been this one's cousin."

Mary nodded casually, as if it made no difference, thinking that perhaps all those cousins had had something to do with the events. Maybe the family ties had pulled her, Ian, and Linda together somehow. Liz didn't know Ian's surname, Mary had never mentioned it, No one else would make any connections and that was how Mary wanted it.

But that night she cried bitterly for the friend she'd loved and lost, and as she wept she wondered – would there ever be someone who loved her that much? Or was love only that strong when you couldn't have it? She slept at last, clutching the silver scarf, and woke to find her hand curved around Ian's Oak Tree medallion.

She held it up to the sunshine pouring in through her window and made out the initials engraved into the trunk. I.G. and L.R. She wept again, then found she was smiling through her tears. It was a wish from both of them, she thought. One day there could be love like that for her. One day.

SOWING ON THE MOUNTAIN

I always liked being on the police force in Wellington. In many ways, being on one beat for a long time is like working in a small town. I know a lot of people around here. They talk to me and sometimes they tell me important things. It helps that I'm distantly related to Granny Ngaire and Patti Paiwai too. Everyone knows them around here. Maybe that's why the police force has kept me on this beat. I don't get promoted but that's okay. I like it where I am and my bosses like me there too so no one has any problems.

And what I do reminds me of the saying that the more things change, the more they stay the same. I started walking a beat in the city when I was twenty-one and just out of police training school. Then they put us into cars for years, and now in 1997 we're back walking a beat again because that's how the public likes it.

So, my partner and I were walking up by the old Bolton Street cemetery around two a.m. on a weeknight when everything was dark and quiet. I was thinking about the latest rash of vandalism in my area – probably ring-led by the Thompson boys who lived up Tinakori Road way and were real little nuisances – when I caught sight of the small figure trudging down the road towards me. Ten futile minutes later I was on my radio to dispatch.

"Constable 147 Olsen reporting. My partner and I have found a child in the street, female, about eleven. We can't find out who she is or where she lives. She does look vaguely familiar to me but I can't quite place her. She's in nightclothes with bare feet and she's freezing."

"Dispatch to Constable Olsen, ask her who she is."

"I've done that, dispatch. She could be in shock. She's shivering very badly and seems unable to talk."

"I'll have a car with you in a couple of minutes. Take her to the hospital. I'll have them drop you back once she's hospitalized and you and your partner look around the area. Do you think she's come far?"

"We're not sure. She looks healthy enough although she's very thin and she seems to have a lot of bruising on her arms. I guess she could have walked quite a way."

"Ask the doctor if he can get an address from her."

"Will do."

* * *

"She was just walking down the street towards the cenotaph, Doctor. I spoke to her. She turned to look at us and passed out on the pavement, just briefly. She was already trying to sit up when I kneeled down beside her."

"But she hasn't spoken?"

"Not a word. Dispatch said we should bring her here and have her checked out. She's so cold I thought she could be in shock for some reason, what with her not talking either."

"She is cold, but it's freezing outside, it could just be that – however shock is always possible. I *am* able to tell you one thing right now though, Bob. I think it probable someone's been beating her over a period of time. These bruises of hers tell a fairly clear tale; some are very recent, others are a few days old, and there are others that are nearly gone, they'd be about a week to a week and a half old. I'll get her into a cubicle with a nurse and take a proper look once you've gone."

Bob went out to see what he could discover and I got the girl into a cubicle. I knew it would take time to examine her properly, and it did. In the end we had no choice but to sedate her so I could make a proper physical examination. I was disgusted at what I found – although I have to say I wasn't greatly surprised.

What had been done to her isn't unusual in a major city. Although even in small towns this sort of thing goes on. I've worked in small towns and in cities and in fact, perhaps it's more likely to go on in small towns without anyone laying a complaint because that's where people know each other and are reluctant to tell tales.

* * *

"Constable 147 Olsen to dispatch. We've spotted a house nearly a kilometer from where we found the girl but I'm fairly sure this is where she's come from."

I was quite sure this was where she'd come from. I remembered her now.

"The front door's been left wide open and all the lights are on. I know the occupants and they'll make a legal fuss if I go in without a warrant. Should we enter?"

"Constable 147, in view of the circumstances you are cleared to enter the house to check status."

I guessed what I'd find as soon as I approached the front door. The smell told me. I sent my partner out to check around the outside of the house to see if there were any signs of a break-in. I entered the hall, looked in the rooms that opened off the passage all the way from the front of the house to the kitchen at the back. I swore, returned through the place, and stepped outside into the clean air on the front porch to phone back.

"Dispatch, there's four bodies in the house. I knew them as the occupants: one adult male in his forties, one adult female around the same age, and two young boys. I'd say they all died in their beds, but there's vomit in the hall by the front door. This has to be where the girl came from. I remember her now and she lived here."

"I have detectives on the way as of right now, Bob. Hand the scene over to them once they arrive, file your reports and go off shift."

"Thanks, dispatch. Constable 147 Olsen out."

One thing about our discovery in the house, I could stop worrying about the current vandalism in this part of the city. I wasn't happy about how it had been stopped, but I was pleased that it had. I didn't appreciate seeing the cenotaph lions wearing black felt-tip moustaches all the time – and I suspected they didn't like it much either.

* * *

"I'm Detective Ainsley, Madam. What can you tell me about the Thompsons, the family two doors down on your right?"

"Nothing much, Detective. They're religious although you'd never know it from the way their boys behave. I think they adopted his dead sister's daughter about three years ago."

"Detective Haddan, sir. What can you tell me about the Thompsons, the family next door to you on the left?"

"Why?"

"There's been an incident, sir. They're dead, everyone but the little girl. What can you tell me about them?"

"Malcolm, who is it?"

"The police, dear. They say the Thompsons have had an accident and they're all dead but the girl."

"It's no more than God's judgment on them."

"Why do you say that, madam?"

"I don't like to speak ill of the dead, but they ill-treated that poor child. She was always working, some jobs were far too heavy for a girl of that age, and he used to hit her far too often. I saw him do it several times."

"Did you ever report this abuse?"

"I couldn't do that, Detective, but I let him see that I knew. I stared him right in the eye last time I saw him by his front gate and I know he got the message."

"How was that, madam?"

"He looked guilty and went hurrying indoors again, that's how."

"I'm Detective Ainsley, madam. Is your husband in?"

"John's in Auckland for several days on business, Detective. Can I help?"

"What can you tell me about the Thompsons, the family next door to you on the right?"

"What's happened?"

"There's been an unfortunate incident, madam. They're all

dead but the little girl."

"Poor child. I'm sure that's a blessing in disguise for her."

"Why is that, madam?"

"Well, the Thompsons used to punish her a lot – and when I say 'punish' I mean that they beat her and that may not have been all. I mentioned it to him once and he said 'spare the rod and spoil the child' and gave me a very nasty look. I asked her to help me move a couple of pieces of my furniture a while back and when we'd finished, I gave her afternoon tea. She was polite, but, Detective – she ate as if she hadn't had a decent meal in days. I'm sure she was starving and that isn't right.

"I didn't say anything to the Thompsons at the time but I saw her adopted mother at the shops a week after that and I just said that Pam seemed to be very thin. Mrs. Thompson gave me a nasty look, said something about fasting and repentance being good for the soul and walked away. I'm afraid the Thompsons really may not have treated the child very kindly."

"Did you tell anyone?"

"Like who?"

"Well – Social Welfare or us, madam?"

"Oh, I couldn't do that. It wasn't really any of my business and neighbors have to get on, don't they."

* * *

"Olsen, check with Doctor Ross at the hospital. He says they have an interim medical report on the child's physical condition."

"Yes, sir."

I love my city, but there are times when the 'don't see and don't want to see' attitude of people angers me. I'd heard about the interviews and what had been said in them from the detectives. That poor kid, half the people in her street knew she was being beaten and maybe starved on a regular basis and no one did anything about it. No, of course not. They might have to testify in court – still worse, if they talked someone might talk about the testifier's own sins and that would never do.

* * *

"What can you tell us about the kid, Colin? What about the bruising on her arms and legs that I noticed?"

Colin Ross is a good doctor, he likes kids and they mostly trust him on sight. He looked angry as he glanced at a report and started talking.

"She's suffered long-term abuse. She's been regularly beaten. She's also been raped repeatedly and she is definitely malnourished. In my professional opinion she's been underfed, overworked, and badly abused for two or three years. She is also suffering quite mildly from some form of poisoning."

I looked up at him sharply at that. "What sort of poisoning? Could she have taken something herself?"

"It wouldn't be surprising if she had." Colin told me bitterly. "Life must have been hell on earth for her. Why didn't anyone notice? What do the neighbors say?"

"That the girl seemed to be overworked and hit a lot but they didn't want to get involved. I can see why, I knew Thompson, and in my opinion, he was a nasty piece of work. All piety and biblical quotes, but using them to justify whatever he wanted."

"Wonderful. It reminds me of the saying that 'the more I see of people the more I love my dog.'"

"I know," I told him. "Is she talking yet"

"A little. I've been told her family were found dead. Under the circumstances the shock of her finding them when some poison had already weakened her could well have produced traumatic amnesia. She might never remember. She certainly doesn't appear to recall anything from the time she went to bed until the time she found herself standing on the street looking at two policemen."

"Could a hypnotherapist help?"

"Possibly, but it's unlikely Social Welfare would agree – either to the experiment or to the expense. They have a foster home arranged for her to go to as soon as she can be discharged. At least there may be money for her once she's twenty-one. I presume that as the only surviving member, she'll inherit whatever the family owned."

"I hear she was adopted, but yeah, I guess so. Under adoption laws it counts as if she's a natural daughter and so far as I know, the Thompsons didn't have any relatives who'd be closer than this girl."

"Well, let me know if there's anything more I can do." Colin offered. "I imagine the autopsies on her family will be interesting."

* * *

"Ainsley, you'll have to interview everyone in the Thompson case again."

"Why, sir?" I was annoyed about that. I'd done a comprehensive job the first time, talked to almost everyone in several blocks and now he wanted me to go over the interviews again?

"The autopsy reports have just come in and they say that they'd all ingested weed-killer. One of the nicotine-based poisons with a very high concentration. The pathologist has identified it as Pestaway. That's a powder concentrate intended to be diluted at a teaspoonful per forty liters of water. It gets sprayed on fruit trees I'm told."

"I see, sir. Yes, I'll talk to all the neighbors again."

I would, although I didn't think they've have much more to tell me.

* * *

"Is your husband home now, madam? He was out when I called three days ago"

"Yes, he got back from Auckland last night, I'll just call him."

"John? There's a policeman wants to speak to you about the Thompsons."

"Detective Ainsley, sir. You'll have heard about your neighbors?"

"Yes, I heard. It's a terrible thing. I'm told they were poisoned?"

"That's unfortunately true, sir. They seem to have eaten or drunk weed-killer in some way."

The Thompsons neighbor looked at me and his mouth fell open in shock.

"Oh, my God. I *told* him. I warned the fool!"

Ah ha, it looked as if I might have been wrong about further interviews being a waste of time. There had been a bit more to find out after all.

"Sir? What did you warn him about?"

"He was chatting to me over the fence last week while he made up the spray for his fruit trees. He turned around without looking and knelt on the plastic bag. It split so he went and got an empty container from the kitchen and he put the remaining spray powder in that."

"What sort of container, sir?" Could this be the explanation?

"He had a sweet tooth, you know, old Thompson did. His wife used to keep icing sugar in the kitchen in one of those shaker containers with holes in the lid. She sprinkled it on half the desserts they ate. I know because my wife had tea there a couple of times in weekends when Thompson was home. She and Mrs. Thompson were on a school committee together for a term last year."

It looked as if it *was* the explanation. That'd be good, it would mean we could stop interviewing and tell the coroner to hold the inquest.

"I saw what he was doing and I said to him that it wasn't a good idea putting weed-killer in a food container. He said he'd label it and then he gave me a very nasty sort of 'mind your own business look' so I did. You know, Detective, he wasn't the sort of man who appreciated advice from anyone – but I really should have said more about it."

"I don't see what more you could have done, sir. You could hardly insist. It was his decision."

"Yes, but I still feel I should have done something. If I had maybe they wouldn't all be dead."

* * *

I did feel guilty, that was true, but only a little bit. As a neighbor, Thompson had been a complete pain in the neck and I'd loathed the way they'd treated their niece who always seemed to be a nice, polite little girl – if terrified of Thompson and his wife. My wife hadn't liked them any better than I did and she said she was delighted when Mrs. Thompson wasn't nominated for the PTA the next term.

Thompson hadn't exactly been chatting to me either. It had been one of his endless diatribes about how I should trim my trees better, cut my lawn more often, and paint the dividing fence on my side to improve the value of *his* property. And I hadn't been nearly as definite about the dangers of weed-poison in a food container as I'd suggested to the detective. In fact, I'd carefully said just enough to put Thompson's back up. He was a man who liked everything his own way and he absolutely hated to be told anything.

When I saw him use the icing-sugar container to put the Pestaway powder in, I must admit that it just crossed my mind how very convenient it would be if his wife made a mistake with it and we got new neighbors. None of the family – apart from the girl, and my wife said she was positive the child never got anything decent to eat and certainly not sweet desserts – would be missed by anyone in the area.

Mrs. Thompson was a spiteful piece of work who loved making trouble on any committee to which she belonged, and the boys were complete hooligans in the making. If the police didn't know who was responsible for the latest outbreak of graffiti around the cenotaph and the cemetery, I did. I also knew better than to say anything to the police – even Bob Olsen - about that.

Friends of mine who lived in the next street had once complained about the Thompson boys' depredations – to their father, and when that hadn't worked, they'd mentioned it to the police as an official complaint. That week their garden shed burned down and nearly took their house and the garage with it. We could all guess who had been responsible for that but this time the silence was deafening.

It would, I thought with some satisfaction, *be a much more friendly area with the Thompsons gone.* And the girl had survived too – which eased any guilt I might have felt about the other four.

* * *

"All right, Ainsley, where are we with the Thompson case?"

I'd been working on it for ten days after we found that the cause of the deaths had been poison – along with everything else I had to do. I'd talked to Bob Olsen who knew the family and knew just about everyone else in the area as well. He'd not been able to suggest any possibilities other than what I was about to tell my boss.

"I think the coroner is going to bring it in as death by misadventure, sir. We've been all over the crime scene several times, talked to all the neighbors, and it seems to have happened like this. Thompson made up the Pestaway powder as spray for his fruit trees a number of times. The last time he used the powder he knelt on the bag and it split. There was only a small amount of the Pestaway left so he put it in one of those icing-sugar containers that have holes in the lid so you can sprinkle the contents on desserts. His next-door neighbor has told us he saw the whole thing and admits he warned Thompson about it. He's made an official statement on that."

"How exactly did they ingest the powder?"

"They had sponge cake with fruit salad for dessert. The neighbor's wife has given us a statement saying that she ate with them on a number of occasions last year when she and the wife were on the same committee. She says that Thompson indulged heavily in sweet foods and they all liked to sprinkle icing sugar on any suitable dessert.

"Thompson told his neighbor that for safety he would label the icing-sugar container that he used for the Pestaway and at first we thought he hadn't done that as he said he would. Then we found the label under the stove and the container shows signs that it did have an additional label originally. They keep their sugar, icing-sugar, and salt in canisters on a shelf above and to one side of the stove.

"It looks as if steam from the kettle may have steamed off the label Thompson used, and it landed under the stove, probably from a draft when the back door was opened. We checked that and it's all possible. The glue on the label he'd used was from an old box of them and the gum was perished. The draft when the door is opened can blow a label – if it's on the floor below the shelf – under the stove.

"I can't believe that the man was so stupid, but there's only his fingerprints and his wife's on that container. And we have the neighbor's evidence that gives us a clear and believable story of why the poison was in the container where it was found.

"The child has talked a little. She still doesn't remember anything at all from that night, but it appears that the Thompsons were in the habit of starving her in punishment for things they saw as sins. Sometimes she was deprived of three or four meals in a row. As a result, she often unobtrusively ate any minor amounts of leftovers from their plates before she washed them, so she would have ingested a tiny amount of the Pestaway too. Enough to make her vomit and become faint and disoriented, but that was all."

"And you're happy with the coroner's decision."

"Yes, sir."

I certainly was. I couldn't find any evidence the deaths had been other than accidental, caused by Thompson's own stupidity. And – I'd seen the doctor's report on the way the Thompsons had behaved toward their niece. I thought that there was a special place in hell for people who treated a child that way. I hoped the Thompsons had had a taste of where they were going before they died and from what I'd heard from Doctor Ross of Pestaway's symptoms, they probably would have.

"Close the case then. I hope the foster parents they found for that kid treat her well. I saw the doctor's report and she deserves it."

"Yes, sir!" I agreed.

* * *

"There's enough money for you to do what you want to, darling. Now you're eighteen all of it is yours."

"I know, Mum, don't worry. I plan to use some of it to get my law degree and the rest can stay in the bank. I'll use it for the deposit to start a practice of my own eventually."

"That's my sensible girl."

I smiled at my foster daughter. She was most of my world these days. My husband had died of a sudden heart attack last year and it was Pam who had seen to everything for me, Pam who'd been my support. I remembered the skinny, bruised, silent child we'd taken in and how, very slowly over the years, she had become the kind-hearted, friendly, and socially conscious young woman that she was now.

She'd known for some years that she'd inherit money from her dead family, but she'd never been foolish about that. She'd worked very hard, gained her high school qualifications, then left to work at the local lawyer's office for a year and save her salary before going on to university. Mr. Bycroft specialized in Family Court problems and Pam turned out to have a talent for dealing with frightened or traumatized people. Now the money from her uncle was released to her she planned to get her degree and work for Mr. Bycroft for a few years before striking out on her own.

Mr. Bycroft was becoming overworked. Once Pam had her degree, she could work with him in Thorndon and consider setting up on her own or buying into a partnership with him once she had more experience. She was a good and loving child to me, so kind and gentle. It was a miracle she'd turned out that way after the years she'd suffered at the Thompsons' hands. It was God's mercy that she could remember little from the time they'd had her and nothing at all of the night they died.

"Mum? I have to go out for the evening. I promised Di I'd try on my bridesmaid's dress. You'll be okay on your own? What are you looking so serious about?"

"I was just remembering how you came to us, darling. Yes, go and try on the frock, I'll be fine. Have you had a reply from your application to the university? It's fortunate you have the money, I couldn't have managed to send you otherwise, not with it being so expensive these days."

"I know, Mum. Isn't it lucky you don't have to try? Yes, I had the letter of acceptance this afternoon. I meant to tell you. And I've decided I'm going to use a bit of my inheritance when I get it next month to trade in my old car and buy a better one before I start at the university."

* * *

I sat on the bed remembering how I'd inherited the money that would give me the life I wanted where I could speak for the powerless ones – the children who might suffer as I had. I recalled the Thompsons' increasing brutality once I was safely in their hands. Even the boys had enjoyed tormenting me – and been permitted to do so without restraint. I remembered my pain and terror, the deliberate blindness of the neighbors and, very slowly, my lips peeled back from my teeth in the sort of smile my mother would never see.

Silence was safest, and from the beginning I'd made everyone believe I remembered nothing at all of that night. Some of what I remembered I knew to have been impossible, but I did remember it and I relished everything that I recalled.

I'd prayed with all my heart and strength to God to help me and he'd done nothing. So, I'd prayed to anything I thought might hear me, even to the cenotaph lions towards the end. I knew my brothers made fun of them, painting moustaches on them with felt-tip, and I'd heard some odd stories about the lions from one of the Paiwai kids at school in my three years living in the area. So I prayed, and someone – or something – may have answered.

I had come out of my bedroom around midnight that night, feeling wretchedly sick myself – as I'd expected – but too intent on other things to really notice. I watched those who'd brutalized me for the past three years writhe and die, in too much agony to even scream for help. They could only gasp hoarsely and whimper, eyes bulging, hands outstretched imploringly to me for the aid I was happily refusing.

It had taken almost two hours for them to die and for all that time I'd watched what happened and let them see me standing there, enjoying their pain as they had enjoyed mine. After that, I'd walked off into the night leaving the door open and all the lights blazing. Something inside my head whispered that a child wouldn't remember to turn off lights or shut doors. I walked until someone found me – and my life was changed.

It wasn't even as if I'd done anything to cause their agony, not really. *He'd* been the one stupid enough to put his poison in a food container; I'd only overheard the man next door warning him about it. *He'd* been the one to use an old label and *she* always boiled the kettle too long. I'd just changed the containers over – at least I think I did. The label fell off when I did that and went fluttering under the stove in the draft from the half-open kitchen door. *He* dumped the usual heavy sprinkling of icing-sugar on his jam-sponge – as did the other greedy pigs on their own plates of the dessert.

I was never allowed anything nice to eat, and often enough I wasn't fed at all. This time I licked his plate carefully, but only a couple of times before I washed up. I was too young to know just how much of a risk I was taking but it had worked. Their deaths were brought in as death by misadventure as the coroner directed.

It was true; it was just their misadventure that *he'd* done most of it to himself and his family. It had been an act of God as their minister had claimed at their funerals. And maybe it truly was a god of some sort because something had looked out for me on that night when I decided I'd rather risk death than stay alive with them.

Fingerprints? There weren't any of those, I think because it was freezing at 3 a.m. so I must have been wearing woolly gloves as I sneaked into the kitchen and changed the position of the tins on the shelf. Yes, I'm almost sure that has to be why there were no fingerprints.

I do have a sort of odd memory of that night where I never touched the containers, they changed over as I watched them move by themselves. The label fluttering to the ground and under the stove in the draft as the bolted kitchen door swung half open and shut silently again.

That has to be wrong of course. I'm remembering some dream I once had. Things like that don't really happen. I was only eleven and I never knew about fingerprints at the time and it was cold so I wore gloves. I'm sure that's the reason there were no fingerprints.

I do remember that at the funeral we sang the hymn that goes, "sowing on the mountain, reaping in the valley, you're going to reap just what you sow." I guess in the end, whoever or whatever was responsible for their deaths, me or something else, they reaped everything they'd sown – with generous interest!

TIGER DREAMING

The beast that stalked me was huge, a sleek golden-furred leopard. Night after night it came to my dreams. Paced through them, watching me, following on soft dark pads wherever I went. At first it stayed back, a shape glimpsed more than seen, felt rather than heard.

It was a leopard I thought, although somehow it was different from the smaller, graceful cats I'd seen on the television. I got my first real look at the beast when, after months, I had a proper nightmare. I was dreaming that something followed me. Not my leopard but an uglier, blacker shape. A human with things on his mind unlikely to be motives shared by a leopard.

The man confronted me and I stepped back. As I watched him, his face ran like wax re-forming and became the face of John, my ex-husband, only his eyes were missing. From empty sockets, the ghoul stared threateningly at me. The fleshless fingers stretched as they reached out for me. They twisted, twining like stiffer vines, hungry to touch, to cling and drain my life again. I retreated until I could retreat no more. While I had backed away, a wall had grown behind me – a wall built of stone, great gray blocks of it that curved around to hold me prisoner.

I prepared to fight. I had no chance. But I'd fight as I'd learned to do in my marriage, hopelessly perhaps, certainly desperately. But I would no longer submit. The skeleton hands reached out, gripped my shoulder and at their touch, I screamed. Short, sharp – and awoke. I got up and made myself a cup of tea. I drank it slowly, relishing the sweet taste of the sugar I'd loaded into it, before I went back to bed. Normally I sleep peacefully, but this time I fell into sleep and back again into the nightmare as if I had never left it.

I writhed in the grip of bony fingers, cried out in rage and despair and then – the leopard came slipping towards us in silence, a darker shadow among shadows, eyes glowing a soft light as he rose up behind the thing that held me. It shook a threatening bony hand at the beast – which was ignored. I was tossed casually behind John for safekeeping as he broke off his fingers, throwing them before the leopard. They burned. The shadows were chased away and for the first time I saw the beast as it was.

It was terrifying and magnificent. It was far larger than a real leopard would have been. This one was the size of a tiger and golden. The rosettes were only a darker gold against the lighter gold of the coat. The eyes too were gold, a molten shade with the pupils carving a contrast through the metallic blaze. It was beautiful and deadly. The fingers burned lower and my husband spoke.

"Go away."

The leopard paced back and forth in front of him in silence.

"Go away. She's mine here."

Then it spoke. I never even blinked at that, why should I? In dreams anyone can do anything.

"In this place she is whoever she wants to be. As are we all."

My husband gave a whining gurgle of amusement. "I want her here, that makes her mine. She stays with me."

I crawled slowly to my feet. The leopard was an animal; at least I hoped it was. In a land of dream anything can be anything. But the beast seemed less threatening to me than my husband had ever been in life or in dream. I half-crouched ready to act when he was off guard.

My husband repeated his words. As he spoke, the flesh began to drop from his bones until he was only a skeleton again. His voice grated, bone on bone. "I want her, she's mine. She came here. She stays with me."

The leopard grew larger, his purr a shuddering thunder that rocked my bones. "I claim her. She is mine. She is mine. *She is mine!"*

The skeleton between us trembled. The bones came apart slowly, falling into a heap. The beast paced forward and with one paw scooped them to fall in flying arcs about us. One bone struck the wall behind me and that wall and all the dreamscape about us was gone. We stood in a desert of blowing sands. Golden eyes studied me.

"Life is not a ladder to climb. It is a wheel from which you learn as you travel. When the time is right, I'll come for you. Until then, learn on the wheel."

He sank into the sand and was gone. I started walking towards the palm trees of a distant oasis hoping that I'd wake up soon. I did when the alarm clock pinged. Until then I'd been walking. I went to work at my Government Department on Waterloo Quay still tired. After work, I went to see my therapist who was fascinated.

"A leopard protecting you from your husband? You said it spoke to you? What did it say?"

I managed a smile. "Something very New Age which is strange because I don't subscribe to most of that stuff."

"Try to remember. In dreams we let go of many of our fears. It was you speaking to yourself and that message may hold a key."

I dredged my memory for the sound of the leopard's voice and nodded. "He said, 'Life is not a ladder to climb. It is a wheel from which you learn as you travel. When the time is right, I'll come for you. Until then, learn on the wheel.'" I looked at her, waiting for clarification.

"That's wonderful. Do you hear it? You are telling yourself that you can put your marriage and your ex-husband behind you soon."

"What about where he says he'll come for me once I've done that?"

"That's you telling yourself that once that happens, you'll be free to be yourself. Now, I want you to try to recall your dreams very carefully and remember even the smallest details. From now on you should also write them down as soon as you wake up."

I promised I would, but the next night I slept without any dreams that I remembered. After that, there were nights in which I never saw my leopard. As I explained to my therapist, I just knew somehow that he was there. I still wasn't too sure that I wanted him around anyway. Despite what she'd claimed, in my opinion there was only one motive a leopard could have for saying I belonged to him and he'd come for me when the time was right. I'd heard about people who died in their dreams.

I ran into my ex-husband twice during that time. Once in Lambton Quay when John held me by the arm and complained at me in an irritating nasal whine. I felt it was a real advance at least that I merely found it irritating and not frightening.

"Dammit, you have to come back home. A decent woman doesn't go out to work when her husband earns enough to keep her."

I shook him off. Awake there was no guardian leopard watching from the shadows, but I felt as if knowing that he was in my nights gave me an increasing strength of mind in the daylight.

"Let go of me." I snapped. John did so, more in surprise that I defied him than in obedience. "Listen to me for once, John. You're my ex-husband. Ex – as in we're not married any more. I left you, I got a legal separation and I'm not coming back."

"You belong to me."

"I belong to *me*." His hand reached for my shoulder as his face took on that patronizing paternal look that I loathed. I knocked away the reaching fingers as I found my rage unexpectedly rising.

"Get your hands off me and get out of here before I call for help. How would that look to your bosses or on your work CV? Jailed for attacking a woman in the street."

John backed away hastily, a horrified look on his face. He worked as an engineer for the government and his job, with the overseas trips it sometimes provided, was all-important to him. It was the most convincing threat I could have made. I spun on my heel and stalked away before he could speak or grab me again.

My therapist was proud of me when I told her of the encounter. "That's excellent progress. You were able to say to him face-to-face some of what you were feeling. You made him release you and you walked away. I really think that we are making solid progress lately."

I might have temporarily rid myself of John in my waking life, but he continually returned in my dreams. He came as a skeleton lecturing me on my duties to our marriage in my dreams. In reality he was the ghoul who'd done his best in the waking world to eat me alive and now in dreams wished to suck even my bones dry.

The leopard circled both of us in silence whenever I dreamed. In my other world of traffic, work and paying the electricity bills I heard about my husband sometimes from people who knew us both. I was quite surprised when I heard that John had taken several years unpaid leave-of-absence from his government job and accepted other employment overseas. There was a well-paid job waiting for him in an Arab country that needed good engineers. He would leave the country to begin that in another two or three weeks. I'd never denied he was good at his job. It was being a husband he fell down on.

I didn't need the leopard to protect me anymore. I could manage my husband when he appeared in my dreams now – and I did. But what I was hearing in the real world was beginning to worry me. John seemed to be always in the corner of my eye as I glanced around. I would see him sitting in a car near my flat. He would come walking past my flat as I drew my curtains at dusk. He seemed to be always eating at the same restaurants as I did. He never approached me directly, but somehow, he was always about. Gossip said he was leaving in another week. I could hang on until then.

It sounded as if he wasn't coming back either despite having taken only a leave of absence – and that was strange. He'd sold the house his mother had left him. The house, in which I'd been so miserable, unable to ever live up to her standards, the standards he expected of me once we'd married.

But with only that final week to go before he flew out, I saw him more and more often. Glimpses of him as he slipped past me in the commuting crowds hurrying to catch transport home. A shadow as he padded past in the dark street when I went to the dairy for a carton of milk. I'd stopped dreaming him and that scared me too.

I'd have got myself a dog. A pit bull for choice – my ex-husband was terrified of those. But I was away all day and the lease on my flat said no dogs, although it didn't ban other pets. Perhaps I could get a cat? Something alive and welcoming to keep me company, to greet me when I got home. I talked to a friend in Lower Hutt. She bred Ocicats with the kennel prefix of Shadowlands.

"They're wonderful animals. Very friendly, lovely to look at, and quite trainable. I have one you'd love. He's harness-trained so you could even take him for walks in the park opposite you."

I was intrigued by the sound of a cat like that. "Why is he for sale?"

"I swapped him for one of my own show-quality kittens with an Australian breeder. I wanted to widen the gene pool with my own breeding cats but he picked up a bug on the plane. He's been very ill and now we've discovered there was some physical damage. He's almost recovered but he's had to be neutered because he's no good as a stud cat any longer.

"You could have him cheap – and when are you going to visit properly anyhow? It's been almost two years since you actually stayed here with us and we're only an hour away. The last time you were here was after Meg had had her hip operation; she often asks when you're coming to stay again. You could do both, come and visit us and buy the cat?"

"Give me a week or two and I'll come and stay with you for the whole weekend," I promised. "I'll look at the cat then."

In a week, my ex-husband would be gone and I'd feel safer. I made the arrangements that lunch time. I'd take the Friday and the Monday off and have four whole days with my friend and her family, and I rang the Railway to make sure I could bring a cat back on the train. I also went out and bought a cat carrier and a small harness and leash.

For six nights of that remaining week before John would be out of my life and gone, I slept peacefully. I had no unpleasant dreams, and saw no more than glimpses of my leopard's eyes peering out from the shadows. But during the days, my husband was still there.

I'd mentioned that to my therapist and she was anxious on my behalf. "Do you think he could be a physical threat?"

"Not really. He was never physically violent during our marriage. He made me miserable in other ways."

"If you ever feel he could be a danger to you, you should ring the police and lay a complaint. They could have a word with him. Or you could take out a restraining order?"

I knew the local constable who patrolled Thorndon – I'd been at school with him and I knew he took his job seriously. I had a quiet word with Bob Olsen, who nodded reassuringly at me.

"I'll speak to him unofficially, Bev. Program the station number into your fast-dial. If you're ever afraid that he's around your flat and it's going to get physical, you phone the station, they'll call me and I'll be straight there to check."

I did that and it gave me the courage to hold on. One day and a night to go. Then only the night. I knew my ex-husband was leaving from the airport at midday on the Thursday and I'd be free of him. The day after that I'd be on a train going north to get my cat. I had almost decided that I'd buy him even if it were sight-unseen.

John had looked almost gaunt the last time I'd seen him. As if he wasn't eating properly or as if there was something preying on his mind. I smiled whimsically. Maybe my leopard had taken to hunting him in his dreams? That last night before freedom I went to bed, fell asleep easily and – there were the desert sands again, and the leopard.

"It is almost time. You are mine. I will come for you."

Somehow, I wasn't afraid of him now. I smiled and for the first time my hand reached out to brush fingertips over soft fur. The leopard purred thunderously, a friendly approving sound.

"Yes! You are mine. I am yours. It is almost time."

A small clatter inside my flat brought me half-awake, dizzy, disorientated as I was swept abruptly out of my dream. I'd been dreaming, my leopard was – there'd been a noise in the bedroom. What...? Fingers like skeletal claws bit into my nightgowned shoulder and a familiar voice hissed at me.

"My dear sweet wife. In the morning I'll be on a plane to Dubai. They won't find you until you're bloated and the flies will find you first. I won't be coming back from where I'm going – and neither will you, for other reasons." He laughed shrilly. "Not for eternity you won't!" He clicked the light switch. There was no answering blaze of light and I found myself explaining to him, a habit grooved into my brain.

"The landlord said he'd fix that while I'm away for the weekend. The circuit blew last week when I overloaded it."

"My dear little stupid wife." Again, the crazily breaking laugh. "I guess you'll just have to die in the dark."

I could see the faint gleam of a knife blade and I readied myself. My small cellphone was beside the bed. I had the police station on fast-dial as Bob had suggested and at this time of the night he'd be nearby. I reached up slowly and unobtrusively under the edge of the bedcovers and pressed the button. Now – what else could I do?

These were old apartments. The walls were thick and soundproof. It was one of the reasons I'd moved here. But if I could break a window, scream loudly enough – that might bring immediate help. I reached silently for the bedside lamp, keeping the movement smooth so that John wouldn't notice, and with an arching sweep of my arm I flung it through the lighter square of glass in a tinkling crashing explosion that probably woke up half the neighborhood. Then I screamed, a long wailing shriek of rage and fear that became words. Words that should also carry on the cellphone to possibly listening ears.

"Don't you dare threaten to kill me! How did you break in here? Put that knife down!"

I screamed again, putting all my fear into the shrill-edged sound and as if I'd lanced an abscess the fear poured out and was gone. I found my hands crooking into savage claws. I'd fight, for my life I'd fight physically as I'd fought my husband verbally only once before. When I left his house and nothing he could do or say had held me back from the door.

My eyes were growing used to the dimness. I saw his shadow closing in and then, from behind him I saw a darker shadow and the soft glow of golden eyes. I screamed again, the shriek more one of incredulous recognition than fear this time. There came a low growl that scaled up into a shuddering thunderous roar. It slipped back down into a snarl so full of hungry menace my husband fell against the bed, scrabbling to get away from the beast that studied him with hungry golden eyes.

My leopard. But not leopard-sized as he should have been in the real world. He was as he always was in my dreams, the size of a large tiger. I stared as he took one slow pace forward. Another measured pace and he grew again, huge, expanding to fill the whole room, looming over us. My husband shrieked in fury and disbelief.

"Not here. You can't be *here!*" He struck out with the knife – futilely. There was no reply but a contemptuous paw flicked out and lines ran blood down my husband's face. His hand came to up touch the blood and his face twisted in sudden belief and terror.

"You, you..." His voice spluttered into shivering silence.

The paw stretched out again, slowly as John backed across the room. I could hear a police siren pulse down into silence as it approached. I'm sure John heard nothing of that, only the soft snarl of the beast that he confronted, pale blue eyes meeting that molten golden gaze.

It was the man who broke, spinning to escape. A paw slashed out, John dodged, leaping for the door, flinging it open to race down the stairs. To the policemen standing there my husband must have seemed a mad-eyed attacker advancing knife in hand. I ran to the top of the stairs, wrapped in the shadows, just in time to see John trip and fall the length of the long steep flight. He landed with a thud that shook the building and under that I heard a dull snapping sound. In the dark I felt soft fur brush back past me. My leopard purred, his tongue flicking out to lick my hand as he passed – and the darkness within my flat was empty.

I scrambled back for a robe, slippers, before returning to walk down the stairs. Below on the stoop two policemen stood over my husband, one already calling on his radio for an ambulance – which would serve no purpose. The outside light shone on John's unscratched face, glittered from the upturned whiteness of his lifeless face.

I made a statement to the police later, carefully leaving out all mention of my dreams and my leopard. Who'd believe *that* in the light of day? The police had seen nothing anyhow, only John tripping and falling with no one and nothing near him, breaking his neck as he landed.

I'd still been legally married, my divorce unfinalized and John had no living relatives, so I inherited a healthy bank balance and a deposit box filled with a listing of his stocks and shares. I accepted the inheritance. It would help me live more comfortably and be recompense for the misery of the years I was married to their owner. I put off the visit to my friend and for five days. I was busy. I'd keep the apartment for another few months while I looked for a house – perhaps in an area nearer her and her family.

But that could wait a while longer. I caught the train from Wellington city, and got off at the station nearest where my friend lives. She met me with a car there and I fell into her arms. Of course, after the weekend I came back with a cat. I met him that first afternoon. Val carried him into the room and put him down. He made a beeline to me, stretched up and implored with gentle paws. I bent to scoop him up automatically and froze.

He was gold. The rosettes were only a darker gold against the lighter gold of the coat. The eyes too were gold, a molten shade with the pupils carving a contrast through the metallic blaze. It was beautiful and deadly. No, not deadly. This small leopard was cat-sized. He squawked affectionately at me and I completed the movement, catching him up and holding him close.

His tongue came out to touch my wrist and his purr rattled in his chest. Val grinned.

"Looks as if he's made *his* decision. You're lucky he's alive to make it. He was so sick on and off for weeks that I was afraid he'd die. He spent most of his time lying asleep in his basket by my bed. I think he dreamed a lot. He'd twitch and growl in the night."

I looked down at my little golden leopard cradled happily in my arms. I remembered the beast who'd claimed me as his own. The huge leopard who'd protected me. "What's his name?"

Val chuckled. "You know pedigree names. He's Tiger Dreaming of Shadowlands."

My Dreaming Tiger reached up to pat my cheek. I took him home with me, bought a house we both liked and we live there happily. But sometimes I wonder. Whose dream were we dreaming? In whose shadow land did we walk? Not that it matters. And if sometimes in my dreams a leopard, tiger-sized, walks with me. Well, we all have our dreams. And in them we can be any size – and anyone – we choose, as we can in the real world. I learned that from a friendly leopard once.

TRUTH AND CONSEQUENCES

When Nerida Paiwai was sixteen, she started work as a cleaner. Not the ordinary sort of cleaner, doing offices at night, but what was to her the more superior sort. Nerida cleaned the house for Mrs. Hale up on The Terrace. It was close enough to Nerida's home that she could walk there and back and have no fares to pay. Mrs. Hale provided all the equipment and supplies as well so all Nerida had to bring was her own all-enveloping flowered apron and comfortable flat shoes in which to do the work.

It was 1991 at the time things went wrong – and of course the Hales were always polite to Nerida, they weren't exactly chatty or confiding, but that was okay with Nerida. She didn't have much in common with a rich blond white woman who spent her time on committees. Nerida was none of those things and she spent her time making a living by cleaning houses for ladies of that sort in five of the big houses on The Terrace. It wasn't a bad living either and Nerida had been doing that for almost ten years – ever since she'd turned sixteen and left school. It had started because of a coincidence.

"But I don't want to work in a factory, Mum."

Patti Paiwai scowled thoughtfully. "Well, no. Guess I wouldn't want to do that either. But you got no qualifications and you have to do something if you're not staying in school. I'm not having you sitting at home all day while I work."

"I've got School Certificate."

"Yes, but you've left school. You could stay on and get university entrance if you wanted. I reckon I could afford to keep you in school another year or two?" Patti offered.

Nerida shook her head. "I'm not stupid, Mum. But all that stuff, it bores me rigid. Better if I find a job like you say. I'll look around, okay?"

Patti nodded. She'd asked Granny Ngaire for advice about Nerida's future. Granny was actually Patti's mother, but everyone who knew her called her "Granny Ngaire," even some of the pakeha who knew and liked her. Granny had thought about it carefully then said that the girl should have a job that changed regularly. Patti had gone off to think about that and decided it was true. Nerida disliked the sort of routine that she'd find on a factory production line. But with the job market tightening and only School C. as a qualification what could she suggest to her daughter?

She was still thinking about that when she was heading home only to run into Joan Hale. She'd been at school with the woman when Joan was Joan Gardener and she wasn't a bad sort.

"Patti? Nice to see you. What are you doing these days?"

"Still working, still a widow, what about you?"

"Still married, still on too many committees, and now I've lost my cleaner."

"Guess you've been careless."

Joan stared for a moment and Patti remembered that at school Joan never did have much of a sense of humor.

"Oh? Oh, no. I mean she got pregnant and resigned. It's rather a nuisance, she was a good worker and she'd been with me for almost seven years. Now I have to go through all the trouble of finding another cleaner just when I'm really busy. It isn't only me who's inconvenienced either. She used to work for several of my friends as well."

And Patti had her idea. "I can tell you someone who's looking for a job like that, if you'd be interested in interviewing them?" It should be ideal. Nerida wasn't afraid of hard work, her headmaster would give her a good reference, and it would be the "regularly changing job" Granny had said would suit Nerida best.

Joan looked first hopeful, then suspicious. "What's the girl like?"

"She has School Certificate but she doesn't want to stay at school," Patti told her. "She's a good kid, a hard worker, and bright enough, she just isn't interested in books and studying very much. She could bring a reference from her headmaster?"

Joan nodded. "Very well. Have her come and see me tomorrow at three o'clock. What's her name?"

"Nerida."

"Tell her to be prompt, I'll just be home from a committee meeting of the Friends of the Wellington Library, and after that I have to start getting ready for a university dinner."

"I'll tell her." Patti promised.

"Well, if it works out, I'll be grateful to you, Patti."

"That's okay, Joan. If it works out it'll suit both of us."

And so far as anyone knew for a long time, it worked out well. Nerida arrived and was interviewed. She showed Mrs. Hale her School Certificate, and her reference – the headmaster had been happy to give her one saying that she was pleasant, hardworking, honest, and sensible – and Mrs. Hale hired her on a temporary basis. One day a week for a month. If she was satisfactory, she'd be taken on permanently and Joan would recommend the girl to her friends.

Nerida *was* satisfactory and Joan, in turn, recommended her. Nerida became the one-day-a-week cleaner for a small group of women, all of whom were old friends and spent a lot of their time together on various committees. That wasn't all altruism. Their husbands found that having wives on prominent committees was often useful either socially or professionally and encouraged the activities.

Nerida didn't care about any of that. She would listen politely to the occasional lecture on the causes the women approved and agree with whatever they said. Often, she did agree – but she'd also learned very quickly that whether she did or not, it was the approval they wanted to hear. It was part of her job to provide it when required.

"So we're sending a medical missionary to this place for a year and a half."

"That's good."

"Yes. She'll look after women. Many of them are Muslim and won't have a male doctor. They'd rather die. So silly. But Joy will help them, and she can tell them about the Lord at the same time."

"But Mrs. Hale, if they're Muslim they'll know about the Lord, won't they?"

"Well, yes, but they aren't Christians. It's really Christ they don't know about. Joy will tell them about Christ."

"I thought they had their own religion?"

"They do, but it isn't Christianity. They're heathens really. Joy will bring them to Christ, she'll save their souls while she looks after their bodies, and she'll persuade them to come to church."

"Their husbands won't like that." Nerida said realistically, having known at least one Muslim family.

"Nonsense. It'll all work out, you'll see. And isn't it about time you finished the lounge?"

There was something in the abrupt way in which Mrs. Hale changed the subject that told Nerida she'd put her foot in it. A few more conversations like that and she understood that she was there as "chorus" to the star. It was her job to listen and applaud, not to find faults in what was said. And very wisely she said nothing at all when she overheard a conversation about fourteen months later between two of her ladies.

"It's a disgrace, saying that she was causing trouble amongst the community. She was simply bringing Christ's words to those poor women. Joy said they're nothing but chattels to their husbands. She even saw one girl who'd been married at twelve. The poor little thing was still only thirteen and she was pregnant. Joy quite rightly complained to the authorities who had to do something."

"What happened?"

"What do you expect? Her family produced a document claiming the girl was sixteen and the case was dropped. After that, Joy found none of the women would accept her help and the men kept making complaints about her to the local authorities. They said she was trying to convert their wives and, in that country apparently that's illegal, so Joy has had to leave."

Mrs. Hale's friend sniffed. "What do you expect."

She changed the subject while Nerida quietly went back to her cleaning; wondering exactly what it was the two women in the Hale lounge *had* expected. She could imagine how well it would have been received if some woman from that country had come here, telling the women in Wellington that their religion was stupid and wrong and they should all change it at once. It wouldn't have been the husbands who tossed her out there. The women would have done that themselves.

When you thought about it, it was a bit insulting and she wasn't surprised that no one had liked it in the country where this Joy had been working.

Life went on quietly after that. Or as quiet as life generally is for a girl in her teens. Nerida was going out with Jim Braddick and eventually, when she was twenty, they got married.

"You're very young to be thinking of getting married."

"Yes, Mrs. Hale, I suppose we are. But we want to, and Jim has a good job at the freezing works."

"I suppose it's your business. Mr. Hale and I will give you a wedding present, and if you want to keep working for me, I don't have any problems with that."

No, Nerida thought. She bet Mrs. Hale wouldn't. She'd heard often enough from her five ladies about how terribly inconvenient it had been when their last cleaner left because she was pregnant. They'd all be happy to put off the evil day when they had to start looking for another cleaner again, for as long as they could. And they do like me. I think they might even be just a little sorry to lose me as me, not just as their cleaner, Nerida thought as she swept a dusty patio.

Her marriage was happy, but there were no children – and just on five years after the wedding there was a funeral.

"On the new motorway extension, yes. He came around the corner and there was this kid in a stolen car on the wrong side of the road. Poor Jim had no chance." Nerida could hear her mum explaining Jim's death over and over to people who wanted the details. "No, the kid was killed as well."

"I'm so sorry, dear. If you'd like to take more time off?"

"No thanks, Mrs. Hale. I'll be back on Monday."

"Well, work does take your mind off things."

Nerida looked after her employer and snorted. What would Joan Hale know about work? She was on committees and Nerida supposed that was work of a sort, but it wasn't the kind of work where you had to earn a living. Joan Hale had been in hospital a month back, but only for ten days and she seemed fine now she was home. And anyway, she still didn't have to work or agree with any dumb thing her employers said. All she had to do was smile at them all the time, and come back to work when her heart was broken, because she needed the money.

"It's been two years now, Nerida."

"Yes, Mrs. Hale."

"And you've started using your maiden name again?"

"Yes." Oh, I see, you want to know why. "It's like this, Mrs. Hale. Granny Ngaire said I should move on now that Jim's been dead for two years, and that being Nerida Paiwai again would help me to do that."

"I see. Your grandmother is a wise woman."

"Yes, she is. She was right too. I feel sort of better about things."

After all, she was only twenty-seven and while she'd loved Jim, she was too young to spend the rest of her life alone. She'd worked for Mrs. Hale and her other four ladies for eleven years and while the job still suited her, she wasn't sure she wanted to do that all of her life either.

She didn't have to.

"Alan Malion? But dear, he has a record!"

"I know, Mrs. Hale, but he's changed. It wasn't anything really bad. When he was sixteen, he got in with a bad crowd. He was in a stolen car when the police stopped them – but he didn't know his friend had stolen it."

Joan Hale pursed her lips. "That may be true dear, but wasn't there more?"

"He was charged with receiving but it wasn't true and the jury said so," Nerida told her. "He says that after that, the police had it in for him and they kept picking on him for everything that happened."

"Picking on a man doesn't get him convicted, there has to be proof for that."

"Alan says that that marijuana wasn't his. The police planted it on him and one of them said that if they couldn't get him one way they'd get him another."

"I don't think the police would do that, Nerida. Don't you have a relative in the police force? What does he say?"

"Nothing much, Mrs. Hale. I'd better go and vacuum the

lounge now or I'll never be finished."

She didn't like to remember what Bob had said. He'd told her that no one had needed to plant anything on Alan. The guy was a crook, plain and not so simple. The charges that had been made against Alan, and the very few times they'd stuck had been only the tip of the iceberg. The guy was bad news and if she were as smart as he'd always thought she was she'd have nothing more to do with Alan Malion.

But she was in love, Nerida thought. There was no use in saying she should leave Alan. She believed him when he said the police were out to get him. Not Bob, he was family – his mother had been a Paiwai, but with some cops you never knew. Maybe one of them did have it in for Alan. Anyway, she believed him and he'd said he'd never do anything like that again. He was going straight now he'd met her.

She wanted to marry him – a lot – and she thought – she hoped – he felt the same. Not that they'd ever talked about it, but if she felt that way then probably, he did too and sooner or later he'd ask her. It was a pity he had to spend so much time up in Auckland, but he said it was business and he hated being away from her.

When she and Jim had married, they hadn't wanted to rent a house forever. They'd worked hard and lived on Jim's pay while all of hers had gone into a savings account. After two years, what with that money and her savings from before her marriage, they'd had enough for a deposit. And just then a Paiwai third cousin had died. He'd had no immediate family left – and he didn't like the government who'd get it if he didn't have a will – so he'd left his old house to Granny Ngaire who'd offered it to Nerida and Jim at a good price.

"The house is only two bedrooms, but you could add one on when the time comes. And it's a good big yard. Old Hemi put in a berry-house with raspberries, strawberries, and red currants all under netting so the birds don't get them. There are half a dozen fruit trees and a good vegetable garden. Hemi had a toolshed too and he's got just about every sort of gear you'd ever need in that. You can buy it all as it stands for—" she named a figure and Nerida and Jim had nodded at once.

"Smart." Granny approved. "Having your own house is

money in the bank. Insurance and rates are less then rent, and you have an investment."

Even after Jim died, Nerida had kept the house. She loved it, the garden, berry-house, and fruit trees helped keep her grocery bill right down, and she often gave the surplus to friends or relatives. Then she had bad news. The council was extending the motorway and it would go through the area where her house stood. She dug her toes in and in the end the council offered her a really big amount of money to sell. Nerida took it, banked the money, found a place to rent for a while and tried to decide if, or where, she should buy another house. Or should it be a smart new flat?

It was funny, but it was while she was trying to decide that, the week after she got the money, that she met Alan. He'd convinced her not to buy another home just yet.

"House and flat prices are up. You'd do better to keep renting for a while and buy when they come down. If you have the cash, you'll be able to knock the price down even further and do a really good deal." It made sense, so she left the money in her bank.

She'd been going out with Alan for ten months when Mrs. Hale lost her purse.

"Nerida? Have you seen my handbag?"

"You left it in the lounge, Mrs. Hale."

"Oh, yes, here it is. Ah, Nerida? My purse doesn't seem to be in it, you haven't seen that too, have you dear?"

"No, Mrs. Hale. It'll be somewhere around though."

It turned up eventually in Mrs. Hale's bedroom when Nerida cleaned under the bed, but Nerida noticed her employer going through the purse as if she was afraid some of the contents could have disappeared while it was missing.

The next day just before she was due to finish, they had a rather strange conversation.

"Why don't you sit down and have a cup of tea before you go, dear, you work so hard."

Surprised, Nerida made them a pot of tea, sat at the kitchen table and tried to make polite conversation. She found they were discussing the sale of her house the previous year.

"I understand the council paid you a good price for that?"

Was she going to suggest some sort of stocks Nerida

should buy? "Um, yes. They did. I banked it. Alan says that I should wait until house prices fall again before I buy another place."

"So you're still seeing him, dear?"

"I think he may be going to ask me to marry him some time soon."

"That's nice, dear. I suppose he takes good care of you. Does he ever come up to The Terrace to pick you up after work?"

"Sometimes."

"Where does he wait for you?"

What *was* this, Nerida wondered? "He waits outside in the car, Mrs. Hale."

"I see, well, I must get on with those committee letters now. Thank you, Nerida. I'll see you next week."

The next thing she noticed was that her other employers seemed to spend more time than usual talking to her – mostly about her romance and the possibility of her marrying Alan – popping in and out of the rooms as she cleaned, or looking out of their front windows. Mrs. Chapman misplaced a rather gaudy pearl and ruby brooch that had belonged to her great-grandmother and made Nerida turn the house upside down until it was found.

Then Mrs. Hale lost her purse again. She hunted for it all over the house while Nerida trailed in her wake, moving furniture for her and doing her best to help her employer think of where she'd had the purse last.

"I'm sure I had it in the kitchen. I put it on the top of the refrigerator because I was looking at the calendar on the front of the fridge. Oh, dear. I have an important committee meeting and I can't waste any more time now. See if you can find it will you, dear. If you do, put it on top of the fridge again. Oh dear, it's such a nuisance!"

Nerida wondered what the fuss was about. Like all of her group Mrs. Hale, a generation older than Nerida or not, mostly used credit or cash cards, and she hadn't lost those. Just the pretty leather purse from her handbag that she usually kept a few dollars in for convenience. Mrs. Hale left and Nerida kept looking. The purse finally turned up in the bottom of the wardrobe and she left it on top of the fridge.

The next week was one of the worst of her life. She finished on Monday afternoon at Mrs. Chapman's home and was handed her money. Then the old lady looked at her.

"I won't be needing you any more, Nerida. I'm making other arrangements."

Nerida stared at her. "Other arrangements?"

"Yes, I've decided to get a cleaning service in to do my house in future."

Nerida could think of nothing to say. She'd cleaned for Mrs. Chapman for twelve years and now she was being fired.

"Was it something I didn't do? Did I forget to do something?"

"No," the old lady's voice was cold. "No, it was nothing you didn't do. I have decided I prefer a cleaning company, they have certain advantages, that is sufficient. Goodbye, Nerida."

Nerida plodded down the path to the street, still struck dumb by her abrupt dismissal. By the time she got home she was seething. After twelve years, to be sacked as if she were someone the old bag hadn't known for five minutes. A cleaning company, what "certain advantages" did they have that she didn't? She went to work at Mrs. Findlay's house on Tuesday and at half past three she had a similar conversation all over again.

This time Nerida protested. "But Mrs. Findlay. I've worked for you for twelve years. If I haven't done my work in some way, if I've upset you, please tell me, give me a chance."

"I have decided to employ a cleaning service, Nerida. It's my right, I imagine?"

"Yes, but..."

"Goodbye, Nerida."

It was the same on Wednesday and Thursday. When it came to Friday and Mrs. Hale, Nerida was numb. She accepted her wages, listened to the same brief speech and left without a word or protest. Mrs. Findlay had said no more than the truth, they had the right to sack her and hire someone else, and there wasn't a damn thing she could do about it.

Alan commiserated. "Old bags. I should go and burgle their damn places, that'd teach them. They'd have enough stuff around to make it worthwhile." There was something in the casual way he said it that rang a minor alarm bell.

"Alan? You wouldn't?"

"Why not?"

"It's wrong, they've been pretty good to me for twelve years apart from this. Maybe if I wait a while they'll find this cleaning service they're so keen on won't be so good and they'll take me back?"

"Look, I've got an opportunity. I wasn't going to say anything, but I've got the chance to buy into a dot.com company owned by a friend of mine. I don't have enough, but if you put in the house money that you got when the council bought your house, we could be rich in a year or two. It'd be like an investment in our future."

"I'm not sure, Alan. It's everything I have."

"You don't trust me." His face fell. "I know I was stupid when I was a kid, but I've changed."

"I know."

"Then you will?" The loving smile he gave her made Nerida want to do cartwheels. Of course she trusted him.

"I'll have to go to the bank and it'll maybe take a week to get the money. I put it in investments that the bank recommended and I can't just take it all out tomorrow. I have to sign stuff."

He hugged her hard. "That's great. I'll get my friend to get the share certificates done ready for you. You know people are making a fortune with dot.com outfits. You and me, we'll be as rich as those old cows that fired you. An' maybe we should think about moving in together."

Nerida went to the bank the next day still glowing. "You and me" he'd said. Them, and "moving in together." She thought that he'd ask her to marry him as soon as the share certificates were paid for. It would be great, she'd be so happy, they'd be so happy. She was still bubbling when she met Granny Ngaire in Lambton Quay and told her all about it.

"Alan Malion. How long you been going out with him now, Nerida?"

"Almost a year. Well, just over ten months."

"And he's the one who told you about this company?"

"Yes, I think he's going to ask me to marry him too. He talked about us moving in together."

"Living together isn't marrying. You make sure what he

has in mind before you agree to anything you aren't sure about."

Nerida almost danced off down the road. She was quite sure about Alan. Granny Ngaire looked after her. She knew about Alan Malion, as she'd known about other men on the fringes of crime in this city, and what she knew she didn't like. Bob Olsen would know more and he'd always liked Nerida. She'd have a little chat with Bob and see what he could find out as well. Two days later she asked her granddaughter to call and sadly started the conversation.

"Nerida, I want you to listen to me very carefully."

"Granny, what is it?"

"I've been asking around about your Alan. It isn't good."

Nerida felt anger race through her. More of that "he was a bad boy as a teenager – which was twenty years ago now anyway – and he hasn't changed" rubbish. But this was Granny Ngaire whom she loved, so she kept her mouth closed and waited politely to hear what would be said. But she loved Alan, he loved her, they were going to get married and be rich and nothing Granny said would change her mind.

"You said he's arranging to invest your money in nzsecurity.com, and you're getting married?"

"Yes." Nerida almost snapped.

Granny looked at her. "That won't happen. Not either thing. For a start, you can't marry him because he's already married. He has a wife who lives in Auckland. They've been married for more than fifteen years and right now she's pregnant with his third child." Nerida's mouth dropped half-open in shock and pain.

"As for your money, if you invest in that company you'll lose every cent of it. A friend of Bob's is on the Securities Commission and he says nzsecurity.com is a shell. The Commission already has two lawsuits outstanding against similar Malion dotcoms – lawsuits brought by women whom Alan Malion persuaded to put their money into one of his Internet companies.

"Oh, yes, he and his wife own the company he told you about; it isn't a friend's company as he told you. The other women lost everything they invested and their lawyers say Alan set the company up to do exactly that. The investors lose their money but, surprise, surprise, Alan seems to come out of his company's crash with all the money himself."

Nerida was fighting back tears and Granny patted her shoulder. "All of us make fools of ourselves over a good-looking boy at one time or another. It isn't your fault he's crooked and always has been. Tell, me, child? How soon after you sold old Hemi's place was it that you met Alan?"

"Oh, God. It was only a week or so. I'd just got the cheque from the council for the sale. But Granny Ngaire, it couldn't be. How would he have known?"

"Men like that make it their business to know." Granny said quietly. "He may have paid someone in an office involved in the compulsory purchases. He targeted you in the cruelest way. He picked when you were down and unhappy to suggest that you could get your own back on those women by becoming rich yourself."

Nerida was crying now and Granny put an arm around her. "Look on it as experience. You won't be fooled like that again, and..." She grinned wickedly. "We found out about Mr. Malion in time. When were you going to give him the money?"

"Tonight, over dinner. He's taking me to Alberts."

"So? You go and eat his dinner, order everything expensive, tell him you have an envelope for him, wait until he's paid the bill then tell him the envelope is a goodbye card. Say you've come to the conclusion that he isn't right for you and neither is his company."

She gave a deep rich chuckle, smiling at Nerida as the girl slowly lifted her head and a watery smile broke out to match Granny's grin

"I will. I guess the money stays where it is for now."

"That's sensible. Alan was right about one thing. House prices are starting to drop and Bob's friend thinks they'll go quite low before they rise again. In a year you could buy a house like the one you had and for about two thirds the money you were paid."

"I need a job too."

"There's work if you look around and you're ready to do most things, find something that keeps changing in the small ways, something to keep you interested. I'll ask around if you like."

Nerida spoiled Alan Malion's evening a few hours later, leaving him staring in outrage and disbelief at a rather pretty floral card which read – in elegant script:

"I'd like us still to stay as friends,

But this relationship has come to an end."

"What's this?"

"What it says?"

He forced his eyes to look betrayed and grief-stricken – although what he really wanted to do was to give the little cow a good smack across the ear. He'd been counting on her money.

"I thought you loved me. We were going to move in together. You were going to invest in our future."

"Yes, well, I don't think your wife would like us doing that, and the two women already suing you don't need me making a threesome. Goodbye, Alan. Next time you start making sheep's eyes at someone you'd better make sure they are as dumb as a sheep." She walked away from the restaurant table, her heels tapping decisively on the floor. Damn, that had felt good! It almost made up for how stupid she'd felt when Granny told her the truth.

On the way, out she passed Joan Hale entering the restaurant and looked her right in the eye. The older woman reddened slightly and didn't meet her gaze. Nerida turned to glance at Joan over her shoulder as she left and wondered as she had ever since Mrs. Hale's group had fired her, what it was that she'd done to cause her dismissal? Then she shrugged it off. Who knew with that sort? There were other jobs and she'd find one.

She found the perfect job only five days later while reading the paper.

A taxi license was offered for sale. Nerida had lived in the city all her life, she knew the inner city like the back of her hand and she could learn the rest. She bought the license, bought not the old car offered with it, but a better newer one and started work. It was always interesting, and she worked different shifts to keep herself from ever being bored.

That was how she met the Salton kid. Nerida liked the girl, she introduced the kid and her friends to Granny, and until Tina Salton went off to university down in the South Island

Nerida was always her taxi driver of choice if she needed one. She was still that whenever the girl came home and didn't want to drive in the city. The friendship hadn't done Nerida any harm either, Tina had recommended her to other girls at the fancy private school she attended and Nerida had almost more work from them than she could handle.

Nerida had bought her own house two years after she started with the taxi. It had been a reasonable bargain and she loved having her own home again. Several times one or the other of the Terrace Five as she thought of them had used her cab. They usually said nothing much of what had happened, and she didn't either. One day Nerida would like to grab onto whichever one was in her taxi and ask again what it was that she was supposed to have done. Even after ten years it still annoyed her not to know.

That third week of July though she hadn't been working. There was a really nasty sort of flu going around and half the drivers had come down with it. She'd managed to catch it on Monday and she'd stayed home for two weeks getting over it. Now that it was the second Friday she felt better; she'd start driving again on Monday. Nerida was clearing the table of her dinner plates around five o'clock when there was a quiet tapping at the front door. She opened it. Outside on the step Joan Hale stood, looking half embarrassed to be there and oddly ashamed.

Nerida frankly stared. Good grief, what was she doing here? She hadn't seen her around the city for several months and, come to think of it, the old girl didn't look that well. Joan Hale's face was gaunt, she'd lost weight – maybe she'd had the flu as well – and she was wearing a very unfashionable sort of turban-hat that didn't suit her at all.

"May I come in, Nerida?"

She hadn't lost all her manners, surprise or no surprise. "Of course, Mrs. Hale. Come in and sit down. Would you like a cup of tea?"

"Not just now, thank you, dear. I couldn't manage one."

Nerida ushered her into the lounge, sat her in the best armchair, and waited. There was a long pause before Joan Hale spoke.

"I'm here to apologize."

"You mean when you and your friends fired me?"

"Yes." There was another pause. "I was wrong, and I'm bitterly ashamed of what we did. It was my fault. I jumped to conclusions and I feel I have to explain. I can't make what we did right again, but I can tell you what happened and say how sorry I am."

Nerida wasn't going to give her much help with what Joan was making clear was an awkward explanation. Being sacked by the Terrace Five had rankled all those years ago and still did when she remembered it. She sat there in silence, waiting.

"My husband had friends in the police force. I heard about that man you were seeing, Alan Malion?" Nerida nodded. "He had a very bad reputation with women, they said he could talk even decent girls into doing almost anything for him and I don't know if you know even now, but three of his girlfriends before you ended up with criminal records because of him."

No, Nerida said silently to herself, Bob had never mentioned that, nor Granny either.

"Then I lost a lot of money." Mrs. Hale finished.

Nerida stared; it was as if dawn had broken in a haze of brutal light. The purse! The second time Joan Hale had misplaced it and made such a fuss, that was the week before she'd been sacked.

"My daughter was going overseas. I was worried about how little money she had so I withdrew a thousand dollars to give to her. I thought she could change it when she got to England. I put it in the purse and then the purse went missing."

"I found it." Nerida said, remembering. "It was in the bottom of your wardrobe. I thought you must have meant to put it in a coat pocket there and missed the pocket."

"I did. But when I found the purse on top of the fridge where you'd left it for me, all the money was gone."

"And you thought I'd taken it. You thought that Alan had persuaded me to rob you first and maybe your friends next? So you all sacked me. You never said a word and I had no chance to defend myself!"

"That's unfortunately the truth. I – we all liked you, Nerida. I was so upset thinking that you'd stolen from me that I told the others and we decided to let you go. We didn't want to talk to the police; we didn't want to ruin your life. I thought

– I hoped – you'd know why we were doing it and never do such a thing again."

"Instead, I've wondered for years what it was that I was supposed to have done. I've racked my brains trying to think how I could have upset all of you." Nerida's voice broke slightly as she recalled the times one of the five had been in her cab. "You said you were bitterly sorry. You know it wasn't me now? Who was it?"

Joan Hale seemed to shrink into herself. "It was no one, Nerida. Or to be exact, it was my fault." She leaned forward clasping her hands tightly together.

"I took the money out of the bank. As you may remember I hadn't been well that year. I'd been on medication and I suppose I was careless. I thought I'd put the money in my leather purse, and I thought I'd put the purse in my coat pocket ready to take with me when I got home after the committee meeting. I was going to see Jessica and give her the money then."

Yes, Nerida remembered that year too. Mrs. Hale had been in hospital for a week or two and come home again. Whatever had caused her stay hadn't seemed to be serious and they'd never discussed what sort of illness it had been. Joan Hale spoke again, abruptly.

"I had cancer. They operated on me and they thought they had it all but this year it's recurred. My husband died two years ago and I decided to sell the house before I had to go back into hospital. I wanted to simplify my estate and it was while we were clearing up the house that I found the envelope with the money in it."

"Where was it?" Nerida was standing now; looking down at this woman whose carelessness could have ruined Nerida's life.

"Where I never thought to look for it until I found it and remembered. I'd put it in the back of one of the small top drawers in my dressing table. There was a false back on one. I recall that I was worried about leaving the money in the house while I was at the meeting, so I put it inside the false back of the drawer and the empty purse in my coat pocket to remind me to take the money out when I got home. I came home and I'd forgotten that I'd hidden the money. All I remembered was having it in my purse and now it was gone."

She looked up at Nerida. "I'm so sorry. I've been worrying about it for days but I haven't been able to get to you to tell you about it. Nerida, please forgive me. What I did, the conclusions I jumped to, were unforgivable, but I hope you can forgive me despite that? I did manage to tell my lawyer before I became so ill. I've left you something, well, not just something - exactly what I owe you. Use it as you like - but it's yours."

She glanced out of the lounge window. "I must go now. I have another appointment."

Nerida nodded. It had been a long time ago and, in the end, she'd probably done better for herself than she would have done if she'd stayed a cleaner for the Terrace Five. She owned three taxis now, and she had almost completed a business degree at the University. She looked at the woman in front of her. Poor old bag of bones, all upset over her mistake, knowing she'd misjudged a woman she'd liked and making herself come here to admit it and apologize. Nerida held out her hand.

"No hard feelings, Mrs. Hale. And I'll accept whatever you've left me. I've been thinking of buying a fourth taxi and hiring another driver." Her smile flashed out at her visitor. "I'll put whatever you've left towards that. I reckon I'll be rich yet."

Joan Hale wordlessly grasped the hand held out to her. For a moment she savored the feeling of peace. She had confessed her stupidity, her cruelty and her misjudgment, and beyond her hopes or her just deserts, a better woman had forgiven her.

"Thank you. Thank you, Nerida."

"It's all right," Nerida was embarrassed. Jeez, you'd think she'd saved the old girl's life or something. "Don't worry about it anymore. It's all forgiven and forgotten, eh?"

She walked her visitor to the door, saw her down the steps and went back to cleaning the kitchen. She'd be back at work on Monday. It'd be interesting to see if she heard from Joan Hale's lawyer too.

It was the Monday, only an hour after she had started work again, that the phone call came. Nerida answered.

"Yes, this is Nerida Paiwai. Yes, I used to work for Mrs. Hale as a cleaner years back. Who else? Well there were four of her friends; I did a day a week each for them. There was Mrs. Chapman, Mrs. Findlay, Mrs.... That's enough? Okay. What do you want me to do? Yes, I can come after lunch. Around two o'clock? Sure. No trouble. I'll see you then. Oh, do you mind if I bring a relative in case I need legal advice? No? Good."

Granny was startled, as she rarely was these days. "Me? What for? You told him you wanted me there in case you needed legal advice?" Her face broke into a huge grin. "Well, I'm no fool if I do say so myself. I suppose I can give you as much sensible advice as any fancy lawyer. All right, you pick me up from my place about half-past one." Nerida was on time and they reached the lawyer's office on the hour.

"Now, Ms. Paiwai. I am informed that my client, Mrs. Joan Hale owed you a sum of money, the debt being owed from some ten or twelve years previous. My client instructed me to take the basic sum she owed you and add compounding interest from the time of the debt and remit that amount to you. One of our clerks has been working on this for a full day. They've had to look up bank information about rates from years ago, and compound that each year." He glanced at Nerida who remained silent.

"With compound interest over the period at the bank rates of the time, the client having also insisted that any tax due on the amount should be paid by her, the original sum is now..." Nerida felt a little faint.

Granny piped up, "Could you repeat that?" The lawyer did so, a very small smile curving his lips.

"It's surprising what compound interest does, but I assure you that the amount is correct as stated. My client wanted you to have the sum immediately. I have here a bank draft. If you would sign here? Yes, thank you. And here? Then that is it. The money is yours."

Nerida stood, the bank draft held in one damp hand. "I'd like to thank Mrs. Hale, can you tell me which hospital she's in?"

The lawyer looked surprised. "My dear Ms. Paiwai, I thought you knew. Mrs. Hale died on Friday afternoon around half-past five. She was buried this morning."

An appointment Mrs. Hale had said. Nerida recalled the words. Mrs. Hale couldn't stay to talk with Nerida any more, she had another appointment – it seemed that she'd had that for sure. The lawyer was still talking.

He sighed. "A lovely lady, I've known her most of my life. She called me into the hospital early one morning and made this codicil to her will. She was adamant I do it at once, really quite agitated about it. I had it typed out at once and she signed it that evening.

"Only the day after that she slipped into a coma. The hospital said it was odd. She was still very restless even then. Several times before she passed away, she seemed to be Mumbling urgently to someone. They thought she might have had something she needed to tell someone. But she was in the coma so she didn't hear what her family were asking her and she couldn't have spoken clearly any longer even if she had heard them."

Silently Granny Ngaire and Nerida left his office. They walked down the street to the bank, deposited Nerida's bank draft and without discussion Nerida took Granny home where she made a pot of tea that they both sat down to drink. There was a long silence. At last Nerida spoke.

"She did have something she needed to say – and she said it. I'm glad I forgave her."

Granny nodded. "It's probably just as well. If you'd refused, she might have stayed around until you did." She smiled at her granddaughter. "Think of being haunted by Joan Hale." Nerida did, and her shudder almost upset the teapot.

COMING HOME

Above the harbor curve, the great Haast's eagles fly. On the ground their prey cowers under ferns, fearing the hiss of wind through wings that is the signal for incoming death. There is no date. Dates are human things, created by people and fueled by their need to know when they are. To the eagles, all times are the present. Only the seasons come and go. This is their land, their place, one day the harbor below them may host a city. That time is not yet, nor will it be for two thousand years.

* * *

The land groans. People in their huts startle awake. In 1847 the city is a jumble of whares, small wooden settlers' cottages, and the occasional larger building made from massive, crude, pit-sawn planking.

"John? John, what's happening?"

"I dunno." John Melford rolled over as the bed shook violently a second time. He yelped as a third shake tossed him to the floor. "What the...? It's an earthquake. Get outside!" He scrambled to the bed, grabbed his wife and hauled her towards the doorway.

"Margaret, get Margaret!"

"I will, you get outside."

His daughter was sleeping still. Her tiny form flat on its back, one small fist stuffed in her mouth. John Melford snatched her up fractions of a second before a lump of the roof smashed down onto the cot. He held her tightly, grateful that she was alive as he ran for the doorway. He exploded out into the sunlight and into the arms of his wife.

He gaped about at a changed landscape. "My Lord, how can such things be?"

The city was aflame in two places, jumbled heaps of what had once been homes showed the lines in which they had once stood – but little else. Land at the harbor edge had risen, to the destruction of many vessels. Everywhere people wandered dazed and bleeding, or sat staring at the ruin of their hopes. Here and there a man wept as he dug desperately, seeking someone or something lost in the wreckage of his home.

John Melford held his wife and baby daughter. Behind him his own home, though damaged, still stood; he'd lost nothing. He owed the Lord everything John Melford owned including three lives. He'd remember it and bring up his daughter to acknowledge the debt.

* * *

"My dear Miss Melford. It can be done of course, but it will take a fortune."

"I have a fortune," Margaret Melford said calmly. "And a recent letter tells me that I have inherited another from my father's English cousin."

"But surely you could build a school for boys. A school for girls is unnecessary. Girls marry, they become wives and mothers, what need do they have for a school that..."

He saw the look in his client's eyes and stopped short. The woman might be eccentric but she was related to nobility in England and she was rich. Very rich – and his only wealthy client. The money she would waste on her foolish scheme was her own and she'd do it no matter what he said. Better to agree and make sure some of what was spent came his way.

"But, of course, I'm sure you have thought carefully about your plan and it shall be my work to ensure that all goes as you would wish."

"I felt sure you would do so."

Margaret Melford's voice was so delicately ironic that she knew her lawyer would not notice it. She'd followed his thoughts quite closely and he'd come to no conclusions other than she'd expected. He'd help her and defend her plans to others, only that way could he remain her lawyer and continue to be well paid. And being well paid in work he enjoyed was his sole aim in life.

A year later she stood outside a sturdy building. Beside her the lawyer pursed his lips. "Are you sure it was necessary to make the building that solid? It has cost you far more than necessary."

"Yes."

She left it at that. He had not come to the new colony until ten years after the later quakes of 1855. She'd been only eight, but she remembered those, and remembered too her parents' tales of the earlier quakes from which God had preserved her life. Her parents had died years ago, her father leaving her everything he had. His cousin, Jane, a strong-minded spinster, had done the same only the previous year. Margaret had corresponded with Jane and confided to her the vision of a school for girls.

"They have little here. It is the boys who receive tutoring or training. Yet I believe it is no waste for some of the girls of this colony to receive an education as well. I plan to start a boarding school for girls. I will also establish several scholarships for girls whose parents are too poor to allow them to attend in the ordinary way. I am setting everything up in a trust so that my work shall continue long after I am gone."

And Jane, a spinster because she preferred it that way, and also believing in the education of women, had agreed. In that she had infuriated the English side of the family, bypassing them and leaving her considerable estate to the Melford Trust.

"Do you wish to see inside the classrooms now?"

Margaret turned to her lawyer and nodded. As they climbed the steps to peer about the first classroom, she decided that she would offer him a seat on the trust's board. He hadn't approved of what she'd planned and accomplished here, but she was his client and so he'd always done his best for her. He'd worked hard, arranged everything with care, and he'd seen to it that her money was tied up very tightly despite his disapproval. No one would easily break this trust, even in the years after she was gone.

"Yes, they have done a good job here. I approve of the work," he said, looking about him.

Margaret Melford nodded. "Mr. Salton? I would like to ask

you a question; will you join the school board as one of the trustees? I believe that a man of your education and principles would be invaluable."

Michael Salton flushed. He'd been against her idea from the first and she knew it, but – perhaps they were building something valuable here after all. Besides, she was still his client, and being on the board would pay him – in a number of ways.

"Certainly. I would be honored to serve."

No, that's not the truth, Margaret thought, *but it will be.* In time, he *would* feel that way.

She was right. By the time she died in 1919, having lived to see the First World War begin – and end – Michael Salton was a devoted believer in Margaret's school. It had grown to prestige, with a roll of almost twenty girls living in the boarding house attached to the school and another dozen attending as day girls. His own granddaughters attended, and when he too died – in 1927 – he left two hundred pounds to the school to build and fully equip a new classroom. His conversion had been complete.

About the school the city grew, expanding outward – safe within that envelope of city center and suburbs. Margaret Melford had foreseen the school's need for more classrooms and playing fields as the years passed, and in her original purchase, she had very amply provided the room for that growth. It was as well she had. The school roll grew with each generation. Girls came to Melford from all over the country now and the school took them in. It prospered, a woman's heart that beat for them in the city.

* * *

"I have to go. I've been called up. Darling, don't cry. The war will be over by Christmas and I'll be back."

"No." Ngaire clung to him. "Don't go, Rewi."

He bent to kiss her gently. "I must. I swear I'll be back."

Rewi Paiwai gave her another kiss, unwrapped her arms from about him and was gone – on the long trail to war and home again. Ngaire looked after his strong, lithely striding figure. She'd always known he'd leave her when this day came.

The heart of the city talked to her and told her many things.

She knew too that he'd return, give her two daughters and die young – from the wounds he'd receive. She'd bring up her daughters alone. She'd take no other man to her heart after him, only now and again to her bed. She wept; slow tears of bitter knowledge and the city took them to itself in return.

* * *

Above the harbor curve a great eagle flew in slow circles, turning, orienting itself before heading downwind. There was something in the wind that called it to the south and it obeyed. Icarus, child of a sideways slip in time, male in search of a mate – a quest whose resolution would be granted in a year that was still to come and by the girl-child who'd been his foster-mother and whose greatest talents were yet to be realized.

* * *

"They've come back?"

"Yes. My grandmother would have been so happy."

The other laughed. "I bet some local farmers won't be. Eagles above the city, all the farmers will see are dead lambs."

"Maybe, but the eagles are a protected species. There'll be an investigation of the disappearance of any stock it's claimed the eagles have taken and the Department of Conservation will reimburse farmers for them if the proof is there."

"Oh? Where are they getting the money for that?"

Jo Salton smiled. "My grandmother and one of her old friends left a considerable sum of money in a special trust with me as one of the trustees. Grandmother Tina believed this day could come and when it did, she expected trouble to arrive as well. There's enough money to hire lawyers too if we have to. But the eagles *will* be protected."

"Who was the friend?"

"Lyn Warne."

He stared at her. "The computer woman?"

"Yes, she never married, and she and my grandmother were friends from the time they started school together." She smiled kindly at the boy. Well, he was a boy to her; she was in her seventies and he was only thirty-four.

"Your grandmother was their friend too, Jim."

"I don't remember her."

"No." But she did. As a girl she'd thought of them as The Three Musketeers. Tina, Lyn and Jan. The first named had been deeply into recreating extinct species using genetics, the second one into computers so deeply that it was as if they embraced her as a lover. And the third woman, who loved and supported her friends – while keeping a good marriage alive, incidentally, carved out a top career in politics when she reached her fifties.

Tina Salton the second smiled at the memories. In 2027 Jan Murall Eggers had slipped bills past her Parliamentary colleagues, bills which – in a deal with some from the opposition – demanded and received complete protection for the Haast's eagles if they ever returned to the city. She would have rejoiced with her two best friends if she could have lived to see this day. None of the three had lived that long, but in 2067 Tina was here to see it, and she could rejoice enough for all of them.

* * *

Some inner areas of the city were crumbling. After the great quakes of 2147 portions of the business district nearest the sea had been largely abandoned. Insurance companies had paid out but the government of the day had refused to let rebuilding take place. The scientists had been saying for almost a hundred and seventy years that the city was overdue for The Big One. That year they had finally been proved correct. It had been a bad century for natural disasters in many places.

New Orleans had been forcibly evacuated at the start of the century when a tsunami coupled with what had been expected to be a minor hurricane and tidal surge had wiped out the whole city – along with most of the sleeping inhabitants as it struck in the early hours of one May morning. The American president had rejected calls to rebuild and had had what few of the city's buildings survived promptly demolished to prevent survivors from resettling there.

In India twenty years after that, an earthquake had been followed by a tidal surge that killed tens of thousands along the whole coastline and for almost fifty kilometres inland. The diseases that followed in the wave's wake killed millions more.

In the heart of the Pacific, another tsunami caused by an undersea landslide near the Auckland Islands had washed into Wellington's harbor and carried away everything near the sea's edge. It was then that most of the inner city's remaining population had packed up and left, never to return. The heart of the city beat more slowly.

* * *

Tina Eggers Paiwai stared about her. "I suppose we must remove the school?"

"There's no other option." Her companion was adamant.

"I'll hate it." Tina said. "This school has stood here for nearly three hundred years."

"Think of it as the city leaving the school, not the school leaving the city."

"I suppose."

She watched as the last of the massive lifters swung into the sky. It was the end of an era. With Melford School packing up, the buildings could crumble and no one would know or care any longer. There would be no one left in a deserted city. She'd held on almost beyond common sense, but even she had had to admit it was time to leave. She looked up then as a long harsh scream echoed from above – and she smiled suddenly. No, the city was not deserted; it had just had a change of ownership.

* * *

Above the harbor curve, the great eagles fly. There is no date. Dates are human things, created by people and fueled by their need to know when they are. To the eagles all times are the present. This is their land, their place. They ignore the settling mounds of grass below, under which the remains of a city turn to dust and shadows.

All times, all places that were, or will ever be, live within the city still. For it is not so much the city that men built that remembers, it is the land. And when all else is gone, the land remains – and everything within the city is remembered – for everything that dwelled within the city has at last come home.

About the Author

Lyn McConchie started writing professionally in 1990, since then she has seen fifty-two of her books published and over three hundred short stories. She has written SF/F, but also true-life humor about her farm and animals (7 books known as the 'Daze' series), children's books, a YA quartet set in her own New Zealand, a western, a dozen Sherlock Holmes pastiches, half a dozen post-apocalyptics, and one non-fiction. Lyn says her imagination is related to the energizer bunny, and she hopes to be writing for many years to come.

Discover more great titles by Lyn McConchie:

The Way-Out Wild West
The Far Side of the Wild West

Learn more at Hadrosaur.com

www.ingramcontent.com/pod-product-compliance
Lightning Source LLC
LaVergne TN
LVHW091144080826
845145LV00008B/2251

* 9 7 8 1 9 6 5 3 1 3 0 2 2 *